Born in Wales in 1930, Terry Nation, novelist, screenwriter and creator of the Daleks and *Blake's Seven*, wrote for such enduring series as *The Avengers*, *The Saint* and *Dr Who*. He began his career writing comedy for the radio for stars such as Tony Hancock, Spike Milligan and Frankie Howard. He soon moved on to write for BBC television, and with early success as creator of the Daleks came the freedom to work on his first novel, *Survivors*, and a highly acclaimed children's novel, *Rebecca's World*. On the wave of his British successes he moved with his wife, Kate, and two children to the States, where he worked for a number of major studios on projects for TV and film. His work remains hugely popular with both cult and mainstream fans in Britain and the US.

SURVIVORS

Terry Nation

An Orion paperback

First published in Great Britain in 1976
by Orion Books,
This paperback edition published in 2008
by Orion Books, an imprint of The Orion Publishing Group Ltd,
Orion House, 5 Upper St Martin's Lane,
London WC2H 9EA

An Hachette UK company

5 7 9 10 8 6

A CIP catalogue record for this book is available
from the British Library.

ISBN 978-1-4091-0264-9

Printed and bound in Great Britain by
CPI Group (UK) Ltd, Croydon, CR0 4YY

The Orion Publishing Group's policy is to use papers that
are natural, renewable and recyclable products and
made from wood grown in sustainable forests. The logging
and manufacturing processes are expected to conform to
the environmental regulations of the country of origin.

www.orionbooks.co.uk

For Kate

PANDEMIC: General, universal. *esp.* Of a disease: Prevalent over the whole of a country or continent, or over the whole world.

SURVIVOR: One who survives or outlives another or others.

HOPE: To entertain expectation of something desired. To trust, have confidence. To look forward to.

PROLOGUE

In the beginning, the Lord said, "My name shall be known to all the peoples of the world." In one hour He spoke his name to ten people.

In the hour that followed each of those people met ten others and said the Lord's name.

In the third hour each of those one hundred and ten met ten more people and spoke the name of the Lord.

At the fourth hour each of those one thousand two hundred and ten disciples whispered the Lord's name to ten more people.

And so it continued:

How many hours will pass before the name of the Lord has spread to all the peoples of the world?

The Good Child's
Book of Pastimes (1850)*

The Boeing inched forward to nuzzle the side of its nose against the walkway.

As though conducting a symphony, the ground controller swept his arms downward in a dramatic gesture that

---

*In 1850 the population of the world was one billion. The answer to the problem was "between seven and eight hours." Today the answer would be "between eight and nine hours."

signaled the finish. The orchestra of the engines died. The
wheelbrakes clunked. The drawbridge and canopy
slithered across to the open front hatchway, tethering the
great machine to the airport.

"There will be a brief delay before passengers can dis-
embark. We apologize for this and would appreciate it if
you would remain in your seats for a few minutes more.
Thank you."

A fuzzy click ended the announcement, and the voice of
the stewardess was replaced by a track of syrup-smooth
music.

In the main compartment the passengers from the aisle
seats were already standing, waiting to shuffle forward to
the exit. Now they seemed uncertain what to do. A few
settled back into their seats, uncomfortable and bulky with
raincoats and packages, flight bags and plastic carriers from
the duty-free shops at Charles de Gaulle Airport.

"Will we be long?"

The chief steward gave his professional calming smile.
"Not more than a couple of minutes, sir." He indicated an
empty seat to his questioner.

The man remained standing. "What's the trouble?"

"A passenger in the first-class cabin was taken ill. The
captain radioed for an ambulance to meet us."

"Is he bad?"

The chief steward assumed a confiding voice. It com-
bined gravity and reassurance. "He's in some sort of fever.
We just want to give the medics a chance to get him off, and
then we'll start disembarking. Now, if you'll excuse me." He
moved on up to the first-class cabin.

The man lay stretched across three seats at the front of
the aircraft. A stewardess knelt on the floor beside him.
The steady blast of cool air from the overhead ventilator
had blown her hair free from the grip of the lacquer, and it
lay in thick strands across her forehead.

She looked up gratefully as the ambulance men appeared
beside her. She got awkwardly to her feet, her legs stiff
from being folded under her.

The ambulance men snapped the stretcher open and laid it in the aisle. They tossed aside the airline blanket that covered the passenger and lifted him onto the taut canvas.

The man was shivering violently, but his face was glossy with sweat. His breathing was swift and shallow. His eyes opened and closed as though he were drifting in and out of sleep.

The red stretcher blanket was flipped over the man, locking his arms to his sides. Then he was lifted and with practiced ease manipulated through the tight angles up to the exit.

"Got his travel documents? Passport? Luggage tags?"

The stewardess who had nursed him pointed back to a briefcase under the seats.

"Better get it. And someone should come with us to deal with the formalities."

The girl glanced at the captain standing in the open door of the flight deck. He nodded. "You go with them, Mary."

By the time she had collected the briefcase the stretcher was already on the cart and starting up the steep ramp. She ran to catch up.

She was still wearing her flat "in-flight" shoes. Her blouse had tugged free from her skirt. She started to tuck it in as she walked beside the swiftly moving cart. She felt hot and untidy. She pushed the hair back from her eyes. One of the ambulance men grinned at her.

"Glamorous old life, isn't it, being an air hostess?"

She didn't answer.

Flight 301 disembarked seven minutes late. Two hundred and eleven passengers filed out of the aircraft, smiled off by the cabin crew.

Forty-three of the travelers avoided customs and immigration and moved to the crowded transit lounge to await connecting flights. The others were filtered through the airport processes and out into the main concourse, moving against the tide of travelers who were starting their journeys.

In that single day more than six thousand people moved through London Airport. Their destinations included every major city in the world.

The man carried from the aircraft was Robert Jorden Mills. He had flown from Moscow to Paris, spent a one-night stopover at the Hilton and then picked up a British Airways flight to London. He had been taken ill within minutes of boarding. Four days later he died in the isolation ward of a London hospital.

British Airways stewardess Mary Saunders overnighted in a New York hotel. She was due to join the morning flight out of Kennedy. She reported sick two hours before takeoff.

BOOK ONE

THE FOURTH HORSEMAN

1

SHE'S in the garden. I'll call her."

Mrs. Tranter carefully balanced the receiver on the pile of directories and hurried across the kitchen to the terrace door.

The gusting October wind pressed the door back against her as she pushed it open. She stepped out onto the wet paving and stared down across the lawns toward the swimming pool. The glass doors of the sun room were closed. Mrs. Tranter moved to the corner of the house. Scent-spray-fine rain misted her spectacles. She directed her voice toward the gate of the walled garden.

"Mrs. Grant!"

She waited a moment and then called again. Louder this time.

"Mrs. Grant. Telephone."

There was no answer. She was about to start along the path when Abby appeared at the gate.

"Telephone, Mrs. Grant." The woman mimed holding a receiver as she called.

Abby waved a hand of understanding, and the housekeeper started gratefully back to the kitchen.

Abby began to run. Graceful despite the knee-high

muddy rubber boots, she wore a bright-red plastic raincoat that was much too short. Several inches of her skirt showed beneath it. A silk square, knotted at the neck, covered her hair. In her hand was a colander half filled with autumn raspberries.

Mrs. Tranter held open the kitchen door. Abby handed her the colander and stooped to ease off the boots.

"It's a personal call. I think it must be Peter."

Abby crossed to the telephone, shrugging out of the raincoat and letting it fall. She pulled off the head scarf and dropped it on the floor. The older woman followed her like a conjurer's assistant picking up the props.

"Hello. Yes, this is Mrs. Grant. Yes, I'll hold on."

Abby noticed the trail of damp footprints across the kitchen floor.

"Those damn boots leak." She reached down to touch her foot. "My feet are soaking."

She pushed her hand up under her skirt, hooked a thumb behind the elastic waistband of her panty hose and edged it down to her thighs. She lowered herself onto the edge of a chair and peeled off the wet stockings.

"Hello. Mummy?"

The connection gave a slight echoing quality to the boy's voice.

"Hello, darling. I hoped it was you. Sorry I was so long. How are you? Is everything all right?"

While her son reassured her that he was well and explained that he was telephoning from his housemaster's study, Abby made a silent signal to Mrs. Tranter and mouthed, "Pass me a towel."

Then it was her turn to answer questions. She rubbed her feet as she spoke.

"Yes, Daddy and I are fine. He's in London today, but he'll be back this evening. Tell me what's happening down there?"

Peter retailed the school news as though he were reading it from a prepared statement. He explained that all the boys were being allowed to telephone their parents. Abby wondered if the housemaster was in the study with the boy.

The picture of her son was very clear in her mind. Tall for eleven but too thin. Like hers, his hair was fair. And as always, whenever she spoke to Peter on the telephone, her image of him began to focus on his wrists. No shirt or blazer cuffs ever seemed long enough to cover the bony wrists.

Peter ended with: "And that's about all."

Abby said, "It sounds quite exciting. Like being under siege. Classes are going on as normal, though, are they?"

"Yes," he said. "Worst luck."

His mother laughed. "Hard cheese. Look, darling, will you ring again before the end of the week?" And then, to make it sound more casual: "I'm not at all worried, but I do want to hear what's happening. They've closed the village school for a couple of days, so I thought they might be sending all of you home."

Peter said there had been rumors about a special holiday for the emergency, but that the Head had decided against it. He finished by promising to telephone on Friday.

"Try and call in the evening, and then you can talk to Daddy, too. And don't you dare go breaking bounds and sneak off into town. Take care of yourself, darling. Talk to you Friday. Bye. Bye-bye."

Abby waited until she heard the connection break, then put the receiver back on the rest. She rubbed the towel vaguely over her damp hair.

Mrs. Tranter waited for a report. "Is he all right?" she demanded finally.

"Oh, I'm sorry." Abby roused herself. "Yes, he's fine." She shivered. "I'd love a coffee, Mrs. Tranter. Instant will do."

The woman pressed the switch in the handle of the kettle.

"Apparently they've closed off the school. Nobody coming in or going out. The tradesmen leave things at the gates, and when they've gone, the boys go down to collect them."

Mrs. Tranter gave a series of nods. "Very sensible." She spooned coffee into a cup and stood with her hand hovering over the kettle, waiting for it to click off. "Any sign of it down there?"

"Peter said there are about a dozen boys in the San', but

Matron thinks it's some sort of stomach bug. Nothing to worry about."

Again the housekeeper nodded approval. "That's good. And the school being out in the country, they might be lucky and miss the worst of it." She moved the cup beneath the spout and in the moment of the water boiling tilted it onto the coffee.

Abby glanced at the wall clock and stood up quickly. "I must have a shower and get changed. I'm picking up David at the station. I'll take that up with me." She reached for the cup and, balancing it carefully, started out of the room.

"I'd like to go home for a day, Mrs. Grant."

Abby halted in the doorway. "Is there something wrong?" she asked. "Have you heard from your sister?"

Mrs. Tranter shook her head. "I tried to ring her this morning, but there was no reply. Then I tried again about an hour ago. There was a funny sort of signal, so I got the operator. She said there had been a big breakdown in the Clapham area. No calls going through at all."

"But that doesn't really mean anything," Abby said. "I mean, nothing to worry about necessarily. They said on the radio that there'd been some breakdowns and that the telephone people were short-staffed."

Mrs. Tranter was a determined worrier. "Yes, I heard that. But the phone was ringing this morning, and there was no answer. Doris never goes out in the morning." The idea of her sister leaving the house before noon was impossible; therefore, an unanswered telephone was ominous.

Abby said, "Well, I'm sure everything is all right, but of course you must go. Just to set your mind at rest."

"Thank you. Of course, if everything is all right, I could be back here tomorrow just after lunch."

Abby was tempted to try to talk her out of going. It was a difficult journey. More than an hour on the train, then a long tube ride and two bus changes.

Before she could speak, Mrs. Tranter said, "I really must go."

"Of course you must. And decide when you're coming

back after you find out what's happening. If you can find a phone that's working, perhaps you'd give me a ring. Now you get ready, and I'll run you to the station."

Abby hurried across the hall to the stairs.

Mrs. Tranter took her purse from the kitchen-table drawer and checked that her return ticket to Victoria was still valid. She made certain she had enough cash and then moved around the kitchen, tidying quickly.

The telephone made a noise. Not a real ring but a series of weak single notes. Mrs. Tranter lifted the receiver.

"Hello?" No sound came from the earpiece. "Hello?" she said again and jiggled the rest. The instrument stayed silent. She replaced it and went up to her room.

Abby shifted the automatic transmission into D1, slid her foot off the brake and touched the throttle. The "E"-type Jaguar edged out of the garage. The tires made more noise on the gravel drive than the enormous V12 engine.

Officially this was David's car, but she enjoyed driving it far more than her own Granada Estate.

For three months she had listened to her husband debate buying the car. The brochure had become his regular bedtime reading. One night he listed the reasons for not owning the car.

"It's a selfish car. I mean, just two seats. And that engine. With petrol the price it is. And anyway, I'd never really get a chance to use all that power. A seventy-mile-an-hour speed limit. No. It's silly."

Abby had waited until they had settled down and switched off the light and then had said, "It's a beautiful car. I love it. We can afford it, and you want it. That's all that matters." David ordered the car the following morning.

Abby stretched across and opened the passenger door. Mrs. Tranter lowered herself in awkwardly. She pulled the door shut. Locked it. Settled her overnight bag on her knees and took a firm hold on the grab handle. She sat rigidly, looking directly ahead.

The women traveled in silence, Abby driving with

relaxed expertise. Her long acquaintance with the road allowed her to position the car perfectly for every bend.

She pressed the cartridge into the tape deck. It was the Mozart they had played on the way home from dinner last night.

Abby thought about her son. Perhaps it would be better to drive across to the school and fetch him. Bring him home until the worst of the flu was over. Then again, as the school had isolated itself, it might be as well to leave him there. She'd talk to David about it. There was no need to make a decision right away. They could wait until they got Peter's report on Friday.

Abby shifted the heating control to "full" and closed the driver's window. She still felt cold. She had changed into a silk jersey shirt and trousers and now wished she were wearing something warmer.

They drifted around a bend onto a long straight section of road. A distant car moved toward them. Mrs. Tranter nodded ahead. "Dr. Stewart," she said, recognizing the Silver Cloud.

Abby nodded and flicked the stalk on the steering column to flash the headlights. The twinned headlight on the Rolls gleamed an answer.

Joe Stewart slowed his car and signaled Abby to stop. She braked gently. The cars halted side by side. The electric window of the Rolls hissed down.

"Hello, Abby. Mrs. Tranter." It was more than twenty-five years since he'd left Glasgow, but his accent was unchanged. His hair was silver and wavy and much too long. He seemed never to look through the half-lens eyeglasses that sat in the middle of his nose. David always maintained that Joe was not a doctor at all, but an actor playing in an A. J. Cronin television series. He was a kind and gentle man, and Abby was convinced that he had discovered a way to halt the aging process. He looked now exactly as he had when he'd saved her pregnancy eleven years earlier.

"Are you and David home tonight?" he called.

Abby nodded. "I'm just off to the station to pick him up."

"Can I come by at about nine o'clock? I want to give you both a shot of the flu vaccine."

Abby looked pleased. "Good. Thanks, Joe. I've been meaning to ask you about it for a couple of days. Bring Gladys with you. We'll have a drink."

The doctor grinned. "I'll drink hers. She's not feeling any too grand at the moment. Really, though, I won't be able to stop. Things are a wee bit hectic."

"Have you had many cases?" Abby asked, after Joe had reassured her that Gladys was "just a bit under the weather."

"There are about a dozen showing symptoms, but I think half of them are just trying to be fashionable. Anyway, I'll give you all the news tonight."

He gave a brief salute and moved his car forward. Abby waved. "See you tonight."

Mrs. Tranter resumed her tight grip on the grab handle.

Unusually, the station forecourt offered plenty of parking space. Abby placed the Jaguar neatly between the white lines that marked a bay directly in front of the booking hall.

A uniformed porter spread tobacco onto a cigarette paper and eyed the two women climbing from the car.

"London train's in if you want it," he said slowly.

Mrs. Tranter was immediately flustered. She hurried into the station at an ungainly trot, paused and turned to say good-bye and that she would telephone when she could, then dashed onto the platform.

On the roadway Abby heard carriage doors slam. A whistle and then the swiftly building roar as the train pulled away. She looked at her wristwatch.

"I must be slow."

The porter lit his cigarette. "That's not the five twenty. That one should have gone through at three fifteen. Timetables have gone all to pot today. All to pot."

"What about the trains out of London?" Abby asked.

The man shrugged. The disruption seemed to please him. "Been nothing on the down line for a couple of hours. They don't know where they are at Victoria. Can't get no sense out of them. Far as we can tell, half the crews haven't turned up for work. Can't even find out which services have been canceled. Right old mess they're in. Even our telephones are all jammed up. All gone to pot."

Abby thought, "He hasn't enjoyed himself so much since the last strike." She glanced toward the telephone box across the forecourt. "That reminds me," she said. "I want to report a fault on my phone." She started toward the box.

"That one's no good," the porter called after her. "Been out of order all day."

She moved back. "I'm expecting my husband on the five forty-five. Any idea—"

"Don't ask me," the man interjected. "Your guess is as good as mine." He relit his cigarette.

Abby settled in the passenger seat of the car. She could drive around and find a working telephone to call David, but that would be pointless. He would already have left the office. She could go home and let David pick up a cab when he arrived. She twisted around to peer through the rear window. The taxi rank was empty. She looked at her watch again and decided to wait.

She lit a cigarette, switched on the radio, and slid lower in the seat. It started to rain again, and the windshield blurred. The windows began to mist over. Abby liked the isolation this brought. The warm cockpit of the car seemed more secure as the outside world vanished. On the radio the music ended, and a voice took over the broadcast. Abby turned up the sound:

". . . and more music in a few minutes. But first the news headlines at five thirty. Reports coming in from motoring organizations say that massive jams are building up in the London area. The metropolitan police advise drivers to delay their homeward journeys for as long as possible to help avoid further congestion. Much of the trouble has been caused by traffic-light failures. Home news today has been dominated by reports of absenteeism in industry. Many shops and factories have been forced to close down. Public transport and services, too, have been badly hit. A ministry spokesman says that it may be several days before the worst of the flu epidemic has passed and things get back to normal.

"And now foreign news. New York is still without electric power twenty-four hours after the breakdown. It's been estimated that more than half the city's work force is affected by the influenza virus, and the mayor has declared a state of emergency. Sources in Rome and Paris report growing concern amongst medical authorities about the rapid spread of the virus. There have been a number of deaths notified in both cities, but there is no direct confirmation that these were a result of the infection.

"That's it for the moment. More news from home and abroad in our six o'clock bulletin."

A bright-voiced disc jockey took over the program and announced that his next record was "dedicated to all those nice folks out there who are in bed with Asian flu and not feeling right up to the mark." The record he played was "Hong Kong Blues."

Abby switched off the radio, leaned back, and closed her eyes. With an unconscious gesture she began to rub the tips of her fingers just below her armpit.

2

JENNY pressed the spoon hard onto the aspirin tablets at the bottom of the glass, crushing them to a fine powder. She added the whiskey and lemon juice. She glanced across the bed-sitter to the girl on the divan.

"Shouldn't be a minute, love. Kettle's nearly boiled. My mother always used to dose me up with this whenever I had a cold or flu. The aspirin helps bring the temperature down."

The electric kettle was beginning to pulse noisily. Jenny lifted the yellowing gauze of the nylon curtain and stared up at the street. The basement window gave a limited view of the cul-de-sac. The solid line of cars parked at the curb still further restricted the outlook. There were lights on in some of the upper windows of the terraced houses opposite. Their glow emphasized the early-evening darkness. There was something different about the street tonight. It took Jenny a moment to identify it. The streetlamps were not on.

She put a teaspoon in the glass and poured the boiling water. She stirred the potion vigorously; then, using a tea towel to hold it, carried it across to the bed.

Patricia's eyes were closed. She was breathing in rapid,

short gasps. Her hair and face were soaked with sweat. She had pushed the blankets down to her waist. She was naked. Her arms were folded across her breasts, the fingers of each hand resting in her armpits. Jenny used the tea towel to dab Pat's forehead. She opened her eyes.

"You ought to have a nightie on."

Pat stared as though she had not heard. Jenny went to a drawer and rifled through her friend's nightwear. All of it was in filmy nylon or shining satin. It came from a shop in Shaftesbury Avenue. Pat always called it the "Whores' Outfitters." That the sick girl should wear them now seemed ridiculous—somehow even improper. Jenny sorted through her own things and chose a cotton nightdress. High-necked and long-sleeved.

Patricia roused herself slightly and with Jenny's help managed to sit up. Like a surrendering soldier, she raised her arms wearily above her head, groping her hands into the nightdress.

Jenny saw the bruised lumps clustered in the armpits, the darkened skin shining and taut over the swellings. She felt her stomach clench in fear and shock, and she pulled her hand back quickly to avoid touching the area. Pat sensed the sharpness of the movement. "What's the matter?"

Jenny made her voice sound unconcerned. "Nothing." She folded the pillow double and lowered Pat onto it; then, cradling her head, she held the glass to the girl's lips. "Drink some of this."

Pat shuddered at the bitter sweetness and turned her head away. Insistently Jenny raised the glass again. Reluctantly the girl sipped it, finding swallowing painful. Only when the glass was half empty did Jenny allow her friend to lie back. Her eyes were closed, and she was sweating again.

"How are you feeling now?"

"Awful. I feel awful." Jenny busied herself straightening the sheets and tidying the bed. She put her hand on Pat's forehead.

"You're burning."

"I feel awful."

Jenny perched herself on the edge of the bed. "Well, at

least you're doing the sensible thing and staying in bed. You should feel better after a good night's sleep. I'm surprised you've got it, actually. You had the injection, didn't you? Didn't they give everybody in your office a shot?"

Pat nodded. "Last week. Couldn't have been much good, though, could it? A lot of the girls weren't in today. Then after lunch I started to feel rotten. I kept going hot and cold and felt a bit dizzy. Then I had to walk home. Couldn't get on the tube."

Jenny said, "The buses are the same. I got as far as South Ken; then the traffic was solid, so I got off and walked."

The sick girl gave a sudden violent shudder. Her body began to tremble. "Cold. Very cold. Get me another blanket, Jen."

Jenny pulled the *duvat* from her own bed and tucked it around the girl, who was shaking uncontrollably.

"I'm going to get the doctor." Pat seemed not to hear her. "I'll be as quick as I can." She picked up her coat from a chair and went to the front door.

She ran up the basement steps and onto the sidewalk. The prodding force of the rain pressed her skirt against her legs. The wind was cold. She hurried forward, head bent against it.

She turned across the brief angle that hid the main length of the cul-de-sac from its junction with the Fulham Road. As she moved to the corner, she saw the traffic.

It stood motionless in nose-to-tail lines in both directions. The wind and rain blended the sound of the engines into a blurred roar. The blaze of headlights created a glowing halo above the cars, showing a swirl of exhaust fumes. Somewhere far back down the line a horn set up a protest. A few more sounded brief replies, then fell silent again.

Jenny turned right out of Seymour Walk and caught the full force of the rain. She walked quickly, staying close to the shop fronts for what little shelter they could offer. She could see the silhouettes of the drivers in the nearside traffic lane. Glowing tips of cigarettes. White faces made featureless by misted windows.

Opposite, outside St. Stephen's Hospital, stood a line of

six empty buses, parked half on the sidewalk, abandoned by passengers and crews. An ambulance had nosed out of the hospital driveway and was now locked in an angle across two traffic lanes.

Jenny started to cross the road, squeezing between two cars. She felt the hot blast of exhaust against her legs. She edged through the second, then third, then fourth line of cars. The drivers watched her—like cripples envious of her mobility.

The traffic lights at Edith Grove were not working; nor the ones beyond, at Gunter Grove. Both intersections were solid with traffic.

The front door of the house was open. Jenny stepped inside. A lighted candle stood on a small table. A dozen or more people were lined against the hallway wall. Beyond them was the waiting room. It, too, was lit by candles and looked very crowded.

The people near the entrance glanced at Jenny as she stood awkwardly in the doorway. No one spoke, and in a moment they had lost interest in her and had resumed their blank gazes at the opposite wall.

The exhaust fumes from the traffic outside had invaded the hallway and mixed with the smell of wet clothing and cigarette smoke. An elderly woman who had the only chair was coughing in regular spasms, trying to muffle the sound in a handkerchief.

Jenny took her place at the end of the queue. A few minutes later a woman with a small child entered and took their place behind her.

"Is he here?" she demanded.

"I don't know. I've only just arrived."

"He should be here," the woman said. "Surgery's supposed to be at six. It's nearly half past now."

A frail man a few positions ahead of them seemed grateful for a chance to break the silence.

"He's not back from his rounds yet," he said. "His wife came down about ten minutes ago and told us he's not back from his rounds yet."

The woman with the child stared down toward the crowded waiting room.

"It'll take him all bloody night to see this lot," she said. "Be quicker to go up to the out-patients at St. Stephen's. I want this one to have the flu injection. She was off school the day they done all the others."

The child looked guilty and stared at the floor. The woman eyed the queue again.

"We could be here until midnight with this lot." She turned and, dragging the child, went back out into the rain.

Jenny, too, decided that to go on waiting was pointless. She moved to the door. The heads turned to watch her. She felt they disapproved of her leaving. To justify herself, she muttered to no one in particular, "I'll come back later."

Outside, the white Advance Laundry van that had been level with the doorway had moved forward three or four positions. Now the traffic line was stationary again.

Back on the Fulham Road Jenny saw a six-car length of roadway had cleared on the inner lane. The traffic waiting to advance into the space sounded horns at the Triumph Spitfire that blocked the way. Clouds of steam milled out from the radiator grille. A girl of about twenty stood beside the open driver's door, trying to push the car. Two men from the car behind got out and ran to her. The girl climbed in and steered the car onto the sidewalk as the men pushed. Within a minute the cleared space had filled with cars and the line halted again.

Three raincoated men moved quickly along the sidewalk toward Jenny. They passed the steaming Spitfire and were briefly back-lit by its still glaring headlights. As the men turned to enter the hospital, Jenny recognized Michael Craven. She called his name and ran forward.

"Hello, Jen."

Michael's companions moved on into the porch and through the swing doors.

Jenny said, "What are you doing here? I thought you were at Brompton Hospital."

He nodded vaguely, then said, "There's a big flap on.

Everybody in research—all our specialists, consultants, surgeons—everybody is being roped in to do a bit of GP-ing. We reckon the ministry is just trying to establish confidence by having a lot of people wandering around in white coats. Let's get under cover. I can only stop a minute."

He took Jenny's arm and led her into the porch. Inside the shelter he shook the water off his coat and started to unbutton it. Through the plate glass of the double doors Jenny saw the corridor was crowded.

"It's packed in there."

Michael glanced inside. "It's the same all over as far as I can tell. I doubt if there is an empty hospital bed anywhere in London. I've been up at St. George's since this morning. They've got cots in the corridors there. Now we've been sent to give a hand down here."

Jenny said, "I didn't know it was as bad as that." And then, quickly, as it seemed Michael was about to take his leave: "Listen, Michael. I've been around to Dr. Marsh, but he wasn't there. Pat's in a bad way. Really sick. She's got a fever, and even when she's burning up, she says she's cold. It's obviously this flu thing that's going around, but she's got it badly. And there are these lumps under her arms—"

"Oh, Christ!" Michael interjected. He looked very serious.

Jenny felt her stomach clench with fear. "The lumps? Are they a bad symptom?" Hurriedly she went on. "Listen, couldn't you come around and have a look at her? There must be something you can give her."

Michael looked at his watch. "I have to report in first and see what things are like here. If I get a break later in the evening, I'll come around."

Jenny was disappointed. She felt she had in some way failed Pat. Perhaps she had not made it clear just how sick her flat-mate really was. Had she made it sound more urgent, Michael might have come back with her at once.

Michael touched her shoulder. A farewell gesture. "I promise. I'll be there first chance I get."

Jenny didn't move. He edged toward the doorway. She

watched him. He put out his hand to push the door and then halted and turned to face her again.

"Jen, have you had any of the symptoms?"

She shook her head and said, "I'm fine."

Michael stared at her for a moment, then quickly pushed the door open and, holding it, beckoned her to enter before him. "Come on in with me. Hang around until I find out what's happening here, and then we'll try and nip away."

Jenny stepped into the crowded corridor, and Michael edged past her to lead the way along it. Only then did it occur to Jenny that the lights were on. She supposed the hospital was using its emergency generators.

What had appeared from outside to be a disorganized crowd was in fact a reasonably orderly line of people. Four or five deep the queue trailed around a corner and stretched away down another corridor. At the far end of this was a table at which two nurses and a young doctor were giving injections.

"Hang on here a sec." Jenny halted, and Michael crossed to an office door. As he entered, she had a brief view of a lot of white-coated people. The door closed.

Jenny didn't like hospitals. There was a smell to them. And a sound—rubbery silence that muffled footsteps. Voices were pitched differently. But mostly it was the people—the patients. Jenny didn't like sick people. Illness was demeaning. Somehow she equated ill health with dirtiness. More than that, it was a weakness. One had to rely on other people, and they would wear special faces. When you were sick, people around you, your friends, changed.

At twenty-four Jenny had never had a serious illness. Once or twice a year she might feel achy enough to stay in her bed. Then she wanted to see no one. Wanted no comforting. Wanted nothing but to be alone. She had read a good deal of pop psychology and believed fervently that all illness was "in the mind." She felt some guilt in being unable to sympathize with the sick, but the guilt didn't change it. This evening, helping Pat into the nightdress, touching her sweating body, seeing the swellings under her arms, hearing her rapid breathing—all these things had repelled her. Sickness was distasteful.

Standing waiting in the hospital corridor made Jenny feel uneasy. The thought of going back to the basement flat and being alone with Patricia was just as unattractive.

Across the hall the door opened, and Michael came out with a group of white-coated men and senior nurses. The group splintered, and Michael started away down the corridor. Then, remembering Jenny, he came back. He looked serious and preoccupied.

"Jen, I don't know what time I'm going to get away from here. They're really snowed under. We've just been given the latest position, and it's a damn sight worse than anybody thought. As of now we're stopping admissions."

"You'll turn people away?" She recognized that her voice had taken on the special, serious sound that hospitals demanded.

Michael said, "I gather it's pretty general. The medical staff are going down with it as fast as the patients. God knows how many people are suffering from it in their homes, but they're no worse off than the ones here. There's nothing we can do for them."

"But what about Pat? Isn't there something you could let me have to give her?"

"There's nothing." Michael glanced at the queue waiting their turn at the table. "We're giving people shots, but we might as well squirt water into them for all the good it's doing. It's just part of the fiction to try and stop a panic."

"Panic?" Jenny felt the word. "But it's only a flu epidemic. I mean, I know it can be bad. Especially for old people. But how long does it last? Four or five days? A week? It's not a long-term thing, is it? And it's not like smallpox or typhoid or any of those things. People don't die from it."

He stayed silent for a long moment, then, not looking at Jenny, said, "It's not flu. That's about the only thing we are certain about. It's not flu. The first cases started to show up about six days ago. That seems to be the time it takes from infection. About six days."

"But the papers. The radio. Everybody said it was flu. The China virus."

"I know what they said. Truth is that it hasn't been identified. Can't even see it under the microscopes yet. We know it's contagious. And infectious. Must be, the rate it's spreading. After the second or third day there is no mistaking it. Buboes. Those are the hard lumps under the arms. You saw them on Pat. After that there's a fever. Then there are blotches that can show up anywhere on the body. Subcutaneous hemorrhages. By now I think everybody here has a pretty good idea what it could be."

Jenny said, "Do you die from it?"

Michael answered with such calmness that it terrified her more than if he had shrieked the answer.

"I've just had the figure for this hospital alone. They've had ninety-seven deaths here today. It will be double or treble that by morning."

3

THE car door opened. Abby jerked awake. Confused for the moment. Dazed.

Her husband smiled in at her. "Hello." Then, with a note of concern at her bewilderment: "You all right?"

She nodded and gave a slight wince at a jab of pain in her neck. She rubbed it. "I've been asleep. Must have had my head awkwardly." It took a moment to shake away the surprise at finding herself in the car. She started to swing her legs across the high transmission tunnel to climb into the driver's seat.

David said, "No. It's all right. I'll drive."

She settled back in her seat, and David rounded the car to slither in behind the wheel. His black cashmere coat was wet and seal-slick. He found a duster and started to clear the mist from the windows.

"What time is it?" Abby asked, wriggling the stiffness out of her body.

"About eight thirty. I had a hell of a time getting here. Lucky to make it at all. You wouldn't believe what it's like in London."

He pressed the starter, and the engine fired immediately. He let it run for a few seconds and set the defogger and windshield wipers into action. The headlights showed the slant of rain.

As they reversed in a neat arc, Abby saw several other cars waiting in the forecourt. What was missing was the usual outward surge of people that marked a train arrival.

"Were you the only one to get off that train?"

"It wasn't from Victoria. It was a local. I picked it up at Chatham. I tell you, I've had the sort of journey that makes Marco Polo look like a stop-at-home."

David powered the car forward into the cave of its lights.

"You know what time I started for home?" he demanded. "Two o'clock. Five and a half hours it's taken to get here. I could get to New York in that time."

As he catalogued his journey, Abby sensed that her husband was beginning to shape the events into a good after-dinner story. She knew that when they were next with friends, she would hear the story again in an edited and colored version.

"There were queues right out into the street from the underground. Then word filtered back that only about a third of the regular trains were running. A few people wandered off, but most of them just went on waiting. Standing in the rain. Astonishing! Well, I started walking. No cabs anywhere, of course, and anyway, the traffic jams were fantastic. Most of the offices seemed to have closed down early. A lot of the shops were shut."

Abby asked, "What about your office? Any of your people off sick?"

"John popped in, but he looked terrible. Arthur Ezard rang to say Andrea wasn't well, and he was staying at home to look after her. Only two of our typists came in. Everybody I talked to seemed to be having the same problems. There was no business being done. It was all. . . ." He sought for the word. "It was confused. No panic or anything like that. Just confusion. People didn't know quite what to do. The routine had been broken. Not just in one area, but right across the board. Or perhaps it wasn't so much confusion as bewilderment. The machine wasn't working properly."

Abby reflected how little of her own routine had been affected by the flu epidemic. That the milk had not been delivered that morning hardly qualified as a crisis. The telephone being out of order was annoying but nothing more. Things might be difficult in the cities for a while, but here in the country she should be able to cope until everything got back to normal.

They left the car at the front door. As David went upstairs to change into dry clothes, Abby called, "It's a bit late to cook what I'd planned. Will you settle for bacon and eggs?"

"Marvelous."

She went into the kitchen and turned on the stove. She gave a shiver and crossed to look at the thermostat. It was set at seventy. She raised it five degrees and heard the dull thump as the boiler ignited.

She was breaking the eggs into the pan when David came in carrying two glasses half filled with scotch. He added ice cubes from the refrigerator. "Isn't it too hot in here?" he asked, handing Abby the drink.

"I didn't think so." She sipped her drink and then started to set a single place at the table.

"Aren't you eating?"

"Not very hungry. I might have a bit of cheese." Abby watched the eggs whiten over the gentle heat.

"Where's your radio?"

Abby pointed to the Welsh dresser. David fetched the expensive portable and set it on the table. He switched on, and they heard an instant hiss of static.

"How do you get Radio Four?"

"Middle button."

David pressed it. There was no sound. "That's odd." He began to wind the needle along the dial. As it moved, it picked up power surges and crackles. There was some distant-sounding very fast Morse from an automatic transmitter. At the end of the dial he was rewarded by a hardly audible voice speaking German. He searched through another wave band. There was some faraway music and then a man's voice speaking in French but much too fast for either of them to understand. David switched off.

Abby set the plate in front of him and then sat opposite while he ate. David recounted some more of his journey. She told him about the telephone call from Peter. She felt warmer now. Unknowingly, she had cupped her hand over her breast. Her fingers circled a gentle massage beneath her arm.

"I ran into Cameron today," David said. "You know his company does quite a bit of business in China. They have agents in Hong Kong. Well, he says that the Chinese government have clamped down on news, but there are rumors that millions have died there."

Abby said, "I heard a news broadcast earlier, but there was nothing about China. There'd been some deaths in Rome. It does seem very widespread. Wasn't there a bad epidemic of something about the time of the First World War?"

"That was influenza, too. Nineteen eighteen, I think. I must look it up. But I've got a feeling that the death toll was something fantastic. Something like twenty million. Mind, I don't think it could ever happen on that scale again. With modern medicine they do seem to be able to limit the outbreaks."

The lights went out with startling suddenness.

"Damn it!"

Abby stood up. She heard David's chair scrape back. He said, "Don't move. I've got my lighter somewhere."

Abby said, "There are candles in the holders in the sitting room."

The gold Dunhill flared to life. David turned up its flame and by its light started toward the kitchen door. "I wonder if it's the whole district or just us?" he said. "Have a look out of the front door. See if the Edgertons' lights are on."

Abby groped her way into the hall, her arms stretched ahead of her. She pulled the front door open and felt a quick scurry of wind. She stared across the road and through the naked trees. There was no hint of light from their neighbors' house.

"They're blacked out, too," Abby said as David came out of the sitting room holding lighted candles.

"I wonder how long it will be? The central heating will be off, too. Well, there's no point in sitting down here in the dark just getting colder. We might as well go to bed."

Abby found more candles while David checked and locked the doors.

Upstairs he showered quickly, and while he was toweling himself, Abby came into the bathroom for her ritual face cleansing. David watched her undress. She pushed down her trousers, panty hose and panties in one movement and kicked them off in an untidy heap. As she reached back to unfasten her bra, she gave a little grunt of pain. She stooped her shoulders forward and let the bra fall. She had small breasts. Her body was long and slim. The hips were narrow. The only weight problem she ever faced was when she lost a few pounds. There was a faded line of a neat scar that ran down from just below her navel, recording Peter's birth by Caesarean section.

She smeared lotion onto a wad of cotton wool. "I've just thought. The electric blanket won't be working. Will you get a couple of the big woolen ones from the landing cupboard?"

Five minutes later they were in bed. Abby shivered at the touch of cold sheets and snuggled deeply under the covers. David tried reading but, with only the light of the bedside candle, found the strain too great. He blew out the flame.

In the darkness Abby tried to put a shape on tomorrow. In the morning she would go to the Cash and Carry and stock up on canned foods. She'd get flour and yeast, too, in case the baker didn't arrive again. Then it occurred to her to wonder how she could bake bread without the electric stove. The power failure started a chain of consequences in her mind. The heating. Well, they still had one open fireplace. David could cut some logs. There was the little butane stove they used for picnics, so at least they could have hot drinks and soup. She tried to remember how they had managed last time when the miners' strike had created a rota of power cuts.

David had turned on his side, his back toward her. She shivered and edged closer to him for the warmth of his body. She felt an ache in her chest and shoulders. She began to drift into the first part of sleep, then wakened suddenly again as she thought, "The deep freeze. The damned thing is going to defrost." She worried about it for a few moments, and then sleep began to take hold of her again. Tomorrow would do. They'd work things out tomorrow.

It was almost midnight when Michael collected Jenny from the hospital waiting room. He looked pale and tired as he led her to a side entrance. In Seymour Walk there was the flickering light of candles from a few windows. They clattered down the steep basement steps, and Jenny opened the front door. The bed-sitter was cold. Damp cold. Michael had a pencil torch. He directed its thin beam across to the bed. Pat lay on her back. Her mouth was open, and vomit trailed over her cheek onto the pillow. Jenny felt her legs tremble. Michael crossed to the bed quickly, mercifully masking the girl from Jenny's sight. His examination was very swift. He sorted the sheet from the tangle of bedclothes and pulled it up over the face, then moved back to Jenny.

"She's dead." Michael put his hands on her shoulders. Her whole body began to shake. She couldn't speak. He guided her backward and sat her on a chair.

"Jen, listen to me. You have to get out of here. Not just out of the flat, I mean. Out of London."

She heard the words, but they had no meaning. More clearly she heard her own voice say, "She's dead."

Michael went on: "Just take a few things. Get out into the country if you can. I doubt that you'll find any transport, so you'll have to walk."

Jenny felt a sudden flood of guilt. "I shouldn't have left her alone. She must have been so frightened all on her own."

"There was nothing you could have done to help. Now, Jenny, get a hold on yourself and listen to me. You should get started as soon as you can. Take some food if you have any and—"

Before he could finish, Jenny flared at him with sudden anger. "For Christ's sake, don't you feel anything? You were having an affair with her. You were sleeping with her! Now she's dead! Can't you even say you're sorry? Isn't there—"

His open hand hit her cheek with well-judged force. The stinging suddenness of the blow brought tears to her eyes. Her head flinched back in fear of another slap. Michael pushed his face close to hers. His hands gripped her arms.

"Jenny, I told you earlier that we didn't know what this disease is. That's true in a way because it still hasn't been finally identified. But going by the symptoms, there's not much doubt about it. It's something very close to bubonic plague. Perhaps some mutation of the bacillus. But to all intents and purposes it's the same as the Black Death."

He paused for a moment and then, in a voice as matter-of-fact as he could make it, said, "I've got it. I've got the disease."

In the darkness he could not see her face, but he heard the involuntary gasp. He gave her no chance to ask questions but hurried on.

"I've worked out that I probably picked up the infection about three days ago. That gives me roughly three more days before it hits peak. Then either I'll survive it or not. I don't know what my chances will be. We just haven't seen enough of it to be able to work out survival odds. And you'd better get used to the idea. You've been exposed to it. I imagine everybody in central London—the whole country perhaps—has been exposed."

Jenny felt her stomach contract in violent spasm. Her skin prickled. Words caught in her throat. She said, "Me? I might have it?"

"I've watched you tonight. You've not shown any symptoms, but that's no guarantee."

"How will I know?" she asked in not more than a whisper.

"You'll know," he said. He released his hold on her arms and straightened up. "There are some people who have a natural immunity. You might be one of the lucky ones."

He flashed his penlight toward the door. "I'm going back to the hospital."

Jenny jumped up. "I'll come with you."

"Damn it to hell, why don't you listen to what I say? Get out of London."

Jenny's fear now was of being left alone. Alone in this room. Her question was like a leash, holding him for a little longer.

"You said I've already been exposed. What difference does it make if I stay here in London?"

He held the beam of the flashlight so each could see the other's face.

"If the mortality rate keeps accelerating the way it is, we're not going to be able to bury our dead. There could be cholera, typhus and God knows what else. They've not had one survival, Jen. In all the cases they've admitted in St. Stephen's, not one has lived beyond the crisis point."

Jenny said quickly, desperately, "But they'll find something, won't they? They'll find a cure. They're not going to let millions of people die."

His voice was very flat. Dulled with weariness and defeat. "From what I've seen and heard, I get the idea they don't even know where to begin. It's all been too fast. Even if they came up with something now, I think it would be too late. When the dead start to outnumber the living, then the cities are going to be like open cesspits. Get out, Jen."

He made a determined move to the door, and she knew that there was no way she could stop him. He paused, then, with what was like a polite but vague afterthought, said, "I'm sorry about Pat."

She heard his footsteps on the sidewalk. Then they were gone. She stood motionless. It was too dark to see across the room, but even so she kept her eyes away from the bed. She remembered there was a candle in the cupboard. Feeling her way, she crossed the room. She found the matches and, by their light, the candle.

In twenty minutes she had changed her clothes and packed a small duffel bag with what she thought were essentials. When she was ready, she put the still-lighted candle on the small table and went out of the door. She had never once looked toward the bed.

Abby clutched at the kitchen door as she felt her legs begin to buckle. The fever surged through her, and she hung on waiting for the wave to pass. Her body ran with sweat. Great damp patches stuck the nightdress to her skin. Gape-mouthed, she sucked at the air. She lurched forward again, catching her hip against the corner of the table, feeling nothing. Barefooted, she took the steps that carried her to the sink unit. In the red blindness she felt for the glass on the draining board, caught it with her knuckles and sent it smashing to the floor. She turned the tap and, cupping her hand, scooped water into her mouth, splashing it into her face.

David's voice came from upstairs, calling her name. She heard nothing.

By the time he had lighted the candle and come down the stairs Abby had fallen to her knees, her head against the cool wood of the sink cupboard.

"Abby, what is it? Why didn't you wake me? What is it?" Swiftly he set the candle on the draining board and from behind slipped his hands under her arms to lift her. She cried out at the stabbing pain his touch brought. He half carried, half dragged her across to a chair. She fell across the table.

Her voice was only a whisper. "Oh, God. God. God. I feel terrible."

He felt helpless. Confused. On the edge of panic. He could think only to reach out and touch her face, and he was shocked by the hot wetness of her.

"Sit a minute. Just sit here."

Abby started to shiver. "I'm going to die." Her whole body quaked, and he realized she was crying. "I'm going to die."

He said, "Stop it. Just stop it. You're going to be all right."

Abby had started to slither sideways out of the chair.

David moved her so she was balanced again. He ran to the telephone and, lifting it, started to dial, then, remembering it wasn't working, let it fall to swing on its cord.

He caught Abby before she fell. She was unconscious. He picked her up awkwardly, badly, lifting her from a kneeling position.

Somehow he got her up the stairs and onto the bed. She lay quite still while he pulled the covers over her.

He was gasping as he pulled trousers and sweater over his pajamas. He moved back to Abby and shifted her head more comfortably onto the pillow, then hurried from the room.

It was after four in the morning. The rain had stopped. Stewart closed the cottage door quietly and started down the garden path. The Rolls was parked at the gate, and he climbed into the driving seat gratefully. He leaned his head back and closed his eyes. He had not known exhaustion like this in many years. He wanted to sleep. Right here and now in the car. He jerked his head forward and shook it hard. Roused, he leaned forward, opened the glove compartment and took out a flask. He gulped at the whiskey.

Headlights flashed in through the rear window, coming quickly closer and then halting behind the Rolls. He turned to squint against the glare but could see nothing. He heard a car door slam, and then his own passenger door opened, and David Grant looked in.

"Abby's got it, Joe. She's bad."

The doctor nodded. "I'll come," he said. "Just give me a minute."

David climbed in beside him and closed the door. "I've been driving all over looking for you. I went to your house. Couldn't get an answer."

The Scotsman stared through the windshield. He said, "Gladys died this afternoon."

"Oh, Christ! Oh . . . Joe, I'm sorry."

The doctor proffered the flask across the car. David took it gratefully.

"They're dying, David, and there's nothing I can do to help. I just go to them."

"I thought we might have missed the worst of it down here."

"I've had seventeen go tonight. Four of them, a whole family, went within the hour. God knows what it will be like in the morning. In another week. . . ." He left the sentence unfinished.

David prompted him. "Go on. In another week?"

"Och, well! I'm tired and maybe getting a wee bit fanciful, but the way it's going could see us with tens of millions of dead."

The two men stayed silent. Then David clicked the top on the flask and handed it back.

"Will you come and look at Abby?"

"Take your car. I'll follow you back."

David climbed out, and Joe pressed the starter.

Jenny crossed Battersea Bridge. The traffic still lay locked in long unmoving lines. Engines and lights switched off now, acknowledging defeat. Many cars had been abandoned, but in some, drivers still waited. Smoking. Sleeping.

There were few people on the streets, and those that Jenny saw were hurrying. They had destination and purpose. On the long steep hill up to Clapham Common a motorcyclist rode past her on the sidewalk.

From the high vantage of the Common she looked back. Somewhere north of the Thames was the glow of fire.

She reached Dulwich and could walk no farther. Parked near the college gates she found a car with its doors unlocked. She curled onto the backseat and fell asleep.

4

THE fever held Abby for three days and three nights. There were periods of consciousness through which she was only aware of pain.

When she wakened on the morning of the fourth day, she had no memory of time. She was limp, drained of all energy. She turned her head and saw the empty space in the bed beside her. The bedroom door was open. She tried to call her husband's name. Her voice croaked.

Abby pushed the covers back and swung her legs off the bed. She tried to stand. A rushing dizziness made her sit again quickly. When it was gone, she rose, swaying, holding onto the bedside table. As she moved, she saw the bed sheets where she had lain. They were stained with urine.

She was shocked by a view of herself in the full-length mirror. Saliva had caked into a brittle streak on her chin and cheek. Wisps of her hair had adhered to it. Her nightdress was soiled. Her face was drawn and thin. Her eyes were dark-ringed.

In the bathroom she stripped off the nightdress and turned on the hot water tap. She waited for the trickle of cold water to run warm. When it didn't, she damped a face cloth and began to clean herself.

David's bathrobe hung behind the door. She pulled it on

and started shakily for the stairs. As she reached the hall, she called his name again and received no answer. She went into the kitchen.

A pool of water surrounded the refrigerator like a moat. Cheeses left out on the table were fuzzed with gray fur.

Abby felt suddenly and desperately hungry. She went toward the bread bin. She saw and avoided the broken glass that littered the floor.

The wrapped loaf of bread was green with mold.

The drinks cupboard in the sitting room held a supply of cocktail biscuits and potato chips. She hurried into the room, rounding the big couch at its center. She rummaged through the cupboard shelves and found a box of salted biscuits. She began to stuff them into her mouth. Still eating, she stood up and touched the wilted flowers in the vase on the side table. Petals showered off.

Abby glanced at the big oval mirror above the fireplace. It reflected most of the room. It showed the couch. And lying on it, the body of her husband.

He lay on his side, his face toward the back of the couch. The lower part of his body was covered with a brightly colored traveling rug.

Abby pulled at his shoulder, turning him toward her. He twisted stiffly and, before she could hold him, slithered onto the floor. His face was cold to her touch.

She stayed beside the dead man for a long time. She felt aching loss. It was compounded with grief and fear and a growing awareness of her loneliness. Finally, she draped the blanket to cover David's face. Then she went upstairs and put on her clothes.

Abby pounded the door at the Edgertons' house. The electric bell wasn't working. When no answer came, she circled the other doors. They all were locked, and she could see nothing through the windows.

It was the same at the Crowleys'. At the third house she found the kitchen door unlocked. She knocked and waited and then went inside. There was no answer to her call, and she found no one in the downstairs rooms. As she started up the stairs, the smell drifted toward her. Sweet-stale and heavy. There was no need to do more than glance into the bedroom. Phyllis Debenham was on the bed curled in a tight fetal ball. Christopher Debenham lay face down on the floor, halfway between the bed and the door.

Abby started toward the village and then realized she would not have the strength to walk the distance. She went back to her own driveway and got into the Jaguar.

There were parked cars spaced along the length of the main village street. An ill-assorted group of dogs ran out from an alley at the sound of the Jaguar's engine. They watched warily as Abby halted the car in the middle of the street. She climbed out and looked around. The dogs were the only living things she could see. She listened to the silence. It echoed around her. Abby stared. Doors were closed. Shops shut.

Farther along the street an upstairs window banged open. A net curtain billowed out like an escaping specter. Abby called loudly.

"Hello. Is there anybody there?"

The window closed slowly, then swiftly banged open again in the breeze.

She put her hand into the car and pressed the horn ring. The long blast frightened the dogs, and they went racing out of sight into the alley.

Abby drove out of the village and turned left into an unpaved lane. Joe Stewart's Rolls stood skewed at an angle across the opening to the stable yard of his house.

Cruft, the Stewarts' big Alsatian, rose, growling, from where it lay beside the driver's door of the car, then, snarling, ran at a low crouch toward Abby as she began to climb out. She pulled her legs back in swiftly, slamming the door. The dog pawed at the window.

Abby angled the car and then reversed so that she was alongside the Rolls. The doctor was in the driver's seat. She could see only the gray hair. His head was slumped against the side window. She was glad his face was hidden.

Still leaping at the car, Cruft chased it out of the lane, then went back to sit guard for his dead master.

She halted the car and looked through the lych-gate along the path to the doors of the church. She had been married here, and Peter christened.

Her footsteps on the flint chippings echoed loud as she walked slowly forward. She turned the iron ring and pushed the door. She looked inside and then instantly turned and ran half the length of the path back to the gate. There were people in the church. In that fleeting look she could not identify them or tell how many. She knew only that they were dead.

She turned. Her eye followed the spire up to the pale blue of the October afternoon. The plea had grown inside her ever since she had reached the village and came now to her lips in terrified awe.

"Dear God, don't let me be the only one."

The cold water of the shower made Abby gasp and flinch. She shivered violently as she lathered her hair and body with soap. Like a flagellant, she bore the lashes of the icy jets. Then, gratefully, she toweled herself and went back into the bedroom. The two packed cases stood on the bed.

She lit the candle on the dressing table against the hurrying dusk, and by its light she combed out her hair. It was long, ending just beneath her shoulders. She started to cut. Close to the nape of her neck. Then the sides and front. When she had finished, there was no more than an inch or two left. Still wet, it lay tight on her scalp. She ruffled her fingers through it. The short hair made her face look even more gaunt. Abby shrugged, then began to dress. As she fastened the trousers, she felt the looseness of the waistband and realized how much weight she had lost. She pulled on the heavy sweater and then the suede jacket. When she was ready, she looked in the glass. Instinctively she reached for her lipstick. Then, realizing, put it back without using it.

The several journeys it took to pack the Granada Estate left her aching with exhaustion. She sat in the kitchen until she recovered. She'd taken most of the canned food out to the car but had left herself two tins. She opened them and ate their contents cold.

It was quite dark when she went back out to the car. She checked that everything was inside, then went up to the garage and picked up the pair of two-gallon gasoline cans.

She took them into the sitting room. Abby had dragged David's body nearer to the window. She had intended to make a grave for him in the garden. After the efforts of a few minutes she had realized that she had not the strength to move him, let alone fashion a grave. . . .

She didn't look at her husband until she had finished spreading the gasoline around the room. Then, standing over him, she said, "Good-bye, David."

She trickled what was left of the gasoline onto the hallway carpet, struck the match and ran to the front door. Before she reached it, she heard the whoof of the bursting flame.

Abby turned the Granada out of the driveway and accelerated hard up the steep slope of Ridge Road. The power steering helped the car around the climbing bends. Three miles later the road leveled out on the top of the ridge.

She slowed the car and stopped. She got out and stared down to the bottom of the valley. The funeral pyre was the only light in that whole distant black landscape.

In the car again she didn't look back as she drove off the ridge and down the other side. She drove swiftly. Peter's school was fifty miles off, and she wanted to get there quickly.

Jenny coughed in a long, racking staccato, her chest aching. This was her second night in the barn. The fire she'd made in the middle of the floor gave little warmth. She broke two squares from her last bar of chocolate. Tomorrow she would have to find proper food.

In her walk from London she had seen only one person—a man. He was asleep in a shelter roughly made from a sheet of plastic. When she had called to him, he had wakened and instantly run from her.

The bitter chocolate caught at her throat, and she began to cough again. When the spasm ended, her head was ringing. Through the ringing she heard the sound. It puzzled her at first, then she recognized it. A car engine.

Jenny ran to the door of the barn. The road lay about fifty yards ahead of her down a slope, and coming along it from the right was the flare of car headlights.

Jenny began to run. Shouting as she went. Waving. The car vanished behind the high hedges, but she could still see its aura of light. She ran. Ran. Desperate to intercept it.

She reached the field gate at the same instant the Granada raced by.

Jenny ran into the road. Shouting with all her strength. Running after the red taillights. Then faltering and slowing as they sped away from her.

Abby saw and heard nothing. She was intent only on the road ahead.

The school gates were closed, fastened at their center by an iron chain and padlock. A square of hardboard had been wired to the ornate bars. Stapled to it was a typewritten notice. The paper was wet. Limp and buckled. The letters smeared. Abby read:

> In an effort to limit the present influenza epidemic the school is closed to all visitors. Please contact the administration office by telephone.

The notice was signed by the headmaster.

Abby stared through the bars at the long straight drive. The night was dark, and she could see nothing of the school buildings. She moved back to the car and turned off the lights, then walked quickly along the road to the green wooden door that she knew led into the lodge garden. It was open, and she entered and followed the paved path that tracked around the house and through the hedge out to the driveway. She walked swiftly. At times she almost ran. Her legs ached. The long days of fever had drained her strength. By the time she reached the quadrangle she was wheezing, her body trembling with exhaustion.

There was no light from any of the buildings. The only

sound, her own gasping. Peter's dormitory was in Chartwell House, the block farthest from where she stood. Abby moved to it slowly. A sudden surge of fear erased the weariness, and she began to run.

The double glass-topped doors of the house were hooked open. The wind had driven rain into the hall, and the fiber matting at the entrance was soaked. She started up the stone stairs, leaving a trail of gradually fading wet footprints. The big windows on the first landing were propped open, a light, cold breeze shifting through them. It was the same on the second landing. Only when she turned along the corridor and out of the moving air did she catch the death smell. Abby retched and ran back to the window and thrust her head out to gulp at the clean, chill air. She stayed for minutes at the window, then turned and went quickly down to the door and into the dormitory. The curtains were closed, and she could see nothing. She had matches in her pocket and by the light of one of them saw the first bed. Mercifully someone had been in the room before her. The blankets had been drawn up over the face of the dead boy. At the foot of the bed was a wooden locker. On it an almost spent candle melted onto a saucer. With a second match Abby was able to light it. There was a neatly lettered card in the name slot on the locker: WILLIAM ROGERS.

Abby moved down the long dormitory, keeping the candle low, not wanting its light to reveal the huddled shapes beneath the blankets. She looked only at the name cards.

She had not been in the dormitory since last Open Day. It was after that that Peter had been promoted to junior prefect and moved his bed space. Abby reached the end of the room and crossed to the beds that lined the other wall. She moved, reading off the names. "John Peyton," "Timothy Brierly," "Phillip Hanwell," "Peter Grant."

Seeing her son's name made her speak it aloud. She said, "Peter." There was no delay. Fear there was, but no reluctance, no hesitation in lifting her eyes to look. The swift raising of the candle almost snuffed its flame; then, as its light steadied and grew again, she saw the bed was empty.

Abby began to shake. To steady herself, she had to press her knees against the locker and hold onto the rail at the foot of the bed. She recognized she was in shock. She had experienced it once before, after a near car accident. Then, as now, she had done what was required with calm, nerveless calculation. She had felt no fear as she used her driving skill to evade a violent collision. Only when she had stopped and climbed out to run back to the other car had the terror of the past moments struck her. Then she'd had to sit on the sidewalk edge, her arms pulled tightly around her drawn-up knees, desperately trying to still her quaking.

It was some minutes before she found the strength to walk from the dormitory. Going down the stairs, she needed the support of the iron banister. As she stepped out into the quadrangle, a confusion of alternatives fell on her like an ambush. The relief she had felt was swiftly whittled away by uncertainty. Was Peter in some other house? In another dormitory? Might he have been taken to the local hospital? Had he tried to reach home?

The sanitorium. If Peter had been among the first to show symptoms, he would have been taken to the sanitorium.

She crossed to the alleyway that led to the back of the school. Halfway along its length it opened onto a small paved square that fronted the science laboratory. As she drew level with it, she stopped. There was a light in one of the windows.

It was the soft yellow glow of a candle, but in this dark emptiness it gleamed like a beacon. Abby ran. The outer doors clattered as she pushed through. A thin vertical of light marked the inched-open door of the laboratory. She went in.

It was a long room. A double row of workbenches running its length. On them, complex arrangements of glass chemistry equipment reflected the candlelight from the far end of the room.

There was a sound. A faint humming noise made irregular by vague crackling like crumpling cellophane.

Abby didn't see the man until she had walked half the length of the room. He was in a chair. His body slumped forward onto a bench, his head resting on his folded arms. On a table beside him was a jumble of radio equipment—a haphazard arrangement of amplifiers, transmitters and receivers. Gentle static issued from a loudspeaker.

She said, "Can you help me? I'm looking for my son."

The man didn't move. Abby stepped closer. "Are you all right?" Then louder: "I'm looking for my son."

She stretched out a hand but withdrew it before it reached him. She knew he was dead.

She half turned to look toward the loudspeaker as it gave a more sustained crackle. She stared at it, willing a voice from it. Music. Some sound that would tell her she wasn't alone.

The touch, the slight pressure of the hand closing on her elbow made her gasp with fear. She spun around to stare into the face of the man.

"I'm sorry. I didn't mean to startle you. I'm sorry." He looked alarmed at Abby's fear.

She knew his face. She had met him on Open Days. His hands made a gesture of apology, and he said, "I'm sorry."

Desperately she tried to remember his name, and sensing her dilemma, he said "Emerson. Dr. Emerson."

Abby nodded, then found her voice. "I thought you were. . . ." She left the speech unfinished and went on, "I couldn't find anybody. I'm looking for my son."

"It's Mrs. Grant, isn't it?"

Abby affirmed it.

"I was always quite good at remembering parents' names."

Emerson pushed the chair toward Abby and indicated she should sit. He was in his early sixties. He wore a heavy brown tweed suit over a thick polo-neck sweater. His thinning hair was untidy, its dark color contrasting with the gray stubble of several days' growth of beard. He rubbed his eyes, still not fully wakened.

Abby said, "Peter is a third former. In Chartwell House. I went to the dormitory. He's not there."

Before she could go on, Emerson raised a hand to halt her. He dug into his coat pocket and took out a large hearing aid. It took him a moment to untangle the wire of the earpiece; then, putting it in position, he switched on. He looked apologetic. "I've had this wretched thing for nearly four years, and I still can't get used to it."

"Do you know what happened to Peter?" Abby found herself speaking more loudly.

"He went off with the group. There were about sixteen of the boys. Mr. Fielding went with them. Yes, he was with the group."

Abby stood up. "Then he's alive. Where is he? Where did he go? I want to find him."

Emerson's hands apologized again, then gestured for Abby to sit. When she didn't, he rose.

"Mrs. Grant. This was four, no, five days ago. The school had been hit very badly. Fielding thought he should get some of the boys away. The ones who were not showing symptoms."

She interjected. Her voice excited. Eager. "Peter was one of them. He was all right. Where did they go?"

Emerson shrugged. "I don't know. Please sit down, Mrs. Grant. I find the effort of standing a little too much at the moment."

When they were both seated, he said, "Fielding's idea was to find a place where they could isolate themselves. They took camping equipment. Food. He thought if they could get into the country, make no contact with anybody, they'd be better off. It seemed sensible. It seemed the only thing to do." He paused for a moment, collecting his thoughts, finding a way to say what he must say. He adopted a practiced parent-teacher voice.

"Mrs. Grant, it would be very wrong of me to offer too much hope. There was no certainty that the boys who went off in the group weren't already infected. Any or all of them might have contracted it a little later than the others."

Abby said, "But there is a chance."

He took a second too long in answering. In that second Abby felt her hope and excitement begin to fade.

"I can only judge chance by what I've seen here. It came so fast. One day it was just a few boys; then, forty-eight hours later, it seemed half the school was down. Some of the older boys went off—trying to get home. A few more were collected by their parents. But all that was before the real peak of the outbreak. For those that remained, over three hundred, I'm the only one left."

Awed, Abby said, "All of them?"

There was something of defiance in Emerson's voice as he repeated, "I'm the only one left."

They talked sporadically through what was left of the night. Emerson told how, by the end, he alone was untouched by the disease. The last to die was a nine-year-old boy. Together they had gone around the dormitories covering the dead. Finally, the boy was taken by fever and died within half a day.

Abby stared at the windows. The sky was lightening. She was reluctant to make any move to leave. She justified her staying by convincing herself it was sensible to wait until full light.

There was a sudden louder surge of the cellophane crackle from the speaker that took their attention, Emerson reached to flick a main switch. The background noise died.

"Batteries are all but gone," he said. "Nobody sending, anyway." He indicated the set to Abby. "The boys built this, you know. It's very good. We used to talk to radio hams all over the world."

"Lately?" Abby asked. "Have you talked with any of them lately? Did you tell them what was happening here?"

"At the beginning. Most nights I put out our call sign. Finally, there was nobody left to answer. I was able to tell them what was happening here, and it was the same for them. Everywhere the same. All across the world." Idly he turned the tuning dial on the silent receiver. "The boys used to listen to police calls sometimes. Aircraft, too. There are official bands as well. I heard some of the reports. There *was* a state of emergency declared, but it came much too late. There was nobody left to implement it. The administrators died along with the rest of them. I'm glad I wasn't in a city. It was bad here. But in a city . . . ." His voice trailed away.

They were silent for a little while, and then, without looking at him, Abby said, "What's going to happen?"

"I've thought about that a good deal. Those of us who have come through—and God knows, from what we've both seen, there can't be many of us—well, in some way, we're biological freaks. Random samples. We have survived by pure chance. We've been left to face the aftermath of this sickness, and it will be more terrible than you can imagine. A real survivor is the one who can come through what must follow now."

Abby was surprised. She had not projected much beyond the future hour. "Terrible? Will it be that bad? I mean, there's food. There must be millions of tons of preserved foods. Clothes, cars, petrol. Everything. Surely, the stockpile of 'things' is enormous."

"Yes-yes-yes-yes-yes." Emerson's voice took on a tetchy schoolmaster-note. The impatient sound of a teacher halted in mid-lecture by a question he considered foolish. "Of course there would be enough for many, many years. Though, incidentally, I'm not convinced that the food would last all that long. But the point is that whilst we live on the debris of civilization, we would simply be scavenging. And scavenging from a constantly diminishing supply. The only real future is in learning again. Learn the old crafts and skills. Teach them to the children so that they can tell the next generation. Learning is what is important."

He glanced around quickly. His eye settled on the still-burning candle. His finger jabbed toward it. "Could you make that?" he demanded. "What's it made from? Where do you get the raw material?"

Her voice showed her uncertainty. "It's an oil product, isn't it? Paraffin wax? And before that, tallow. Animal fat."

"But could you make it?" His finger was jabbing toward

her now. "Something as simple as a candle. Make it from scratch?"

"I could find how to. It will be in a book somewhere."

"That's right. You'll have to learn it." There was something of triumph in making his point. He hurried on, the enthusiasm smoothing the weariness from his voice. He moved quickly to a workbench and picked up a glass test tube. "Look at that. We've been making things of glass for thousands of years. But could you make it? It's silica, potash, high temperature and a great deal of skill. Don't you see, our civilization has the benefit of knowledge that has been accumulated since the beginning of time, and yet most of us are less practical than Iron Age man."

She felt that she was on trial. That she had to defend herself, deny her ignorance. She answered back with a tone that was usually reserved for political discussion after a well-wined dinner party. "But all the information is there for us. We shan't have to discover anything."

He hardly heard her. "A carpenter. He doesn't fell the trees. He doesn't forge the steel for his tools. Could he make a saw? A plane? Nails?" The old man stopped suddenly. The excitement that had galvanized him seemed to drain away. He sat down again, and his shoulders hunched. When he spoke, he was gentler. Softer. "I'm sorry, Mrs. Grant. It was a hobbyhorse even before this. It's incredible, isn't it? We are of the generation that landed a man on the moon, and we talk about the difficulty of making a candle. What you called the 'stockpile of things' will merely allow a little breathing space. Perhaps several generations. But in that time all the skills must be learned. We must learn."

Abby said nothing. After a few seconds she glanced toward the window. She could see the building across the courtyard clearly now. It was light enough. Time for her to go. She stood up.

"I must try and find Peter."

Emerson nodded, "I hope you can." He stood up and stretched out his hand.

Abby took it. "What will you do?"

He shrugged. "I don't know. Stay here for a little while."
He pointed at the hearing aid. "I have two more batteries
for this. I suppose I might find some more. After that I'll be
almost totally deaf. I won't make a very good survivor.
Good-bye, Mrs. Grant."

5

THE wind worked against the tide, chopping the sea into brief white-topped waves. Seabirds hovered and banked on the gusting updrafts from the chalk cliffs. The drizzling overcast obscured the distant French coast.

About a thousand yards from the shore the helicopter started to rise, gaining altitude to lift it over the cliff top, the clatter of its rotors sending the gulls shrieking away in alarm.

It swept inland, still picking up height, banked left over the Dover ferry terminal and harbor, then swung to the right across the town, tracking the main road.

Greg Preston piloted the machine with the concentration of uncertainty. With only four hours of instruction behind him no control came naturally or casually to his hand. His body was tense, straining against the harness. His neck was stiff and aching, his head thrust forward like that of a man driving a car through fog.

He wore a sheepskin coat over a thick sweater and heavy trousers, but despite them, he felt cold. Today was his thirty-second birthday.

He allowed his eyes away from the instruments for a brief second to glance down at the town.

The streets were lined with motionless cars. There was no sign of any human life.

Dover fell away behind him as he tracked the A2 road, swinging with it right and left as it snaked through wooded country, taking no shortcuts lest he should lose it.

Only when Canterbury Cathedral loomed ahead of him did he deviate from the road, banking left a little, knowing that he could now easily locate the London motorway.

The helicopter clattered over the empty main street of Boughton and on to the traffic circle that marked the junction of the Thanet Way.

The oiled highway made its gentle curves through neat orchards and hop fields. Greg saw movement on the road ahead. As he drew closer, he allowed himself a long look away from the instruments and out through the side window of the cabin.

A hundred or more sheep were wandering aimlessly across both lanes of the road, grazing on the banks and central reservation.

At the high stilted bridge that spanned the valley, Greg eased the helicopter left and up to cross Detling Hill. Maidstone and the great spreading Weald of Kent lay before him. It took him several seconds to realize why it looked different. There was no smoke.

He swung right along the ridge of the hill, watching now more carefully for landmarks. He was almost there.

Abby lay curled across the rear seat of the Granada. She slept deeply, fully dressed and with two blankets wrapped tightly around her.

The sound disturbed her. The heavy beating throb was growing louder. She opened her eyes. The light in the car was diffused by the heavily misted windows. She pulled a hand free from the blankets and smeared a view through the moist glass. Then suddenly she knew the sound: a helicopter.

She swung her feet down, impeded by the binding blankets. She threw the door open. Half crawling, half falling onto the wet grass of the road verge. The helicopter was directly above her, the rotors stirring the branches of the hedge. She kicked herself clear of the blankets and ran onto the crown of the road, waving both arms.

But the machine had already passed. It threshed on, leaving its sound for many seconds after it had vanished behind a stand of trees.

Abby stayed motionless in the middle of the road until the sky was silent again. Then, when it was evident that she had not been seen and that the helicopter wasn't coming back, she returned to the car. She picked up the blankets and began to fold them.

Greg made a textbook landing on the rough tufted grass of the pasture. He switched off the power and leaned back in his seat, his eyes closed. He didn't move until the rotors had totally stopped. Then, wearily, he unclipped his harness and stepped out. The long exposure to the noise and vibration, the tension, had left him unsteady on his legs. The new silence made his head feel muzzy. He closed his nose with thumb and forefinger and blew hard. His ears popped, and he heard the natural sounds around him with a clarity that was almost painful.

He looked across at the cottage. The Toyota was parked on the driveway. He felt a nudge of annoyance. "Why the hell can't she put it away in the garage?" he thought. It was always the first thought he had when he came home.

Then, quickly, he moved down to the stile, across the lane and up to the front door. As he searched his pockets for the key, he tried to peer through the translucent glass square that ornamented the door. He could see the shape of the hallway. The stairs. Nothing moved inside.

He found the key and was about to insert it in the lock when he hesitated. In the ten days since he had understood the scale and severity of the sickness, he had thought only of how he could reach his home, not of this moment of finding what was inside.

With a determined gesture he put the key in position and turned it.

The hallway felt damp and cold. All the downstairs doors were closed. Greg called, directing his voice up the stairs.

"Jeannie!" Then again at the closed doors of the ground floor. "Jeannie!" No one answered.

He moved to the living-room door and opened it. In the hearth were the ashes of a long-dead fire. On the rug in front of it was the body of a girl, a cushion from the settee under her head, a fur coat draped across her legs. Her left arm was fully stretched, the fingers of the hand locked into a claw that death had not relaxed.

Greg thought, "Thank God her eyes aren't open." He crossed to her and dropped to his knees. He seemed to focus on her diamond-and-sapphire engagement ring and the ornamented gold wedding ring beneath it. The metal and stones seemed to have taken on a greater luster against the gray tinge of the flesh.

There was an uncapped bottle of aspirin beside Jeannie. A decanter half filled with whiskey. A glass lay on its side. Its contents had spilled out and now, having dried, stained the carpet.

It seemed clear to Greg what had happened. Too weak to get upstairs and cold with the fever, she had lain here beside the fire. Whiskey and aspirin were the only medicine either of them had ever used. Their regular cure-all.

Greg wondered why he didn't feel more. No shock. No grief. Perhaps he had seen too many dead in the last few days.

He reached forward, drew the fur coat up to cover her face and then rose. He stared down at her and said out loud, "I was wrong, Jeannie. I thought you were the sort of bitch who would survive just to spite me."

He left the room quickly, picked up the car keys from the hall table and went through the front door.

Even with full choke it took a few minutes to start the car. Then it fired, and Greg pulled it out of the drive and turned left. He covered more than a mile before he wondered where he was going.

Abby spread her top coat on the grass, then, kneeling on it, pulled off her sweater. The quick chill of the wind made her shoulders hunch. She stooped forward and, cupping her hands, scooped water from the brimming stream. Its impact on her face and neck made her gasp aloud. A trickle of water ran down her spine and made her throw back her shoulders in shock. After the third scoop of water she was so numbed by the cold that it seemed less painful.

Her cheeks glowing from the splashing, she gratefully toweled her face and pulled the sweater on. Growing warm again, she felt refreshed and fully awake.

She moved back to the little fire she had built to heat the can of soup. The sides of the saucepan were soot-blackened. There was an unenthusiastic glow at the base of the piled damp twigs but no flame. Abby cautiously dipped the tip of her finger into the soup. It was cold.

Half a mile down the same stream Jenny cupped water into her mouth. As she raised her head, she saw the smoke: a thin white streamer lifting from behind a scrubby copse of saplings. She felt a quick lurch of excitement. There was somebody else. She snatched up her bag and looked left and right along the stream, searching for a place to cross. She ran down to the shallows and, uncaring, splashed ankle-deep across the shingle. The ground rose in a gentle billow toward the copse. She was panting hard when she reached the brier entanglements that fenced the trees. Pushing through the overgrowth, she felt a rush of panic as she lost sight of the smoke. She crashed and blundered through the whipping branches and out into the open again where the ground fell away, then rose again to another ridge. "Just over that hill," Jenny thought. She forced herself on, like a marathon runner coming in sight of the finishing post. The smoke beckoned her on.

It was just ahead now. A fold in the ground still hid the source of the fire, but she was almost there. Another twenty yards. And then she saw it.

Unable to resist any longer, the twigs had taken flame and were burning with a reluctant crackle. Above the sound of her own breathless gasping, Jenny heard the receding sound of a car engine.

Total despair draped over her like a cloak. Stiff-legged, she paced out the last few yards and stood beside the fire, feeling nothing of its warmth.

Greg slammed at the brake and swung the wheel hard right. He felt the tail of the car come around as the skid took control. The tires on the locked back wheels gave a Grand Prix scream as they left five thousand miles of their life scrawled on the tarmac. When the car finally halted, it had made a complete circle and was facing back the way it had come.

The woman who had caused the violent stop had thrown herself back against the hedge. Greg could hardly believe he had missed her. She had seemed to appear from nowhere. Bursting onto the road just a few yards ahead of him.

He clambered from the car, his concern quickly turning to anger as he saw the woman was unhurt. As she started toward him, he began to shout. "What the hell do you think you're doing! I had no chance—you just ran. . . " But before he could rise into full righteous flow, she stopped him with the desperate urgency of her voice.

"You've got to help me. I can't do anything by myself. The tractor turned over. He's pinned underneath. I can't get him free. Come with me, please. Please. . . . It's up that lane." She pointed to the concealed gap in the high hedge from which she had appeared.

Before Greg could question her, she had run around to the passenger seat and was climbing into the car. Greg was briefly aware that he was being given no choice in the matter. The woman's demand for help had dramatic insistence that stemmed from the reality of her need. But there was something more in her voice: a command and assurance that she would be obeyed.

"Be quick," she said as he started the car. Greg steered onto a potholed muddy track. There was a signpost that announced: THREADMAN QUARRIES—PRIVATE. The car lurched as the front wheel sank in a deep crater. Greg slowed down, weaving a route between the worst of the holes.

The woman said, "You'll have to hurry. I tried to move him, but he's in terrible pain."

"What happened?"

"We'd just unhitched the trailer. He was turning it, and it just went over. Over on its side."

"Your husband?"

"No."

While watching the track Greg managed a few sidelong looks at his passenger. He thought she must be about twenty-eight. Very attractive. On his second look he realized what it was that seemed strange about her. Her hair was neatly combed and positioned. Her makeup was so skillfully applied that it was scarcely discernible, but the long black eyelashes were evidently false. She wore a sealskin coat and beneath it a beautifully tailored pantsuit.

"What the hell is she doing dressed like that in the middle of nowhere?" Greg thought, then immediately felt uneasy at his own grubby unkemptness.

She turned to him suddenly. "By the way, I'm Sarah Boyer."

"Greg Preston."

They said nothing more until the track started downward between the limestone walls of a cutting. Then they were in the quarry, surrounded by its carved cliffs.

Narrow-gauge rail lines ran up to a shed of corrugated iron. Rusting hoppers and machinery littered the area. Off to one side was a long low wooden hut with a notice above its door announcing "Site Office." Caked limestone dust had settled on everything, giving the whole place a cast of white. A grubby frosting.

Greg saw the tractor at once. The bright red of its paintwork was like a pool of blood on the quarry floor. He sped the car toward it. Almost before he had stopped, Sarah climbed out and ran across to the man who lay pinned beneath the machine.

Greg started to follow, then turned back to the trunk of

the car. He lifted out the wheel jack and the winding brace.

Sarah knelt beside the injured man. She glanced at Greg as he joined her.

"He's unconscious."

"Probably as well." Greg lay on his side and pushed his arm beneath the tractor, feeling for the point where the main weight lay. The contorted leg was crushed for its entire length. No clearance above it. Its violent angle disagreed totally with the natural line of the body. When Greg pulled his hand back, it was wet with blood.

Greg said, "Jesus Christ!" Then, quickly, he found a rigid point on the chassis and shoved the car jack beneath it, hammering it into position with his fist. When it was solidly in place, he started to crank quickly. It took several turns before the tractor edged fractionally upward.

Sarah said, "It's lifting."

Greg nodded. "Let me get another inch or so. . . . Get your hands under his arms and try to ease him back."

Sarah positioned herself behind the man's head and started to pull.

"Wait! Wait a minute! It's not clear yet." Greg's arm worked like a piston. He gained another inch of height. "Try now."

Sarah heaved at the man's shoulders, and he slithered backward. Greg moved to help her, and between them they hauled him out and clear of the tractor. In the same moment the jack angled over, and the big machine crunched to the floor.

The right trouser leg was heavily stained with blood midway between knee and hip. From the inward angle of the feet it was obvious that both legs were broken in more than one place.

Sarah said, "Can we get him up to the hut? There's a bed there."

"Get the backseat from my car. It'll do as a stretcher."

She ran to the car. Greg tentatively tried to straighten the left leg. The flesh around the ankle had ballooned into a livid swelling. He expected the foot to be limp, but it resisted his gentle efforts to turn it, staying firmly locked in the unnatural line. Greg's mouth was set in a permanent wince as he started to unlace the heavy boot.

Sarah laid the car seat on the ground, and between them they eased the injured man onto it. The seat was too short, and lifting and balancing were difficult. Greg backed toward the door of the hut, taking small shuffling steps. Sarah's face showed the strain of carrying the heavy man. She shifted her grip, and the seat canted slightly. Greg jerked to correct the balance.

"Careful! You'll have him off."

"It's cutting into my fingers."

He elbowed the door open and edged inside. Between them they maneuvered alongside the bed and tilted the man onto it.

Gasping, Greg straightened up. The inside of the hut astonished him. Apart from the bed and a small table with two chairs, the space was almost totally filled from floor to ceiling with an incredible assortment of goods. It was like a supermarket warehouse: cartons of food, paper sacks of flour, cardboard cases, bottles, jars, plastic containers. There was an enormous heap of clothes. Several sporting guns stood propped in a corner. Glistening new boots, shoes and Wellingtons made another untidy heap. Before Greg could mentally catalogue the hoard, his attention was taken by a low groan. He glanced back to the man on the bed. His eyes were still closed, but his head was moving back and forth on the pillow.

Sarah said, "I think he's coming around."

Greg made a sweeping gesture that encompassed the stores. "Do you have any drugs amongst this lot? Some sort of painkiller?"

She shook her head.

"Spirits, then, Brandy? Whiskey?"

"In the trailer. We picked some up on the last trip."

"Get it. He'll need something. If he really becomes conscious, he's going to be in agony."

Sarah started away. Before she reached the door, Greg said, "Scissors. Do you have any scissors?"

Sarah pulled one of the chairs from the table and stood

on it to reach up to a cardboard carton at the top of a pile. She lifted out three of them before she found what she wanted, then handed down a smaller box.

Greg opened it. There were a dozen pairs of kitchen scissors. Each on a stiff plastic display card. He pulled one free and set about cutting the trouser leg on the injured man.

"Get the spirits."

Sarah went out to the trailer. She pulled back the tarpaulin sheet, uncovering a cargo of boxes and bags. She clambered onto the trailer to sort among the cartons. It took her several minutes to locate the bottles. She checked the labels, selecting some single-year brandy and some malt whiskey. She picked out two of each, then, almost as an afterthought, added a bottle of Dom Pérignon. Climbing down from the trailer, one of the malt bottles slipped from under her arm and shattered on the ground. She gave it no more than the briefest uncaring glance and walked back to the hut.

The man on the bed looked obscenely comic. The upper part of his body still clothed in a heavy jacket, pullover and shirt; then, from the waist down, naked. The damage to the left leg seemed to be below the knee. The entire length of the right leg was blackened and swollen. Blood from the open wound was seeping onto the blankets.

Sarah said, "How bad is he?"

"Bad. The bone has pushed out through the skin. Both ankles are done in. God knows how many oher breaks there are. It's hard to tell under all the swelling. I don't know what the hell we do about it."

"Splints or something," Sarah said vaguely. "You bind splints on breaks, don't you? I'm afraid I don't know much about first aid."

"He needs a damn sight more than first aid. The breaks have to be reset. It's more than I can cope with. First thing to do is stop the bleeding. A tourniquet, I suppose. I'll need cotton wool and bandages. Have you got some?"

"Somewhere." Sarah started searching among the boxes again.

After twenty minutes Greg had done all he was capable of. With Sarah's halfhearted help he stripped the stained blankets from the bed. She brought new ones from the trailer and ripped them from their polythene wrappers while Greg removed the man's upper clothing. When he was finished, he moved across to a chair and slumped into it. He picked up the brandy bottle.

"I think I could use one of these myself."

Sarah found some glasses, and while Greg poured himself a treble measure, she struggled to uncork the Dom Pérignon. Since Greg's arrival she had gradually become less concerned with the injured man, allowing Greg the responsibility for his welfare. Now she seemed almost disinterested.

"What's his name?" Greg nodded toward the bed.

"Vic. I don't think he ever told me his other name. I met him about a week ago. We sort of teamed up."

Greg gulped the brandy, enjoying its smooth bite. Then he said, "Did you lose anybody?"

"My father and my brother. There were just the three of us. I had a couple of days when I felt really awful. I stayed in bed. Daddy had sent the servants away, so there was nobody to look after me. Then, when I felt a bit better and could go downstairs, I found them both. Do you know, I'd never seen a dead person before." She pushed the champagne bottle across to Greg. "Could you open that? It's a bit tight."

He twisted the cork, and the warm wine bubbled over his wrist. He handed it back. She poured some into a glass and sipped it.

"It's not cold. Champagne is disgusting if it's not cold." She added a measure of brandy to the glass, then tasted it again. "That's better." Casually she asked, "What about you?"

"My wife died."

"I'm sorry. Were you with her?"

He shook his head. "I was in Holland. I'm an engineer. I've been working on the Maas reclamation."

"Was it bad there?"

Nodding, he said, "It was slow at first. Just a few people

sick. . . . We all thought it was some kind of influenza bug. Then it came all of a rush. They started dying. I mean, hundreds of them. Everybody seemed to be sick. Nothing happened to me. I was all right."

Sarah looked toward the bed. "It was the same for him. Everybody he knew died, and he wasn't even touched."

Greg said, "In the beginning we tried to bury the dead. Me and a couple of others who were still on their feet. We were using the big bulldozers. Just trying to scoop out trenches and cover the bodies over. But by the end of the week there were too many, and I was the only one left. There was nothing I could do."

"How did you get back?"

"There was a company helicopter. I saw Rotterdam burning. Just miles and miles of fire. I suppose something happened at one of the refineries. Oil storage tanks were going off like bombs. I've never seen anything like it. I came down the coast almost as far as Calais. I saw no traffic. No people. I had to land at Ostend for fuel. That's the only place I saw anybody. A man with two children. I tried to talk to them, but they wouldn't let me get near. Kept moving away. I suppose they thought I might be carrying the disease. I had to wait a day and night for the weather to calm down; then I came across the Channel." He shrugged, ending his narrative.

Sarah emptied her glass, then refilled it with equal parts of brandy and champagne. She said, "Where were you going when I stopped you?"

"Nowhere. Just driving."

There was a long silence that was broken when Vic gave a sharp groan of pain.

Greg stirred himself and stood up. "We'd better do something about getting splints on him before he wakes up properly."

Sarah didn't move. She said, "I suppose so. You'll probably be able to find everything you need somewhere amongst this lot."

The Rolls-Royce Corniche stood parked in the middle of

the village street. The top was down, the driver's door open. Frank Sinatra's voice blasted at full volume from the speakers of the eight-track stereo. The car was opposite a shop that proclaimed itself to be "R. Moodey and Son—Gentlemen's Outfitters."

Inside the shop Tom Price had stripped down to his grubby vest and pants. He pulled on the crisp new shirt, then, still buttoning it, moved to the rail of suits. He chose a two-piece in light gray flannel, nodding approvingly at the £60 price tag. When he was finally dressed in it, he admired himself in the full-length mirror. The suit gave nothing of its respectability to the man.

He went back to the rail and picked out another half dozen suits from the same size range. With these draped over his arm he scooped up the ten boxed shirts he had already selected and went out to the car.

Price was pleased with himself. This new world had become a vast department store where everything was free.

In the first days of the aftermath he had been nervous, choosing only small isolated shops and then only daring to enter them when he had watched for two or three hours to be certain there was no sign of life. In the beginning he had taken only what he needed, quickly collecting cans of food and drink that remained unconsumed until he had put a safe distance between himself and the shop. Later his scavenging had become more daring. Like a leisured shopper, he made his selections carefully. Sometimes he would eat his meal in the shop, choosing his first course and then browsing through the stock to find the next. He had one bad experience when he broke into a shop with living quarters above it. The stench from the dead had driven him quickly back out to the roadway. After that he concentrated only on lockup shops. For two full days he had stayed in an off-license shop, reelingly drunk for the whole time. Price covered a wide area in his foraging, and it never occurred to him to use a car. He had nowhere to go and was in no hurry. He stayed mostly on country roads, sleeping in barns and outbuildings. Perhaps because there were so few dead to be seen in the open or in public places, it had taken him some time to fully realize the scale of the disaster. He had seen bodies in cars and had twice found dead people in tents pitched in open fields. But for the most part the victims seemed to have died under cover.

The Rolls was in the showroom window of a garage near Sevenoaks. He stood and admired it through the plate glass; then, as he walked away, he realized that it was his simply for the taking.

He jimmied the door and walked around the car, respectfully stroking the paintwork. He climbed in behind the wheel, and as the car conferred its importance upon him, he sat more stiffly upright. His confidence grew as he accustomed himself to the switches and controls.

After opening the showroom doors, he drove out onto the forecourt. He saw himself reflected in the span of the big windows of the garage. He giggled. Then, his Welsh ancestry strong in his voice, he shouted loudly.

"Damn! Look at that! There's old Pricey in a bloody Rolls-Royce!"

He drove for miles over empty roads, reveling in his new status. It was then that he decided he needed new clothes to complete his image. He circled the area until he found a village where the death smell was barely evident.

Staggering slightly under the weight of his new wardrobe, Price went back out to the car. On the sidewalk he halted sharply. A girl was standing motionless beside the Rolls.

He felt a sudden wave of fear. Nervous and guilty at being seen in the act of looting.

"What do you want?" he said sharply.

Jenny shrugged. "You're the first person I've seen. I've been on my own for more than a week. I think it's a week. A long time. I haven't spoken to anybody."

She seemed so unsure of herself, so helpless and vulnerable, that Price felt his confidence returning. His voice took on a more aggressive note.

"I've seen a few people. Didn't let them see me, though. I'm staying away from them. I don't want their germs. I don't want to go catching nothing. I'm not mixing with nobody. Now go on! Clear off!"

Price advanced and dumped the clothes onto the backseat. Jenny didn't move.

He said, "You take a tip from me, miss. You keep away from people, and you'll be all right. Just stay away until the doctors get this all cleared up."

"There aren't any doctors! They died along with all the others! There's noboby left to clear things up!"

"But that's only here, isn't it?" He gave a series of sage nods that implied special information. "The Yanks will have something, don't you worry. Like in the war. They sent us stuff then. We've only got to hang on a bit, and the Yanks'll fix us up." He moved to climb into the driver's seat.

She put her hand on the car as though to hold it back. "You said you'd seen some people. How many?"

He started the engine. "Four. Six. I don't know. Now come on. Get away from there. I'm going."

She felt the car edge forward beneath her hand. She gripped the top of the door and moved with it. "Take me with you! Please, take me with you!" She found herself starting to run beside the car as it picked up speed. She shouted, "Please! I don't want to be by myself anymore."

As the pace quickened, she was forced to release her hold. Her momentum carried her along for a few more paces.

Halting, she stood and watched the car until it was out of sight, then turned and walked slowly back to the clothing shop. For a few minutes, hope had driven out the weariness and despair. Now they returned to her awareness. She was no longer hungry. Only tired. Desperately tired and cold.

In the shop she lifted overcoats and suits from the rails and piled them in a corner to make a bed. She draped coats over her feet and shoulders. But still, she couldn't sleep.

Abby stared as she drove past the army transport depot. A fence of wire mesh lined the road. Beyond it were the neat ranks of trucks. There were shrouded guns, searchlight vehicles, half-tracks and armored cars. The tools of war. And for the first time she wondered if she was a survivor of a war. Had The Death, as she now thought of it, been the victory? Had the virus that brought it been the weapon?"

Sarah stood with her hands pressed over her ears, trying to muffle Vic's screams.

Greg was sweating, doggedly binding the splints into position. He tried to keep his eyes from Vic's face, not wanting to see the agony he could hear. As gently as he could, he eased the left foot forward and turned it back into its natural position. Vic shrieked, the sound ripping his throat.

Sarah turned and ran from the hut.

As he finished the bandages, the screams turned to gasping sobs, Vic weaving in and out of consciousness. There was blood on his lip where he had bitten through the skin. Greg took a cloth to wipe it away.

"Can you hear me?" he asked.

Vic's eyes flickered, and he turned his head a fraction. Greg spoke slowly and distinctly.

"That's about as much as I can do. God knows if it's enough."

The injured man tried to speak, but no words came. Greg wiped his face again and said, "Do you want a drink?"

There was a movement of the head that Greg took to be a nod. He poured some Malvern water into a glass and held it to Vic's mouth. He made an attempt to swallow, but most of it trickled down his chin. His voice, when it did come, was grating and forced.

"It hurts like hell. It hurts. It hurts."

The words Greg spoke sounded as helpless as he felt. "I'm sorry. I don't know what else I can do."

A new spasm of pain seemed to advance over Vic, drowning his voice as it enveloped him.

"Oh, Jesus Christ, it hurts. It hurts. It hurts. It hurts." And the words became grunts, and he sobbed into grateful unconsciousness.

Greg went outside.

Sarah was standing beside the still-laden trailer. She had torn open a large carton of cigarettes. The individual package from a two-hundred container lay scattered at her feet. She proffered the started package to Greg.

"You want one of these?"

He took one, and she flicked her lighter. It gave a small flame, and she said, "We'll have to put gas-lighter fuel on our next list. Remind me, will you?" And then: "Is he going to get better?"

"I don't know. But if he lives, he's going to be crippled. He might be able to get around on crutches or something. I just don't know. It's the wound that worries me most. What if it goes gangrenous?"

Sarah made a small movement with her shoulders that seemed to disclaim knowledge or concern. She took a final puff at her cigarette and dropped it on the ground, then drew another one from the package. She said, "It's going to be like this from now on, isn't it?"

"What do you mean?"

She lit the cigarette. "Accidents. Even little things. A bad cut. Burns. They'll become really serious."

"I hadn't thought about it. I suppose there'll be some people left. I mean, ones with medical knowledge. Nurses . . . some doctors."

Sarah said, "Even if there were doctors, how much could they do? Oh, all right, perhaps set bones, put in stitches and things like that. But all they ever do nowadays is diagnose and overspecialize. Most of the time they depend on drugs. There'll be none of those."

"I think you're being a bit pessimistic. Somebody who has worked in medicine is bound to be able to make up a few things."

"I doubt it. Not even a pharmacist would be able to do too much. I mean, really starting from scratch. All their raw materials are supplied. Manufacturing drugs is a huge industrial process. I tell you, God help us if we get something as simple as a toothache."

Greg stayed silent. He had no wish to investigate the future. Most of his life had been dominated by forward thinking. Working hard at school to pass the exams that would get him a good job that in turn would provide for the future. Insurance policies. Savings. Mortgage. Installment plans. Always for something ahead. He had taken on all the traditional responsibilities with a reluctance slightly less demanding than the pressures that made him conform. His strong need to be liked had made him courteous and polite. Rather than offend, he succumbed to what others thought was best for him. He seldom had the courage to rise to anger. As a result, he had been known as a "very nice boy," then later as a "pleasant young man" and now as "solid and reliable." Marriage to Jeannie had added to his burden, and she had forced her ambitions through him. When he had seen Jeannie lying dead in their home, he had felt that burden lift from him. In this new world he was alone. Responsible to no one. No need to plan. No need to go anywhere or do anything.

Sarah said, "I really think we will have to look after ourselves. Take care of our health. Things could be very hard otherwise."

"It'll be hard anyway, won't it?"

She looked surprised. "Oh, it needn't be. Different, perhaps. But not all that hard. Living may not be gracious, but it can be comfortable. There's an abundance of everything. One way or another I'm going to make damn sure I get my full share."

Greg felt that this might be a good moment to make his farewell. There was no more he could do for Vic, and he wanted to be away from this confident, demanding woman. Before he could speak, she glanced up at the sky and said, "I think it might rain. We'd better get this stuff inside."

She selected a small box from the trailer and started for the hut. After a few moments Greg picked up a sack of flour and followed her.

It was dark, and the rain was beating loudly on the roof of the site office. Earlier Sarah had suggested that she would prepare a meal while Greg finished unloading the trailer. It had taken him the best part of an hour. Sarah had opened a can of cooked ham and a packet of Ryvita. As an afterthought she added some pineapple chunks from a six-pound catering can.

Now, the plates empty, they sat at the table drinking brandy. A paraffin lamp circled them with light, the shadows beyond the glow discreetly hiding Vic who now slept.

Their conversation had been spasmodic, filled with long pauses. Sarah seemed to have accepted the fact that Greg had moved in as a permanent guest. She remained totally unaware of his unease. She yawned, then said, "We'll have to get some more beds. There are plenty at the warehouse where we found that one." She waved a hand toward where Vic lay, without ever looking at him. "I'm sure we can make do tonight. There are lots of blankets and pillows. I'll make out a list in the morning. I'd like to get some books. I like reading, don't you? Anyway, I think the three of us might get very bored with one another if we don't have some other interests."

Sarah's reference to the three of them seemed to give Greg the opportunity for which he had been waiting.

"Look, Sarah. Well, you and Vic seem to have got yourselves pretty well set up here. But I intend—"

Before he could finish, Sarah interjected, "It's not bad, is it? Vic chose it. He said it was isolated and easy to defend. And there's plenty of storage space in the other sheds. A bit like camping out, at the moment, but given a little time, I'm sure we can make it very comfortable."

Vic gave a long whimpering sigh. He stirred in his sleep. The sigh became a groan. Greg looked toward the bed and then at Sarah. She ignored the sound and concentrated on recharging the glasses.

Greg moved to the bed and wiped Vic's face with a moist cloth. He adjusted the blankets and waited until Vic calmed and fell into sleep again.

Sarah lit two cigarettes and handed one to Greg. She said, "Can you cook? I'm awful at it. Daddy once offered to send me to Cordon Bleu, but there never seemed to be time. It was three afternoons a week. Do you think we'll be able to get the tractor turned back on its wheels?"

"I should think so."

"Oh, that's good. Because Vic said we should go out every day and get things. Right through the winter if needs be. He said we should collect everything we can lay our hands on. I mean, really lots and lots of things. Then, you see, later on, we might be able to find some people who'd be willing to work for us. They could grow vegetables and things like that, and we could pay them with goods."

Greg said, "Was that Vic's idea, too?"

"No. I suggested that. Honestly, I don't think we're going to be too badly off. I mean, from now on money is not really going to be worth anything. The rich will be the ones who've got things. I should think there'll be plenty of people who'll be glad to work for warm clothing or guns or something."

"Oh, they'll be queuing up," he said with irony that was lost on Sarah.

"So you see, in those terms we can be quite well-to-do."

They talked for a little while longer, but Greg found no chance to broach the matter of his leaving. He drank some more brandy and listened to the beating rain. Slightly drunk, he decided that he would be better off spending the night here. He stood up.

"I'd like to get some sleep."

She said, "I'm tired, too."

Greg busied himself arranging the folded and packaged blankets to form a mattress, then opened a couple for a covering. He stood up, intending to help Sarah make up her bed. She was close behind him. Naked. Her clothes dropped carelessly on the floor around her.

He shifted his gaze away quickly, embarrassed. Feeling that he had surprised her before she could get into her nightclothes.

She said, "Don't you want to look?"

He turned to face her. She was big-breasted and narrow-hipped, but the sight of her stirred nothing of desire. Instead, he felt awkward and uncomfortable.

Gauche. Never in his life or in his lonely fantasies had he played out this scene. Had she come to him in the darkness, needing his warmth and strength, it would have been different, but her offer now was too blatant. He was actually frightened by her.

He mumbled and then, feeling stupid as he spoke, said, "I've had an awful lot to drink. I don't think I'd be very good."

Sarah showed no displeasure at his rejection. Almost as though to comfort him, she said, "It's all right. Don't worry. Don't worry. I just thought you might want to." She turned away and from somewhere beside Vic's bed found a nightdress. She pulled it on and then moved across to the improvised mattress and climbed under the blankets. She looked up at Greg.

"I told you. It's all right. Another time, when you want to. Now get into bed and let's get some sleep."

Greg took off his jacket and shoes and climbed in beside her. He stayed rigidly away from her until he realized she was already asleep.

6

ABBY was still driving, long after dark. It had become routine to end her daily search by parking at the roadside before nightfall. But today's rain, continuous since late afternoon, had made the lighting of a cooking fire seem impossible. Now it was her intention to find a farm or outbuilding where she could shelter to prepare her meal.

The road she followed was flanked by high hedges. Uncleared drains and culverts had caused it to flood for long sections. It occurred to Abby that a few weeks of rain would make many roads impassable.

As she rounded a bend, the hedge on her left gave way to a long low wall.

Abby stopped the car quickly and stared. Across the lawns behind the wall was a house. Some two hundred yards off the road. From three of the downstairs windows came the unmistakable glare of electric light.

It took her some time to comprehend the sight. What, a few weeks ago, had seemed so commonplace was now quite remarkable. "A generator," Abby thought, and then, with more excitement: "If there are lights, there are people."

She hurried the car forward to the gate and turned into the drive. As she followed its curve, she realized the lighted windows were at the rear of the house. The front and entrance were in darkness.

She halted on the broad macadam parking area near the front door and switched off the lights and engine. Climbing out, she looked at the house. There was no sound or sign of movement.

Accustoming her eyes to the darkness, she started toward the porch. Something was sprawled across the path. Dark and shapeless. She didn't recognize it until she reached it. It was the body of a man. Even before seeing the wound, Abby knew he was dead. She edged around him, her changing angle revealing his face. In the middle of his chest was a hand-sized wound. The white shirt displayed it like an order of merit. From its dark center trickles of blood had been diluted by the rain to an insipid pink.

Still staring at the man, Abby took a few more steps toward the house. Only when she reached the porch did she see the front door was slightly ajar. She froze. There was a movement behind the door. No sound, only a barely discernible change in the density of shadows.

She called out, "Hello. Anyone there?"

No answer came. She tried again. "Hello?"

After another moment of silence Abby began to back away, her only wish now to reach her car and drive away from here. She was tense in the absolute certainty that she was being watched.

The darkness that separated her from the car seemed filled with menace. She moved slowly, warily, switching her glance left and right but seeing nothing.

There was a scuff of a footstep on asphalt. Abby felt fear scuttle across her neck and scalp.

"Who's there?"

She stood still. There was another sound. It took her a second to identify it. The car door was being opened.

She said, "There's somebody there!"

The sudden glaring flare of the headlights seemed almost violent. The impact blinded her, and she threw her forearm across her eyes and took a pace backward. She felt trapped and defenseless. Imprisoned in the beam.

A man's voice said, "Stay where you are."

She tried to see beyond the lights.

The voice demanded, "What do you want? Why are you here?"

"I saw the lights."

"You on your own?"

Abby felt herself nodding vigorously. "Yes, I'm on my own. I saw the lights, and I thought there must be somebody here." Then, lamely: "I just came to see."

"You're not sick, are you? You've not got the sickness?"

"No. I was. I did have the disease. But I'm not sick now."

She felt the beginning of resentment at the questions. She took a step forward and was instantly halted by the voice.

"Stay where you are." Then, more inquiring than demanding: "All right. Now what is it you want?"

Abby's resentment fused into anger. "Oh, for God's sake, how many times do I have to tell you? I saw the lights. I just wanted to make contact with somebody, that's all."

She saw a movement at the side of the car. The man came forward but stayed behind the lights. Projecting into the beam was the barrel of a shotgun. The voice said, "You're sure you are on your own?"

"Look, I'm not going to stand here answering damn silly questions. Now, please. If you'll let me get to my car, I'll go."

The figure stepped forward. He was a man of middle height. He wore a raincoat and a felt hat. He let the barrel of the gun swing down toward the ground. He said, "I'm sorry. I just wanted to be sure. I had to be sure. Come on back to the house."

Before Abby could reply, he called past her toward the porch. "Put the lights on, Dave."

A light went on over the front door.

"Like I say, I'm sorry if I was a bit cautious, but I can't be too careful. Had a bit of trouble here yesterday." He jerked his thumb toward the body on the pathway. He started for the door. Abby held her position. He glanced at her impatiently.

"Well? Are you coming in?"

She decided. "Yes. I'll put the car lights out. I don't want the battery to go flat."

He waited for her, and they went into the house.

He handed his shotgun to the man waiting in the hallway and made an awkward introduction.

"This is Dave. Dave Long."

She nodded and said, "Abby Grant."

He put out his hand and introduced himself. "Arthur Wormley."

Abby thought she had heard the name before but could not place it.

Wormley said, "Come on through to the kitchen. We were just getting something to eat when we heard your car. Come on through."

He led the way down the hall. Abby followed. She brushed her hand against the radiator. It was hot. Dave looked warily out of the front door. Closed it and went after them.

There were bubbling saucepans on the burners of the gas stove. From the oven came the unmistakable smell of roasting meat.

Wormley said, "Let me take your coat." He helped her remove it as she looked around.

"This is nice. Everything working."

"Yes. The stove runs off cylinder gas. There's a generator for the electricity. Central heating. There's even water. It's pumped up from a well."

"You're very lucky."

There was a hint of house-proudness as he agreed. "Yes. Yes, there can't be too many places that are totally independent of outside services. Would you like a drink? We've got most things."

"I'd love one. Vodka?"

Dave opened a cupboard. Abby saw a selection of bottles as he asked her, "Anything with it?"

"Tonic, please."

"Ice?"

Abby laughed. "Thank you. It's all so . . . well, it's all so odd because it's so normal."

Wormley smiled and nodded. He said, "Normal. Well, that's it, isn't it? I mean, that's what we've got to get back to as quick as we can: back to normal. That's the job in hand, isn't it?"

Abby couldn't quite place his accent. It was northern, she thought. Perhaps Yorkshire. And it was a voice that was used to authority. It had a tone that suggested it was making statements rather than conversation.

"Will you stay and have some food with us? We're not the best cooks in the world, but you're welcome to what there is."

"If it's not too much trouble, I'd love to. Thank you."

Dave put her drink in front of her. She calculated he was in his mid-twenties. He had neatly combed long hair, and she noticed his hands were calloused, darkly grained. Automatically she catalogued him as a mechanic.

Wormley took off his hat and coat. He wore a neat blue suit, a white shirt and dark tie. What was left of his hair was carefully positioned over the balding area. A small shopkeeper, a clerk. He could have fitted into a dozen categories.

He opened the oven door and looked inside. "Shouldn't be long now."

Dave had poured two more drinks. He handed one to Wormley, who raised it and said, "Cheers."

Abby sipped her drink. She was certain she had seen Wormley before. He noticed her staring.

She apologized quickly. "I'm sorry. It's just . . . I don't think we've ever met, but you do look familiar. I'm sure I've seen you somewhere."

"It's likely. My picture's been in the paper at odd times. I've been on the telly quite a bit."

Then she remembered. "Of course. Arthur Wormley. You're the union man. The chairman, isn't it? I'm sorry I can't remember which union."

He was pleased. He said modestly, "National president,

actually. Well, I was, anyway. There's nothing to be president of now. Not for the moment."

They settled at the table while Dave busied himself with the saucepans. They talked, Abby answering his questions about her own experiences. He listened politely, nodding gravely at appropriate points. Then, in his turn, he told Abby what he knew of the events of the last few weeks. His contact with government departments had allowed him a knowledge of the official action that had been taken.

He said, "Of course they knew it was some sort of plague, but because they couldn't do a damn thing about it, they followed the line that it was flu. They didn't want a panic. Then it was all so quick. They did declare a state of emergency. And I know some damn fool in Whitehall ordered the army out to try and bar people leaving the cities. As though they could stop it spreading. Stupid, that was. There was a bit of looting, so they declared martial law, which meant that under certain circumstances the army or police could open fire. But as far as I can tell, people just crawled away and died."

Abby said, "So now there's no authority. Nothing."

"Not as such. Not yet. But there will be. People are just wandering at the moment. Aimless. Lost. But before long they'll start joining up, making little groups. It's up to somebody to unite those groups, bring them together under one central control. They'll need leadership. Guidance."

Abby stared at him. His voice had shifted out of conversation into oratory. He left no doubt that the leadership and guidance of which he spoke would be provided by him. Staring at Abby, he went on with growing intensity.

"There has to be authority. Someone to organize. Take over and conserve what's left. There'll be no place for individuals wandering around haphazardly. We have to unify. In these circumstances it's up to someone to assume responsibility. To take the power to lead." He stopped suddenly. Perhaps sensing Abby's unease or realizing he had revealed too much of himself, he slipped easily to a new vocal tactic. His voice was softer, even gentle. "I've never been much on churchgoing and religion, but I do believe in God, and I think He might have spared me to give what help I can to those who are left. I mean, if I have got a skill, a talent, then it's for organization." He faltered over some of the words as though his uncertainty added sincerity.

She nodded. Noncommittally. She had no wish to debate with this man, yet she felt he was waiting for her approval. She distrusted political fervor, suspecting it always concealed raw ambition. She did not doubt that Wormley sincerely believed he had an important role to play. What alarmed her was that his conviction hid his motives even from himself.

Dave ended the debate by announcing that the meat was ready. He lifted an enormous rib of beef from the oven. To Abby's look of obvious approval Wormley explained, "Out of the deepfreeze."

Both men busied themselves with the serving. Abby's offer to help was refused, and she asked if there was somewhere she could clean up. Dave directed her to a bathroom in the hall.

While she was out of the room, Wormley cut several thick red slices from the joint. Dave asked, "What about the others?"

"Put it back in the oven. Keep it hot. They can have some later."

There was little conversation during the meal. It had the polite, stilted quality of strangers seeking common ground. Abby found that her capacity for food had grown smaller, and she finished her meal before her plate was empty.

Dave pured brandy, and they lit cigarettes. Wormley had learned the conversational art of being a good listener, and he seemed genuinely interested as Abby told of her search for Peter.

Wormley said, "I hope you find him. We're going to need the youngsters. Anyway, as things get a bit more settled, I might be able to help you. See, like you, there must be quite a few people who've become separated. As we come into contact with them, I want to compile a list. A sort of register: who they are, where they've come from, where they're going. Make this house a sort of central clearing point for information."

She said, "That's a marvelous idea. Something that's badly needed."

"We all have to do what we can," Wormley said. "But apart from looking for your boy, do you have any other plans?"

Abby did have plans. During the long days of searching she had considered the future many times. Her ideas had been random, her thoughts disordered, and now the discipline of explaining them in a coherent flow was difficult.

"To begin with, I'm looking for a place to make a home, a farm, I think. No, it's more than a home. It's a settlement."

Dave said, "You can have your pick of farmhouses."

Abby shook her head. "No, it's not just any farmhouse. It has to be, well, old-fashioned, I suppose. Open fireplaces. Wood stoves. Spring water. You see, I think we're going to have to get back to being agriculturalists very quickly. Most of our energy is going to be spent in growing food. We won't be able to waste time on trying to adapt a modernized place to our needs. I mean, this is lovely"—she made a gesture that embraced the house in which they were sitting—"but even if I could find one just like it, I'd reject it. Because in a year or so, perhaps more, you'll have to concern yourself with finding oil for your central heating. Petrol for your generator. They are going to become very scarce commodities, and when they've gone, this house really won't function at all. Anyway, I think that by living in a place like this, one is only hanging onto something that has already ended. It represents a way of life that no longer exists, and trying to maintain it is wrong." Then, realizing her implied criticism, she added, "I'm sorry, I'm sure you have your own plans and that you'll adapt to suit the circumstances."

Wormley said, "No, no. Go on. What you say is very interesting. I happen to think that with a large enough group working around this area we can maintain this place for a very long time. There's certainly enough left to see us through our lifetimes."

"But isn't that the point?" Abby demanded. "Our lifetime is not enough. We have to start now to provide the next generation with some sort of future. If we go on depending on what is left, we'll just slip back and back and back. But if we accept the fact that as of now we are virtually in the Middle Ages, we can start coming forward again, learning the survival arts as we go. Oh, I'm sorry, I know this must sound confusing. I can't really explain it very clearly."

"Won't you use anything that's left?"

"Yes. Yes, of course I will. I'll have to. But the aim must always be to become more self-reliant."

"You're not making it easy for yourself, are you?"

"Perhaps not. But then it's not going to be easy. The man I told you about, the teacher at Peter's school, started me thinking about it. There's nothing in this room, nothing, no artifact, that is the exclusive creation of one man. Our reliance on technology has robbed us of the simplest, most basic skills. I think we have to look ahead to the time when the last axhead cracks, the last saw breaks. There's no doubt in my mind that we're going to regress very quickly. If we start being self-sufficient now, then perhaps the regression won't be so hard to bear. The sooner we stop depending on the past, the greater our chances of making some new kind of life."

Abby stopped herself. She was flushed and felt suddenly embarrassed by her enthusiasm. She gulped at her brandy and avoided looking at the two men.

Wormley considered. Then, after a moment, he said, "You've looked a lot farther ahead than I have. And I think there's a lot of good sense in what you say. But you realize that you can't do any of the things you've said on your own."

Abby's was quieter now. The passion was spent. "No. But I hope there'll be other people who think like me."

"I'm sure there will. And it's a first-class idea: a community working for the general good, sharing equally. It's what socialism and the trade unions have been trying to achieve for a long time. Not to put too fine a point on it, it's what Christ was preaching, too. I admire your thinking, Mrs. Grant. And when you do establish this, this"—he groped for the word—"this commune of yours, well, that's where I'll be able to help."

"In what way?"

"Well, in making sure you can get on with it without outsiders interfering. Providing some sort of law and order. We have to establish a form of government. There'll be other settlements besides yours, and they'll need to be unified. And that takes leaders. Later, perhaps, when things are a bit more organized, we could even have elections. A sort of central council."

Gently, Abby said, "I should have thought it would be a long time before we need any governing body."

"It's never too soon. We've already begun in a small way. Locating food dumps. . . . We have to be sure that things get shared out. We don't want one person cornering the market or hoarding. If we handle distribution from here, then we can see that nobody goes short. Of course, we've only looked around the immediate vicinity up until now, but as we grow in numbers, get stronger, we'll start to spread out, expand."

"That's how the old feudal barons operated, wasn't it?" Abby said softly.

"Perhaps, perhaps. But that was the way that ultimately led to the finest democratic society in the world."

She nodded. "I suppose. It's just that I hadn't seen a political system as being one of our priorities."

"You're wrong there," said Dave, joining the conversation for the first time. "There are little mobs forming up already. Trying to take over."

She glanced at Dave, but it was Wormley who continued.

"Remember, I told you when you arrived we'd had a spot of trouble. Well, it started the day we took over this house."

Abby interjected, "It's not your house?"

Wormley dismissed her question "No. But we needed a headquarters." He went on with a hint of outrage in his voice that he invited Abby to share. "We'd just settled in when a rat pack of toughs came marching up. Ex-army chap leading them. Retired major. You know the sort. Been in civvy street for twenty years and still use their rank. Well, he said they were a vigilante force of citizens, and he reckoned one of his mob—there were about six of them— owned this house. Well, I offered to let them join up with us. Couldn't have been fairer. Then, right out of the blue, they started shooting. I tell you it was a nasty do for a while. That was one of their blokes you saw lying in the drive. Anyway, we gave them a taste of their own medicine. They won't be back in a hurry."

He nodded with satisfaction at the memory of the encounter. He noticed Abby's glass was empty. "Let me pour you another drink."

"No. No, thank you." She pushed her chair back and, like a good guest, began to make her thanks.

"You've been very kind. The food was marvelous, and just being able to talk to somebody again was. . . ."

Before she could finish, Wormley said, "You don't have to go on tonight, do you? Wouldn't you like to bed down here? Plenty of room, and you must be tired after all that time on the road."

Abby made the meaningless gesture of looking at her watch. Then: "Well, if it wouldn't be imposing."

"Of course not. Certainly not."

She said, "There's one thing I would appreciate. I noticed you've got hot water. A bath would be just about the greatest luxury I could think of."

"No trouble at all." Wormley rose and led the way to the door. "All the hot water you can use. Come on, I'll show you where the bathroom is."

Abby turned the taps and watched the water steam out. In the medicine cabinet she found shampoo and a fresh bar of soap. There were large towels on the heated rail. She undressed quickly, and despite the fact that the water had risen only a few inches, she climbed into the bath. She lay at full stretch, watching the water ascend like a slowly rising flood. The skin on her knees and thighs became islands, changing in shape and growing smaller until they were finally engulfed.

She didn't move until the water had climbed over her

breasts, then she reached forward and turned off the taps. She lay back, her eyes closed. It was ten minutes before she could rouse the energy to sit up and start to soap herself.

She used the hand shower to wash her hair, then, standing, sprayed the soap from her body. She stepped out of the bath and bound herself in a huge blue towel. There was a collection of scent bottles in a glass-shelved alcove. She considered carefully and then selected a Givenchy spray cologne and directed its misty fragrance over her neck and shoulders and wrists.

She picked her clothes off the floor and dressed slowly, then moved to the mirror to comb her still-wet hair.

The glass of the bathroom window shattered with such resounding violence it almost drowned the blast of the shotgun. There were three more deafening shots from somewhere close outside the house. The suddenness of the assault locked Abby into immobility. Then, whimpering with fright, she dropped to her knees out of the line of the window.

There were more shots. Farther away now. And men's voices shouting, though she could not hear what they were saying.

Abby crawled on all fours to the door and, reaching up, pulled the switch cord, plunging the room into darkness. There was the distant sound of a car engine.

She stood up swiftly and heaved the door open. On the landing she pressed against the wall, fear still pulsing through her.

Through the open front door a chill updraft of air carried the murmur of voices. Cautiously she moved to the top of the stair and looked down. The hall and porch lights showed every detail of the body that lay sprawled in the doorway. The shotgun blast that had killed him had struck just below his chin. The wound was like a scarlet cravat at his throat.

From the blur of talking outside the house Abby recognized Wormley's voice. She went cautiously down the stairs and, edging around the dead man, out into the porch.

Wormley and Dave stood with their backs to Abby. A

third man was with them. They all held guns. Two more men appeared, advancing into the fringe of the light. They walked either side of a figure who was evidently their prisoner, firmly gripping his arms.

Abby stood, silently watching, partly hidden by the bushing honeysuckle that draped the porch.

From another angle two more men came in to join the group. As they approached, Wormley called, "Did you get them all?"

"Couple of them got away in the car. I had a shot at them but couldn't swear I hit them."

Wormley said, "Pity," then looked around the faces of the men who had gathered about him in a loose circle. Missing somebody, he demanded sharply, "Where's Frank?"

The man who had spoken before said, "He's had it. He copped it when they arrived."

"Bastards!" Wormley spat. He made a hitchhiker's thumb over his shoulder toward the house, directing their attention to the body in the hall. "They got Norman, too."

They saw Abby in the shadows, and to make it perfectly clear she was not hiding, she stepped out into the open. "What's happening?"

Wormley gave a quick glance and said, "Go back inside, Mrs. Grant." Then he turned his attention to the prisoner. Abby stayed where she was.

The captive was a tall gaunt man. He stood very still, only betraying his nervousness by the swift and regular flicking of the tip of his tongue over his lips. Wormley placed himself directly in front of the man, and when he spoke, his voice took on a very formal sound.

"I have assumed the authority to establish and maintain law and order in this area."

The tall man said, "By what right?"

Wormley continued, the words sounding as though they were being read from a prepared speech.

"The government announcement of a state of emergency and the introduction of martial law provides all necessary powers to protect life and property."

The prisoner's voice was louder now. "That power was

invested only in the recognized authorities: the services and the police."

It was as though Wormley had not heard. "You are guilty of leading an armed attack upon peaceful citizens."

"Peaceful citizens! You're a gang of thugs," the man interjected while Wormley continued to speak without falter.

"You have caused the deaths of two men who were carrying out their duty in defending this area."

Wormley paused, then slowly stared around the circle of men, looking directly into each face. Then he said, "Now, you men, listen to me. Since we have assumed responsibility for this area, it is our duty to administer such laws as are necessary for the general welfare of the public. This man has committed murder. We are completely within our legal rights to pass judgment on him. It is not only our right but our duty. Do you understand that? Do you clearly understand that?"

There was grunting assent from the men. Wormley wanted more. Again he demanded, "Do you understand?"

This time he received a chorus of clear yesses. Satisfied, he again confronted his prisoner.

"You are guilty of murder. By the statutes contained in the declared state of martial law the punishment is death. You will be executed. The sentence to be carried out immediately."

The men tightened their grip on his arms as the prisoner tried to jerk free.

Abby started forward. "No! No! You can't do that. You have no right."

Before she could reach the group, Wormley lifted the muzzle of his shotgun until it was level with the prisoner's chest and only six inches from it. The action was very deliberate. Calculatedly free of emotion. He pulled the trigger.

The impact of the shot hurled the man back, jerking him free of his captors' grasp, his dead body reeling four or five yards backward before crumpling to the ground.

Abby was gasping with horror. She threw her hands over her face.

Wormley looked toward her. Staying where he stood, he said, "He was leading an armed gang of men who were trying to take over this house. His execution was perfectly legal."

Abby said, "You murdered him." Then she started to run, making for the car.

Dave made a movement as though to stop her, but Wormley caught his arm.

In the time it took her to climb into the driver's seat and start the engine, Wormley called after her, "I'm sorry you had to see that, Mrs. Grant. But we'll never get law and order while men like him are trying to grab power."

His last words were lost in the revving roar of the engine. The car jumped forward, swinging around in a tight circle, making the men leap from its path. Driving blindly, Abby lost the edge of the drive, and the nearside wheels churned through the soft earth of a flower bed. She had almost reached the gate before she swung it back onto the hard surface. Then she was on the road and driving away with all the speed the car could give her.

Wormley and the rest of the men watched her out of sight. He said, "Stupid bitch." He looked around. "Get the place cleared up. We'll have no more trouble tonight." He started back to the house.

7

THE grimy light of a wet dawn filtered through the window of the site hut. The sound of a churning car engine failing to fire intruded into Sarah's sleep. She wakened slowly as the sound persisted: then, recognizing it, she sat up quickly. Greg was gone. She threw back the blankets and, barefooted, ran to the door. Vic was already awake. He called to her, but she ignored him and was out of the hut before he could speak again.

Hobbling on the sharp stones, she hurried to the car and bent to speak into the open driver's window. Greg gave her only a brief glance. Again he pressed the starter, and the engine turned, sounding weary now as the battery began to lose power.

"Where do you think you're going?" Sarah demanded.

"I don't know. I'm just going."

The engine fired and ran for a few uneven revolutions, then died.

Greg muttered, "Come, come on, damn you." He thumbed the starter again.

Sarah felt the damp chill of the morning as the misty rain soaked her nightdress. Her feet were icy cold.

"You're coming back, aren't you?" There was more demand than question.

"No."

"You can't just leave. What about me?"

"I'm sorry. You'll have to look out for yourself."

The engine caught and started to run. Tentatively he put some pressure on the throttle, and the sound grew more confident.

Sarah's voice edged up toward hysteria.

"You can't leave me. How do you expect me to manage on my own?" She nodded her head toward the hut. "He's useless now."

Greg grated the gear into reverse and started to shift backward to allow himself room to turn. Sarah moved with the car. She grasped the door and pulled it open.

"You can't go!"

Greg jerked the door from her hand, slammed it shut and pressed the inside lever to lock it.

He tried to make his voice sound reasonable. He wanted to explain. Wanted her to understand.

"I just can't take on the responsibility. That's what I've had all my life. I don't want it anymore."

He moved the gear into first. Then, as though to justify himself, to placate, he said, "If I can find some drugs, medicine, something to help Vic, then I'll bring them back. I can't promise. And even if I do, I won't be staying."

The car started forward. Sarah ran beside it, her face ugly with rage, shrieking now and hauling at the door.

"You have no right to leave me! You shan't go. I won't let you! Get out of the car! You hear me? Get out of the car!"

Determinedly, he jabbed the accelerator. The sudden burst of speed threw Sarah clear of the car, and she fell, sprawling to the ground, scraping the skin from her knees and elbows.

Her fury anesthetized her pain. She screamed after the car as it vanished into the cutting. She got to her feet, her nightdress torn and muddied. Her sobs had no tears as she limped wincingly toward the hut.

She slammed the door with all the violence she could muster, then hurled herself face down onto the makeshift bed. She began to pound the blankets with clenched fists.

Vic forced the words through his parched throat.

"Sarah. Will you get me something to drink?"

She screamed back at him. "Shut up! Shut up! Shut up! Shut up!"

Abby braked gently and drew to a halt beside the Rolls. The big white car was canted at a steep angle, its curb-side wheels in a drainage ditch. The top was down, and the doors were wide open. The soft rain had darkened the pale leather of the upholstery to a muddy brown. For a moment she thought there was a body huddled on the backseat; then she recognized it was a bundle of clothing. There was no trace of the driver. Abby stared across the hedge beyond the car. The ground fell away gently for almost a quarter of a mile, then rose again as a wooded hill. Near the crest was a church, half hidden in the trees. She leveled the binoculars. Even at this range the neglect was evident. There were dark holes in the spire where slates had fallen away. Nature had counterattacked across the land long ago cleared for the site. Ivy had scaled the walls. Ash and elder had advanced among the gravestones. An infantry of weeds had surged forward.

Abby panned the glasses left and right. There was no other building to be seen. On the map she located the symbol that marked the church and then traced the route that would take her to it.

Jenny had slept badly. Her stomach muscles ached from the prolonged spasms of coughing. Her breathing was rapid and shallow. Like a woodwind reed, mucus at the back of her throat added a wheezing note to every gasp.

She sat up painfully, straining to hear. The noise that had alerted her might have been breaking glass. Her own loud breathing had distorted the sound. Her legs trembled as she rose. Her balance was uncertain. She held onto the counter and edged down to the shop door. Across the street and off to one side there was a sports car, parked in front of the pharmacy. It had not been there earlier.

Jenny reached the car at the moment when Greg stepped out of the shattered plate glass of the pharmacy door. He was carrying a carton filled with drugs and medicines.

Jenny said, "Help me."

Vic watched Sarah dress. She had not spoken or looked at him since Greg had driven away. She spent some minutes arranging her hair and applying makeup. Then she pushed several packages of cigarettes into her shoulder bag and pulled on her mink coat.

"Where are you going?" There was alarm in his question.

She pointedly avoided looking at him and crossed to the door and walked out.

"Sarah. For God's sake, don't go. You can't leave me on my own. Stay with me."

He twisted his body across the bed until his hands could reach the floor, then, clawing forward, dragged his legs off the bed. On elbows and hands he shuffled to the still-open door. Sarah was already starting up the steep slope to the cutting.

Vic crawled almost twenty yards across the quarry floor, calling, whimpering, begging and lastly shrieking. When he finally knew she was gone, he started to cry. The unendurable pain seeped back into his shattered legs. The pain that made him know he was still alive. He began to inch his way back toward the hut.

Sarah stepped out onto the main road as Greg slowed to make the turn. Jenny was beside him in the passenger seat.

"I've got some drugs. I don't know what they all are; I just brought what I could find. There must be something that will ease the pain. Get in. I'll drive you back."

Sarah said, "There's no point. He's dead."

They drove aimlessly for the rest of that day. They spoke very little. Greg contributed only variations on one theme.

They could stay with him until they found some more people. But they saw no one. Jenny sipped from a bottle of cough medicine she had found among the drugs. Sarah smoked a good deal. At dusk the car ran out of gas, despite the fact that the gauge still showed a quarter of a tank.

"Well, what do we do?" Greg resented that neither woman answered him. He was being forced to make decisions, to take charge.

"We passed a cottage back down the road. We could shelter there for the night." He waited for an alternative suggestion. Instead, both passengers climbed from the car and obediently waited for him to take the lead.

They walked back the way they had come, then crowded gratefully into the shelter of the cottage's porch while Greg put his shoulder to the locked front door. The doorframe splintered at the third assault, and Greg stumbled forward into the tiny hall. The stench of the rotting dead seemed more substantial than the door itself. He wretched and lumbered blindly back outside. The women had retreated from the door, their hands covering mouths and noses. Greg felt that the perfume of death was clinging to his clothes, and he was glad of the sweeping rain that washed him clean.

It was Jenny who suggested the barn. It was half filled with bales of straw. There were dry logs piled in one corner. Sarah watched while Jenny and Greg started a fire and broke bales open to provide dry bedding.

Long after midnight Jenny wakened, shivering with cold. There were still traces of red in the wood ash of the fire, and she rose silently to bring more logs. Through the half-open barn door she saw the searchlight: a tall column of light beaming straight up into the darkness. A beacon. Its only purpose to attract attention. To be seen.

She roused Greg and at the same time shook Sarah's shoulder. With a petulant grunt Sarah shook off the hand and turned on her side, refusing to wake.

Greg stood up. "What is it?" She led him to the door. There was no need to point. He stared in silence.

Jenny said softly, "Let's find where it's coming from."

Greg tried to estimate their distance from its source. "Hard to tell how far away it is."

"I'm going there." She said it with a determination that surprised him.

"Now?"

She nodded. "It's a signal. There must be people there, and they want others to see it."

He stared again. "It's a fair way off. And it's still raining."

"I'm going anyway."

"Then we'll all go." He moved back to Sarah and touched her shoulder. "We're going, Sarah. Come on."

Ill-tempered, she pushed off his hand and wriggled away from him.

"I said we're going."

She gave no sign of hearing him.

Greg gave up. He said loudly, "If we find anybody, we'll come back for you in the morning."

They took as direct a route as possible, crossing fields and woods and deviating only for the highest hedges or deepest streams. The rain ended with the dawn. The growing light paled the beam until at last it withered and became invisible. But by that time they could hear the throb of the generator coming from beyond the brow of the next hill.

Jenny pushed through the scrub into the overgrown churchyard. An army searchlight truck stood on the muddy track that led to the church, its great lens pointed upward. A woman was climbing into the cab of the truck, and a moment later the generator was switched off. As she stepped down, she saw Jenny. She hesitated briefly, then came toward her. Greg waited a few yards back.

Jenny said, "We saw the light."

"I hoped someone would. You're the first."

"Will there be others?"

Abby shrugged.

BOOK TWO

THE SILENCE

8

THE first winter came hard. In late October the rain ended, and there were several days of pale-blue skies. The sun was generous with its warmth, and there was no breeze to stir the mists that came morning and night. They talked about an Indian summer.

Then the wind started. Blowing directly out of the north. Like a chisel, it cut the last leaves from the trees, dried and hardened the ground and chilled an edge of ice onto open water. The first snow came at night, settling instantly on frozen ground. It crouched against defiant walls and hedges, building into drifts, smothering and finally overwhelming all but the tallest obstacles. Speechless telephone wires bowed beneath its weight. It snapped branches from trees. Unprotected by antifreeze, the cylinders of car engines cracked in the sub-zero temperatures. Countless birds and animals died and gave life to the carrion eaters.

There were brief periods of thaw that ended at nightfall when the surface snow refroze and formed a crisp icy shell. Movement became all but impossible. They stayed by their fires, burning whatever timber they could find. When there was no more firewood, they used the furniture and even ripped away parts of the fabric of the places where they sheltered.

When the little stocks of plundered food were finished, they were forced out into the snow to forage in the dead houses and shops. Their journeys were short, limited by the distance they could walk in the brief daylight hours. Limited, too, by what they could carry on their backs. Roads were unpassable to vehicles. The intense cold slowed the decomposition of the bodies, making close contact with the dead at least tolerable.

Many long-held principles and ideals shriveled in the chill of that long winter. Illusions were shed, and the simplest truth became profound. To sustain life, you needed only two things: warm shelter and food. Fulfilling these two needs became the total preoccupation of the survivors. For food they competed with the other animals: dog packs, rats and . . . one another. Those who had sought protection in isolation were hardest-driven. In the remote areas accessible supplies ran out quickly. When there was nothing left, some conquered their disgust at eating human flesh and lived on.

The cities were both mortuaries for the masses of dead and great treasure-houses of food and clothing. Their wealth had been protected by festering disease and the stench of corruption. The long cold checked the decay and provided a key that opened up the urban areas.

The ones who moved back lived well through that winter. It was a time of abundance. As groups or individuals they laid claim to whole sections of shops and houses. Late-comers seldom disputed ownership. They simply moved on to unoccupied areas. There was treasure enough for all.

By Christmas there were more than a thousand people living in London. They housed themselves in the department stores or near shopping centers, feasting on canned and bottled foods. Lacking only fresh meat and green vegetables, some cautiously supplemented their diet with vitamin pills. Fresh water was a constant problem. Washing clothes became pointless. They discarded garments and replaced them with new ones.

They lived fatly and warmly but afraid. Every day they

watched the sky, dreading the return of the sun and the thaw that would drive them out again. But through January and February the cold persisted and the air stayed clean.

The group of twenty people who had taken territorial rights to Piccadilly and the surrounding area made some preparation for evacuation. Using a bulldozer from a building site, they cleared snow from stretches of roadway. They serviced and fueled dozens of vans. These they loaded to capacity with food, clothes and equipment. Ready for the retreat from the city.

It came on the first day of March. The wind had come around and was blowing in heavy rain from the west. The lock of ice broke swiftly, and the hard snow softened to a mash. Drains blocked since the autumn were holding the waters. Low-lying areas flooded quickly. Basements and cellars filled. Heavy slides of snow off rooftops broke guttering and dragged off slates. Broad cracks in roadways and masonry revealed themselves.

And with the rising temperatures the stink returned: the putrefying dead and the damp molder of the decaying cities.

The survivors who had overwintered were driven out, leaving the towns to the rats and the flies.

The convoy of vans moved down Piccadilly toward Hyde Park Corner, the bulldozer clearing a path through the abandoned cars. It took them two days to reach Vauxhall Bridge Road. Here the traffic-spread from Victoria Station was so dense that they could make no more progress. They left the vehicles and, taking what they could carry, retreated on foot.

The treasure-houses were again locked and deserted.

The church didn't work. Abby was sure of it soon after the first big snow. There was no economical way of heating it. Despite the huge fires, the cold lived in the walls. It was too far from any building that might contain food stores. When the stream froze, they had no water. The qualities that made it appear so attractive—its isolation, its defensibility—no longer seemed important. She planned to move out during the first break in the weather and marked several places on the map as worthy of investigation.

There were eight of them now. Like Greg and Jenny, other survivors had been drawn to the church by the spire of the searchlight. They made an ill-balanced community: five women and three men. The enlarged group quickly depleted the small cache of food, and through even the worst of the weather they were forced to hunt and forage daily. The women spent many of the daylight hours bringing in firewood, but despite all their efforts, their stockpile was seldom more than a few days ahead of their needs. The men hunted and burrowed in the snow in fields where undug root crops still remained. Abby imposed the strictest rationing which allowed them to eat every day while remaining hungry. Only once that winter were they sated with food when Greg located the carcasses of four sheep, deepfrozen in a snowdrift.

Early in the new year Abby realized that the effort expended in collecting food and wood exceeded the energy it provided. They were starving.

In late January Greg took the six remaining shotgun shells and set out alone. In the afternoon it started to snow again. Light flurries became heavier and more sustained as darkness fell. The hours passed, and Greg had still not returned. Concerned that he might have lost his way in the storm, Abby insisted that they light a fire outside. Shoveling cinders from their fire, they established a beacon. They fed it with what remained of their timber store and were able to keep it burning for several hours.

The two remaining men set out to search for Greg at first light. The fresh snow had wiped out all trails, and the physical effort of walking through the heavy drifts quickly exhausted them. They abandoned the hunt.

By the second night the group was divided. Abby and Jenny believed Greg had suffered some accident. The others concluded that he had abandoned them. From the very first day of his arrival at the church Greg had maintained his stance as a temporary member of the group, never joining in discussions of long-term plans, making no commitment to a joint future. There was little consolation in the fact that there was one mouth less to feed. Greg had been a determined and dogged forager. His going seemed to rob the two remaining men of the will to seek out food. They returned empty-handed after only a few hours of searching. Abby did what she could to rouse a new enthusiasm but could do nothing to dispel the sense of defeat that had settled over them. She imposed the strictest rationing, limiting them all to one sparse meal a day. On the morning of the fifth day after Greg's disappearance Jenny wakened Abby with the news that the two men and two of the women had gone. They had taken all that remained in the food store.

Abby sat crouched beside the fire, made helpless by her total despair. Ruth, a girl a little older than Jenny and the last to arrive at the church, made an attempt to comfort her but was answered with brooding silence. The black depression surrounded Abby like a protective shell that neither of her companions could penetrate.

After a few hours Jenny tried to break through. "Will you help us collect some firewood, Abby?" Then, after receiving no answer: "What are we going to do?"

Not looking at her, Abby said, "You'll die if you stay here. You'd better find somewhere to settle. A place with food."

Jenny nodded. "I'll put our things together. We won't be able to carry it all. Anything in particular you want to take?"

"I'm not going."

"But you can't stay here on your own."

Abby's voice flared with a violence that frightened Jenny. "For Christ's sake, get out and leave me alone! I'm sick of being responsible for all of you! Just get out and leave me alone!"

The two girls talked in quiet voices beyond Abby's hearing. When they had finished, Ruth packed a bag with her extra clothing. Ready to leave, she asked Jenny, "You're sure you won't come?" Jenny shook her head. "Good-bye, then." She called across to Abby, "Good-bye." Then she went out into the cold still of the afternoon.

Jenny fed what was left of the firewood onto the flames and took a place opposite Abby. Neither spoke. The silence they shared was a balm to Jenny's fears. She had made a decision to stay, and that single positive action was enough to free her from concern about the future. She was certain that sooner or later Abby would decide what to do for both of them. Until she did, Jenny was content to sit and wait.

The church door was thrown open swiftly and loudly, bringing both women to their feet in alarm. Ruth came quickly inside, her excitement making it difficult for her to speak. "There's a signal. Outside. A signal." She backed to the door again, beckoning them to follow. "Smoke. A big smoke signal."

They trailed a few yards behind Ruth, running to the crest of the hill. They came up beside her as she halted and pointed.

The column of smoke was a long way off but clear and straight like a black pencil stuck in the snowy landscape. As they watched, the spire seemed to topple sideways for a few seconds, caught in some light breeze, then slowly it leaned back into the vertical.

"There. There, can you see it?" Ruth demanded. "It's a signal. Can you see it?"

Jenny felt herself caught up in Ruth's enthusiasm. "It must be a signal. Like your searchlight, Abby. They want people to see it."

Abby held check on her own excitement. She ordered her words carefully. "It could be. But it might just be a fire. It doesn't follow that it's there to attract attention."

"Even so, there must be people there, and they're not making any secret about it." Ruth turned to face them, her voice belligerent. "I'm going there anyway. Are you coming?"

Abby stared for an instant longer and then nodded. "We'll get our things."

The walk across the snow was slow and exhausting. The light began to fade, and the wind started to rise, smearing the smoke and finally erasing it. It was quite dark when they breasted a wooded hill and saw the glowing source of the smoke. It took them another hour to reach it.

They approached the fire cautiously, staring at its still brightly burning heart. The wind swirled a billow of smoke that briefly engulfed them, and they coughed and retched on the stink of charred flesh. As it cleared again, they say the body at the edge of the flames, one blackened arm grotesquely reaching upward, the fingers extended.

They moved quickly from the fire toward the clustered houses some hundred yards beyond, then halted, alarmed at the sudden roar of a tractor engine starting up. They saw its lights and were blinded by them as the tractor swung toward them. It halted, and Greg climbed down from the driver's seat. His face was ashen. His every movement showed his exhaustion.

He said, "I've been clearing out the dead. There were a lot here. It will be a good place for us. There's plenty of food. A shop. But I wanted to get rid of the dead before I came for you." His voice was so soft they could hardly hear him above the throbbing beat of the tractor. "All the bodies are gone now, but we must keep the fire going. It'll be clean here then. A good place for us."

9

THE winter was slow in ending. In sheltered places the snow lingered until early April. In later times events were remembered by names and not dates. They called that period the Winter of the Death.

There were eleven houses in the hamlet that Greg had cleared of bodies. They formed a central point for a fairly widespread agricultural area. The village store that had served the community was heavily stocked with canned and dried goods. There had been little modernization of the houses, and the one they chose to occupy had open fireplaces and solid-fuel stoves. Well water could be hand-pumped to a roof storage tank, and when the freeze ended, they were able to enjoy indoor plumbing. Most of the houses had good stocks of coal and timber, so finally, warm and well fed, they were able to consider a future beyond the next day.

Abby started what she called her Shopping List for Survival. In a notebook she jotted down the items that seemed essential. The others contributed their own ideas, and in a week the book was filled. From the diversity of the list it was obvious that none of them had any clear idea of where their future lay.

As they settled down after an evening meal, Abby rather

formally announced that they should start to make plans.
The others looked at her expectantly.

She began hesitantly, looking directly at Greg. "If we stay
together as a group, then we have to decide what our aims
are."

Greg looked uneasy, feeling he was being forced into a
commitment. He shrugged. "I don't have any particular
plans. I'm not sure what I'm going to do. So count me in, at
least for the moment."

Jenny said, "I think we should stay together."

Ruth nodded, a little less certain.

"All right then," Abby went on. "It seems to me we have
very few choices. We can work like hell all year round to
forage and bring in everything we can lay hands on.
Everything on this list"—she waved the notebook—"and a
whole lot more besides. There must be millions and millions
of tons of canned and preserved foods. Clothes. Oh,
everything. There is no point in listing things. Everything is
available except fresh food."

Greg interrupted. "Everything is there, but I'm not so
sure it's available. Not for a while, anyway. The biggest
stores will be in what were densely populated areas. Stink
and disease are going to keep us out of them for a long
while."

"I agree. But it depends how badly we want things.
Sooner or later somebody is going to start plundering the
cities. But that's really not the point. What we have to decide
is, are we simply going to go on using up what is left, or are
we going to try and create a totally new life-style?"

Nobody answered for a moment. Then Ruth asked,
"What kind of life-style?"

Abby had her answer ready. "Farming. Or at least market
gardening. We have to become a peasant society that
produces virtually all it requires—in terms of food, that is.
We grow all our own meat and vegetables. If we could do
that, if we could just do that, it would give the next
generation enough time to learn the other skills. From
books they'll find out how to make things. Things that will
have run out by then." Abby's voice took on a fervor that

had her listeners nodding with agreement. "We, and I don't mean just we four, but all the survivors in this country, could probably live out our natural lives by simply scavenging, but what about the next generation and the one after that?"

Like an apostle, Jenny caught the spirit. "It's a beginning, isn't it? I mean, it's not as though we have to invent or make the tools we use. For a while, until the petrol runs out, we'll even have tractors to do the hardest of the work."

"Hold on," Greg interjected. They all turned to look at him. "We're going to go out and collect all the things we need. Petrol, tools, seed and so on and so on. Is that right?"

Abby nodded. "We'll pick and choose carefully, but yes, that's the general idea."

Greg picked up again. "And we're going to grow crops and keep livestock. Right?"

"Right," Abby confirmed.

"Then it can't be done." Greg settled back in his chair with the confidence of a debater who had just scored an irrefutable point.

"Why?"

"Because there aren't enough of us. If the four of us worked like dogs all year round, we couldn't do much more than scratch a living. Look, in this country we have only about six months when the ground is workable. In that time we have to grow enough to eat day by day, enough to set aside for a six-month winter. Provide winter feeding for our stock. Collect fuel. There's no way it can be done."

"Then we'll have to find others to join us." It was Ruth who spoke. Abby glanced at her in surprise. Of all of them Ruth had seemed the least concerned about future plans. She went on. "I think you're both right. Abby's right in that we have to grow things. Greg's right in that we are too few in number. The answer is obvious."

They had so long shared the company of one another, been so long without seeing other people that the idea of enlarging the group came as a mild shock.

Jenny was cautious. "We'd have to be very careful about who we let stay."

"Of course," Abby said. "We'd make it clear what our aims are. If people weren't willing to share those ideas, then they wouldn't be welcome."

They began to explore the idea. What numbers would they need? How many could they house? How would the work force be divided? How many farming, how many scavenging? As they talked, their sense of excitement grew. They shared an enthusiasm they had not known for many months. They were starting on a long-term plan. They were going somewhere.

A fortnight later Tom Price wandered in. His clothes were filthy. His hair was greasy and grown to shoulder length. His face and hands were flaked with dry skin. He gratefully accepted their offer of a meal and, while it was being prepared, reluctantly agreed to Greg's suggestion that he take a bath. Ruth found fresh clothes in one of the abandoned houses. They burned the verminous things he was wearing, despite his insistence that there were "years of good wear in them yet."

Eager to hear news from outside, they sat with him while he ate. He spoke through mouthfuls of food, emphasizing and gesturing with his fork. He had wintered with Arthur Wormley and his group. Abby was fascinated and concerned to learn that the group had grown to number more than thirty. According to Price, Wormley had titled himself Acting President and called his organization the National Unity Force. Before the big snows the force had worked in an ever-widening circle collecting food and essential materials, which they stored at their base. New recruits who did not want to serve with the military arm were offered parcels of land. Their crops would become the property of the force. In return they enjoyed the support and protection of Wormley's "army." Price seemed impressed and a little afraid of what he had seen. "Disciplined they are, see. And organized. They don't stand no nonsense. Mr. Wormley—Arthur I called him—he said to me, 'Tom,' he said, 'these people have got to have leaders. For their own good they've got to be told what to do. There's no place for individuals.' That's what he said. Anyway, I told him a few of my ideas, and right away he offered me an important position on the executive. Officer he wanted me to be. High-ranking. Lot of people working under me."

Greg interrupted before Price could enlarge on his fantasy. "Sounds pretty good," he said. "Why didn't you stay?"

Without hesitation Price shifted to a new tack. He was a man to whom lies came more easily than truth. His voice took on a solemn note. "Well, we had a bit of a disagreement, see. A matter of principle, it was. Mind, later on he came and apologized to me. Agreed with everything I'd said. Begged me to stay on, he did, but I said no. I said, 'There's a lot of poor devils wandering around the countryside who could do with a bit of help. And that's all I want out of life: the chance to help people.' "

Price smiled around at his listeners, trying to look humble. "I mean, that's what we're all here for, isn't it? To help one another."

The meal finished, Price settled in a chair in front of the fire. The others went about their chores.

Later in the afternoon Ruth struggled in with a heavy armful of logs. Price eyed her sympathetically. "You shouldn't carry too many at a time," he said, not moving. "You'll strain yourself."

Mildly Ruth suggested he might like to help.

He gave a little grimace and clutched at his thigh. His voice had a wince. "I'd do it like a shot, see, but the old leg is playing up a bit. War wound. Gives me gyp now and again. Probably better tomorrow. Then you'll see some work done. Thrive on it, I do. Never know when to stop."

At the evening meal Price made certain there was no scrap of food left uneaten, then returned to his chair. He quickly fell into a snoring sleep and had to be wakened to go to bed.

Jenny helped Abby clear the dishes. "Well, we've got our first recruit. What do you think of him?"

Abby grinned. "If we get any more like him, God help all of us."

The melted snow and the early-spring rain made the land heavy and unworkable. Their first attempt at plowing a piece of ground for a potato crop had ended with the tractor being buried hub-deep in the mire.

Greg found a Range Rover undamaged by the freeze. At a garage only a few miles from the houses there was a good supply of gasoline. The hard work of hand-pumping ended when they wired in power from a portable Honda generator.

Price seemed happy to stay behind as caretaker while the others went out to collect items from Abby's Shopping List for Survival.

At a garden center they found vegetable seed. Abby made a point of mentioning that they would have to set aside a small part of each crop to provide seed for the following year. Ruth noticed that many of the packets carried the warning that the variety was a hybrid and that seeds saved from it would not breed true. The thought struck all of them: Many plants were going to regress faster than they.

Within a month they had covered a radius of about five miles. At first they had avoided areas where the smell of decay was strong, but later they devised face masks that they impregnated with disinfectant. Wearing these, they penetrated village shops. At times they found signs of post-Death foragers: doors and windows smashed open, empty food cans and bottles littering the floors. But they saw no one.

They drove over roads cracked and potholed by the frosts, silted and muddy and thick with the decaying leaves of autumn. In fields where the sharp green of new grass was beginning to show there were the carcasses of cattle and sheep. The winter had destroyed the livestock as effectively as the disease had killed the people.

One afternoon they halted at what had been a neatly maintained farm. Row after row of low brick buildings had housed intensively farmed pigs and chickens. Greg peered in through a window. Hundreds of the animals lay dead in their pens. . . . In the broiler houses the chickens had died in huddled piles that looked almost orderly.

Driving away, no one spoke until Greg said, "I wonder which suffered the heaviest death toll. The animals or us?"

They had extended their range and were driving over unfamiliar roads some twenty miles from their base. Greg drove swiftly and confidently, ignoring traffic signs and never pausing or slowing at intersections. When the sedan pulled out ahead of him from a high-hedged lane, Greg was so shocked that his reactions were slowed and he hit the brake a fraction too late. The big Range Rover hit the rear corner of the car, shunting it onto the grass verge. Greg stopped and climbed out, instantly reverting to the urban driver of a former time.

"Why the hell don't you look where you're going? If you can't drive, you shouldn't be on the bloody road." He advanced toward the sedan, shouting angrily. He had a sudden realization of how ridiculous he seemed. He grinned. "I'm sorry. Conditioned reflex." And then, with more concern: "Are you all right?"

He was only a pace or two from the car when he halted. A big Colt .45 was poked through the window of the car. Its muzzle, like a black cave, wavered slightly, pointing at his face.

The man holding the gun said, "Keep back." Instinctively Greg raised his hands to shoulder height and took a pace backward. By this time the women had climbed from the Range Rover and stood in a huddle beside the door.

The voice said, "Are you armed?"

"No."

"Have you had the sickness?"

Greg tried to give his voice a note of authority. "Some of us. We've all had contact with it."

There was a pause. Then the man with the gun opened the door cautiously and started to climb out. He kept the revolver pointed. There was a second man in the front of the car, and on the backseat a woman and a child. Even in his own tight fear Greg felt relieved to recognize that they looked tense and frightened.

The barrel of the gun dipped toward the ground. The man behind it said, "We don't want any trouble." He was in his early forties, tall and stoop-shouldered. He wore eyeglasses in which one lens was missing.

Greg said, "We don't want trouble either." Then, in a forced conversational tone: "Where have you come from?"

The man gave a vague wave of direction. "We have a little farm. That way. It's a good place. A lot of greenhouses. We've started planting things." He paused again, studying Greg carefully, then: "I think we can make it work, but we need more people."

Abby took a step forward. The gun rose again warily. She said, "I'm Abby Grant," and extended her hand. The gesture confused the man, and he awkwardly transferred the gun to his left hand, wiped his palm on his trousers and shook hands. He said, "William Faber. Bill."

Ruth and Jenny came forward, and Abby continued with the introductions. Bill Faber beckoned to the others in his car, and they seemed grateful to climb out and join the group.

Philip Patterson was eighteen. He was bearded, and his hair fell below his shoulders. His smile was eager and nervous as he did the round of hand-shaking.

The woman was Elaine Corman. She remained slightly withdrawn and formal. Abby noticed with surprise that she was wearing makeup, and that her hair was arranged in unnaturally tight curls. She set her age at around fifty.

The frightened little girl who clung close to Elaine was six years old. Her name was Claire. Faber had found her living in the bar of a public house. She had survived alone for three weeks, living on chips and biscuits and lemonade. He'd had the greatest difficulty in persuading her to leave the bar, because of her insistence that her parents would be coming to get her soon.

Jenny brought the Primus stove from the Range Rover and set it up in the middle of the road. From the sedan

Faber brought a can of condensed milk and a jar of instant coffee.

The sharing of food and drink ended the reserve that both groups had maintained. They talked freely, matching experiences, exchanging news.

Faber invited them to follow him back to their farm. "Just to look it over. See what you think."

Abby countered with the same invitation. Greg settled the matter by pointing out they were closer to the hamlet than Faber's farm.

On the way back Jenny and Greg went in the sedan. Faber, Elaine and Claire traveled in the Range Rover.

Price came out to welcome them. He looked heavy-eyed, like a man just roused from a deep sleep. He apologized for the fact the fire had gone out, claiming that he had been working outside all day long.

Jenny and Ruth started to prepare a special meal, opening cans of soup, corned beef and peaches. They mixed large pans of instant potato and set the table with pickles and sauces.

While the food was made ready, Abby and Greg took the visitors on a conducted tour of the hamlet. They carefully pointed out the ample accommodation offered by the other houses. Faber admitted that his farm had only the one building with just three bedrooms. He explained that he intended to tow in several big trailers to house newcomers who might join them. Greg found himself talking like an enthusiastic real estate agent, listing the advantages of the settlement.

Abby waited until the meal was over. Greg offered brandy to the guests, and they settled around the relit fire. She had difficulty in keeping the formality out of her voice.

"I think I'm speaking for all of us. I know I am. We'd be very happy if you would join us here."

Greg said, "Right. With our two groups we could really make a go of this place."

Ruth and Jenny nodded. Price cleared his throat. He assumed a serious look and began ponderously, "Discipline is what we've got to have, see. Got to be able to take orders. . . ."

Before he could continue, Abby interjected, "We'd work together. We wouldn't be two groups—just one. From what you've said I think we have roughly the same aims. But we'd be glad of new ideas. One thing I'm sure of: We'll all stand a much better chance as a single unit."

Faber said, "We were going to make the same offer to you. Our farm is a good place, and it has a lot of potential. I think it could be more easily defended than this. But it is limited for space. The land is hillier, and that makes it more difficult to grow a crop. I'll be perfectly honest with you: I think you have the edge on us. For myself, I'd like to join you."

Unable to contain herself, Jenny said, "That's marvelous."

Faber held up his hand. "Hang on a minute. I want to hear what Phil and Elaine think." He glanced at them.

Phil said, "I don't mind moving. But I'd want to go back to the farm and get all my gear."

Faber reassured him. "Of course." And then, to Abby: "We've got a lot of food we could bring with us. And something better: we've got three pigs—a boar and two sows; and six chickens. No cockerel, though."

Excitedly Greg said, "My God, livestock must be worth its weight in gold. If we could get a litter from a sow, we'd really have something to trade with."

Ruth looked at Elaine. "You haven't said if you want to come yet."

Unsmiling, she gave a noncommittal shrug. "I do like my privacy. I always do my share, but I do like my privacy. I've got a room of my own at the farm."

"You could have that here." Jenny was quick to satisfy her. "I know what you mean about privacy. It's nice to get away on your own once in a while."

Elaine nodded seriously. "It's just that I don't think it's good for people to be always living on top of one another. You need a bit of privacy."

The whole group suddenly fell silent. Abby waited a moment, then asked, "Is that it then? Are we agreed?"

Faber said, "If you'll give us a hand, we could get most of our stuff moved up tomorrow."

10

IT was late in the year before the ground was dry enough to plow and rototill. They planted several tons of potatoes in what had been a meadow near the houses. They worked long days, setting them by hand. In another field they worked the ground to a fine tilth and spread seed for cabbage and sprouts, peas and beans.

The gardens attached to the houses had served as vegetable plots to previous occupants, and they were easily brought to order and used as nursery beds and for salad crops.

The enlarged group became quickly unified. There were minor disputes, occasional arguments, but in general they resolved their differences easily. The one resort to violence was brief and quickly settled. Tom Price had taken to working beside Philip Patterson. Whatever task the boy undertook, Price would be close at hand, offering advice and criticism. After several weeks Price had reduced the boy to the position of unskilled apprentice and taken upon himself the role of employer. It ended when Abby asked Price to cut some logs. Price turned the request into an order and passed it on to Phil. Then he sat on a wall and watched the boy piston the saw back and forth. "You want to speed it up a bit, boy. We'll be here all night, the rate

you're going. Put your weight into it. Good saw that is. I'd
get twice as many logs off as you in half the time. There's a
knack in it, see. You got to get the rhythm. Push, pull. Push,
pull." Price lit a cigarette. Wheezed. Coughed, then took up
the beat again at a swifter tempo. "Push, pull. Push, pull."

Phil stopped cutting. He withdrew the blade from the log
and laid the saw on the ground and then, with great
deliberation, walked across to Price and hit him full in the
face with his clenched fist. Price fell backward off the wall
and lay on the ground, blood streaming from his broken
nose. For a moment he was dazed and shocked. He rubbed
his hand across his mouth and saw the blood. He jumped to
his feet and squared away, hands milling in front of him in
sparring style. "You little bastard!" he said. "You idle little
sod. You're going to get a damn good hiding now." Phil
took a step forward and hit him again in the same place,
flattening the nose still more. Price looked surprised and
bewildered. There was hurt in his voice. "What d'you want
to do that for? I been like a bloody father to you. There's
gratitude for you." Phil moved toward him again. Price
backed off quickly, then turned and hurried toward the
house. When he was safely out of range, he turned and
called back, "Bloody vandal!" Phil went back to sawing the
logs.

Faber and his group quickly adopted the habit of looking
to Abby for orders and instructions. There was no dispute
or any question that she made the decisions. Nobody
doubted her authority, and no one even considered chal-
lenging it. That she was their leader never occurred to her.
Beyond Abby the line of command established itself easily
and naturally. Greg and Faber shared responsibility, and
neither made a decision without consulting the other.
Philip was a natural follower and an eager worker whose
confidence had grown since his victory over Price.

There were sharper edges to the relationships between
the women. Ruth found herself particularly irritated by
Elaine Corman. The older woman was extremely fastidious

about her personal appearance. Her hair was always neat, her makeup carefully applied. At work in the kitchen or the fields she seemed able to keep herself looking immaculate. She was conscientious in doing her share of the work and carried out every task with slow, painstaking thoroughness. In contrast, Ruth worked swiftly. Elaine cleaned every pan and dish as it was used. Ruth piled them up for an assault at the end of the day. Ruth peeled potatoes. Elaine subjected them to surgical scrutiny. The clash of temperaments came when Ruth was waiting impatiently to get to the taps and then realized that Elaine was carefully washing out empty food cans before dispatching them to the waste bin. Jenny heard the shouting and arrived in the kitchen in time to see Ruth slam out of the back door. Elaine stared after her, slightly flushed. "She's slovenly, that girl is. My house was always spotless. My hubby always used to say how nice I kept the place. Spotless, it was. We wouldn't have had that disease if everybody had kept their places as nice and clean as mine was."

Later Ruth apologized. After that they made a point of arranging the schedule so that they spent no time together in the kitchen.

Claire was never able to tell them with any certainty if she was six or seven years old. She was able to read quite well and enjoyed simple sums. The women made time each day to give her lessons of a kind, and she showed a remarkable skill at drawing. She was a happy and friendly child, and it seemed she had adapted more easily than any of them. Sometimes at night she would wake up screaming.

Finally, all the seed they had was set. The planting had occupied them so fully that they had not had time to make any forays for supplies. Abby's shopping list had risen to several pages.

Philip and Bill Faber went on the first trip. It was dark when they returned, the back of the Range Rover piled high with rolls of wire and garden tools. They decided to leave the unloading until morning and went straight into supper. Faber was very satisfied with their day. They had easily found what they had wanted but, more important, had met two more people.

"They have a cottage about thirty miles west of here," he explained. "We saw smoke, so we thought it was worth a look. Very cagey they were at first. Had a shotgun pointed at us from an upstairs window. Anyway, we talked a bit, and after a while they opened up the door, and we went in. Decent sort of chap, he turned out to be. Name of Christopher. Malcolm Christopher."

Phil took up the story. "He's got a fair-sized garden there. Reckons he can grow enough to keep the two of them going. Anyway, we told him about our place. Invited him to come and have a look if he wanted to. He seemed interested."

It was Faber's turn again. "He'd be a handy chap. He was a rose grower before the Death, so he knows a fair bit about horticulture. You could see that from his garden. A treat, it was."

"Do you think he might come?" Jenny asked.

Faber shrugged. "He might. Seemed he was playing things very cautiously. I told him there'd be no strings if he did come and visit."

"You said there were two of them. A woman?" It was Abby who asked the question.

"No. A lad. Boy about ten or eleven. Something like that. Nice kid. Christopher found him camped out in a field. He'd been at a school, apparently. The only one who'd survived, as far as he knew."

Abby felt her stomach contract in a sharp spasm. She spoke quickly.

"What was his name?"

Faber frowned and then shook his head. "Damned if I can remember. I'm not even sure he said his name."

Philip looked up from his food. "Peter," he said. Then: "Anybody want the rest of those potatoes?"

"Peter what?" Abby's voice was urgent.

Phil scooped the remaining potatoes onto his plate. He was casual and vague. "Don't know. Just Peter."

Driving the Range Rover, Abby left before dawn. Jenny sat beside her with the map on which Faber had marked the location of Christopher's cottage.

They hardly spoke in the hour or so that it took them to cover the thirty miles. When they were close, Jenny checked the map again. She said, "We take the next left. It's only about a mile then."

Abby nodded and watched for the turn off. The secondary roads had been made narrower by the burgeoning hedges. Intersections were difficult to see until you were level with them.

As they made the turn, Jenny said quickly, "Abby, you know the chances are against it, don't you? I mean, don't expect . . . what I'm saying is, don't be too disappointed."

"I know what you're saying, Jen. And I know you're right. It's just that I've got a feeling. I can't explain it more than that."

The cottage lay on the right of the road. It was built in brick and white weatherboard with a steeply pitched roof. Smoke was rising from the chimney to mingle with the hazy mist of the early morning.

Abby braked and turned off the engine. She and Jenny started to climb out. A man's voice called to them. "Stay there."

He was standing at the gate, slightly sheltered by the brick pillar. He held a twelve-bore shotgun directed toward them. "Have you had the sickness?"

Abby said, "We're both well." And then in hurried explanation: "You talked to some of our people yesterday. They told us about you."

Christopher stepped from his cover out into the roadway, lowering the gun. He remained cautious.

"What can I do for you?"

"You have a boy with you called Peter. That's my son's name. He's eleven and a half."

The man nodded. "Pete must be something like that."

"What's his other name?"

He looked puzzled. Then he grinned wryly and shook his

head. "Isn't that funny? I don't know. He's always been Peter." Christopher turned and pointed across the meadow behind the cottage toward a distant line of trees. "He's up there fetching timber. Do you want to see him?"

"Yes. Please."

He leaned the shotgun against the wall, cupped his hands to his mouth and called. "Peter!" His voice was clear and echoing in the silence.

The three of them stared toward the far trees. After a moment Christopher called again.

Abby stared unblinking. There was a movement at the edge of the trees, and a small figure stepped into the clear.

She began to run, through the gate and across the garden, then into the meadow. She knew now with absolute certainty that this was her son. Her eyes flooded with tears. As she ran, she softly called his name over and over again. Her arms extended toward the boy. She was within fifty feet of him. Then she halted. The boy, too, stopped, staring at her. Polite but bewildered. Then he smiled. "Who are you?" he asked.

The kettle began to boil, and Christopher scooped it off the hob of the open fire and carried it to the table. He filled three of the cups, then paused before topping up the fourth. "You're sure your friend won't join us?" he asked Jenny. She turned from the window. "I think she'd rather be on her own for a little while." She gave another glance out the window. Abby stood leaning against the front of the Rover, motionless except for the quick jerking motion of her hand as she snatched smoke from a cigarette.

"Why don't you sit down?" Jenny took the chair that Christopher proffered. He pushed the steaming cup of black coffee toward her. "I'm sorry, we have no sugar. And the last of the condensed milk went a few weeks ago."

Peter said, "We've got some bees. Later in the year we might have honey for sweetening."

"She's taking it hard, isn't she?" From where he sat Christopher could see Abby through the window.

Jenny said, "I tried to prepare her for a disappointment. It was just that she seemed so certain."

They sipped at their coffee. Christopher said, "The people we've met, not a lot admittedly, but the ones we've met—none of them were related. And as far as I know, none of them had even known one another before the Death. Mind, if her son was eleven and he did come through the disease, then I suppose he'd have a chance. God knows what the odds against it are, though. Millions and millions to one, I should think."

"Abby just won't accept that. I thought she had for a while. She hasn't talked about Peter since the winter. Then today I realized that he's never been out of her mind. All she's doing, all the work at our commune, is only so that she can have a place for him when she finds him."

"Well, it's some sort of future to work for, I suppose." He looked at Peter. "I'm not sure I wouldn't have quit if it hadn't been for him. When we met, he seemed to need me. Now we need each other." He tousled the boy's already untidy hair.

Peter ducked his head aside and with embarrassed pleasure said, "Get off!"

They were silent for a moment. Christopher stared into his cup. Then, quietly, he said, "Know what occurred to me the other day? There's going to be a big, big gap in the generations. I mean, any babies who didn't get the disease couldn't have come through. And how long could five- or six-year olds manage on their own?"

Jenny shuddered. "Poor little things. It doesn't bear thinking about."

Peter chipped in brightly. "There's a few kids of my age about, though. Boys and girls. We met some of them at Waterhouse."

"Waterhouse?"

"It's a place out in Sussex. One of those marvelous old estates. Stately-home style, you know. We happened on it by chance. Fair-sized community they've got going there. Something like thirty people. That's counting the kids, of course."

"Sounds good," Jenny said.

"They're doing all right. Bit of gardening, but mostly scavenging. They said we could stay if we wanted, but I didn't really fancy it. A bit too military and disciplined for my liking. Showed, too. When we said we weren't staying, they told us to drive out of the area. And they had a jeep follow us to make sure we did."

Jenny considered for a moment and then, deciding, took the map from her pocket. "You say there were children there?"

"Yes."

"Well, just in case. Could you mark where this Waterhouse place is? It's always handy to know where other communities are setting up."

Christopher unfolded the map and spread it on the table. With help from Peter he traced a route across it and then jabbed a point with his finger. "Here. Just about here."

Peter found a pencil, and they marked the spot with a large cross.

They finished their coffee and walked to the door. Shaking hands, Jenny said, "I hope you will come and visit us."

"The garden keeps us pretty busy," Christopher said. "Perhaps a bit later on. We know where you are."

Abby stayed silent on the drive back. She smoked incessantly, lighting one cigarette from the other.

Jenny resisted the temptation to tell her about the children at Waterhouse. On the one hand, she realized that it would give Abby another reason for hope. But if, as was almost certain, the clue again led nowhere, Abby would be plunged into black depression.

When they arrived back, Abby went straight to her room. Jenny showed Greg the map and told him what Christopher had said. Greg was adamant that the information should be kept from Abby.

"You'll just start her going again," he said. "Look, you know as well as I do that it's a ninety-nine-point-nine certainty that Peter is dead. If only she was honest, she'd probably agree. Tell her about this, and she'll be off like a flash. She won't find Peter, but they might tell her about another place where there are kids. She could keep wandering for months. We couldn't let her go on her own, so that means the work force here gets cut. I don't think any of us, me included, would put up with that for long. Anyway, she's too valuable here. If she knows it or not, she holds this place together."

Jenny agreed with Greg. Absolutely. As the day went on, she seemed less certain.

Abby came down to assist with the evening meal. She only joined in conversation that was directed at her, staying withdrawn and guarded. After the meal, which she didn't share, she went back to her room. Jenny stayed beside the fire long after the others had gone to bed. On her knee was the map, folded to the section where Waterhouse was marked with the cross.

The door to Jenny's bedroom blasted open with shuddering violence. Terrified, she sat bolt upright, the sheets falling away from her naked breasts. Greg stamped across to her bed and glared down at her. His voice was tight with rage.

"You told her, didn't you?! You damn well told her!"

Jenny was still dazed by the fear and sudden awakening. "What is it? What's the matter?"

She started to climb out of bed, and only when she stood up did she become aware of her nakedness. She slithered back into the bedclothes and pulled the sheet to her chin. From the window was a thin pale light that only hinted at dawn.

"You stupid bitch. You told her."

Jenny understood then. She nodded. "I thought about it a lot. When I came past her room last night, I heard her crying. I had to tell her, Greg. I had no right to keep it from her."

"If you'd cared about her at all, you'd have said nothing. Anyway, she's gone. I heard the Rover about ten minutes ago. I couldn't get out in time to stop her."

"You wouldn't have, anyway. Shall we take the other car and go after her?"

The anger seemed to seep out of Greg. He sighed and made a helpless gesture with his hands. "We'd never catch her now. Anyway, I suppose she's perfectly capable of looking after herself."

He turned and started for the door. He didn't look back as Jenny said, "I'm sorry, Greg. I had to do what I thought was right."

Abby climbed out of the driver's seat and walked to the tree that lay across the road. She considered fixing a cable to it and attempting to pull it clear with the Range Rover. She wasn't sure that the cable or the car would have the strength to move it.

She reversed the Rover back until she drew level with a fallen field gate. Then, shifting into forward, she advanced into a meadow already high with grass and weed. She drove cautiously, looking for an exit that would allow her back onto the road beyond the toppled tree.

The slow-moving Rover thudded against something and stalled. A swarm of glinting blue flies swirled around the windshield. She started the engine and backed off. The decomposing carcass of a cow lay half hidden in the grass.

She swung around and moved on carefully. There was no gate, but the powerful four-wheel drive pushed the Rover through the wooden posts of a barbed-wire fence. Back on the road again, she drove swiftly to make up for lost time.

11

GARLAND threw himself into a clump of deep bracken. He was panting from his long run. Slowly and with a conscious effort he controlled his breathing, taking long, slow inhalations. Calmer, he turned and parted the bracken to stare back the way he had come. Five hundred yards away a man stood on the crest of the bare hill. From the other side of the hill another man appeared and halted on the crest. Then another and another. Finally there were eight figures silhouetted against the afternoon sun. They stood in a line, each separated from the next by about fifty feet.

Garland pressed himself closer to the ground as he caught a glint of light from the binoculars that one of the men was using to scan the area. The man with the glasses raised his hand, and the line started to advance slowly down the hill.

Still keeping low, Garland angled his head to check the ground behind him. The most direct line to the edge of the woods offered little cover, and he would be in clear sight of the hunters. He calculated that he would be out of the range of shotguns but an easy target for anyone with a rifle. The alternative was to work his way through the cover and, taking the longer route, reach the trees unseen.

Cautiously he raised himself into a sprinter's starting crouch, paused, then bounded forward across the open ground. Distantly he heard the sharp cries of alarm from the line of men, then the muffled report of a shotgun as somebody wasted a cartridge. Legs pounding, he started to zigzag. There was the crisp, clean sound of a rifle being discharged. Now his pursuers were running, the line converging on him. Thirty yards, and he'd be in the trees. There was another rifle shot, and he fancied he heard the whine of the bullet near him. Excitement surged through him. There was no fear. Simply the exhilaration that he had always found when he put himself at risk. He made another sharp turn, and then he was among the trees.

He slowed to an easier pace, weaving through the woods, changing direction frequently. He jumped down a steep bank and splashed his way across a shallow stream. Then he halted and listened. The sounds of the hunters were far behind him, muffled and indistinct. There were more gunshots.

"They're nervous," he thought. "Shooting at nothing." He scooped a handful of water from the stream and splashed his face, then moved on at a gentle jog trot.

As he entered a clearing, a figure stepped from behind a tree. There was a shotgun at his shoulder pointing directly at Garland. He said, "Stop. Stop there."

Garland halted. His challenger could have been no more than sixteen and looked terrified. Garland said, "Where the hell did you come from?"

The boy said, "Just you stop where you are." His voice was thick and nasal. His eyes were red-rimmed and moist. His nose was running.

Garland took a pace forward and grinned at him. "Hayfever?"

The boy backed away, keeping the gun leveled. He yelled as loudly as his husky voice would allow. "Over here," he called. "I've got him. Over this way." And then to Garland again: "You just stand still."

"What are you so nervous about? You have the gun. I'm not likely to try anything with that pointed at my chest."

"You'd better not." Then shouting again. "Over here."

A hardly discernible voice called, "Which way?" The boy glanced toward the sound, and Garland leaped at him. His hand closed around the muzzle of the shotgun and deflected it toward the ground. In the same instant the boy pulled the trigger. The blast ripped through Garland's trousers, the shot searing a shallow wound across his outer thigh. He pulled the gun from the boy's hands, unaware that he'd been hit. With the gun free, he swung it toward himself and then sharply back, jabbing the stock hard into the boy's stomach. The boy doubled up with a loud gasp and fell to the ground.

Only when he started to run did Garland feel the surge of pain. He clasped his hand to his thigh and felt the oozing hot blood.

There was a crashing in the undergrowth to his right, and he veered away from the sound. Two of the hunters appeared almost directly ahead of him and set up a cry as he again changed direction. They were close around him now, their voices loud and violent.

Limping from the wound that was already stiffening his leg, Garland headed for the edge of the woods. As he cleared the thinning trees, he heard an excited voice call, "He's gone into the open. We've got him now."

The downward slope over the open grassland gave him some speed, but a swift glance behind him showed that at least four of his pursuers were coming up fast. Garland eyed the barrier of the hedge in front of him. He veered to the right, aiming for a point where it seemed less dense.

Abby had heard the shooting but could see nothing for the high green walls that lined the road. Garland seemed to fall out of the hedge directly ahead of her, landing on his knees. Had she not braked swiftly she could not have missed hitting him. She halted only a yard from him. He bounded to his feet, flung open the passenger door and hauled himself into the seat.

"Drive! For God's sake, drive, and do it fast!" There was such urgency and command in the voice that without question Abby shifted into gear and raced the car forward. Before she reached third gear, she saw, through her rearview mirror, two men scramble out through the hedge and onto the road. With no hesitation they raised their guns and fired at the Rover. Abby put her foot down hard. In the same moment a man slithered down the road bank some twenty yards ahead of them. He found his balance and leveled his gun.

"Drive through," Garland ordered. Abby swerved the car toward the gunman. His nerve broke before he had time to pull the trigger, and he threw himself flat against the bank as Abby roared past, missing him by inches.

There was another shot from the couple behind, and the Range Rover lurched as the rear tire blew out. The steering wheel jerked and juddered in Abby's grip. Garland put out a hand to help steady it. He said, "Just keep going. We'll be all right now."

They covered another three miles on the racketing flat tire; then Garland pointed to some flat ground beside the road. "Pull off over there." As they halted, he turned and grinned at her. "Thanks."

Abby lifted her hands off the steering wheel. Her fingers were trembling. Now that the tension had eased she felt the fear crawl across her body. She leaned back and closed her eyes.

Garland took a cigarette package from his pocket. He offered it to Abby. "Cigarette?" She opened her eyes and nodded. She reached for one, but her hand shook so that she could not grip it firmly.

"I'll do it." Garland put two cigarettes in his mouth and lit them. He handed one to Abby. She drew on it gratefully.

She turned to take her first good look at her passenger. She guessed he was in his very early thirties. He had a good face, the bones making clean firm lines. His hair was fair and chopped raggedly short, but what came over to Abby most strongly was the incredible good humor of his smile.

Abby said, "What was all that about?"

"It was the first time they've really organized a proper search to try and catch me. They did it very well, too.

They've had me on the run since dawn. Had you not come along, they'd have got me."

"They were trying to kill you?"

"That would have done if they couldn't have caught me."

"Why?"

"I suppose you could say we don't see eye to eye over a few points. So, as far as they're concerned, we're at war."

She thought he meant the word as a joke, but looking at his face, she saw he didn't.

He said, "Historically, that's what it's always been called. Two or more groups with opinions at variance who resort to force of arms. That's war, isn't it?"

"How many are you? I mean, there seemed to be a lot of them. How many with you?"

"Oh, there's just me."

"You're on your own?"

Garland nodded. He took a last deep pull on his cigarette and pressed it into the ashtray. As he opened the door, he said, "I'll change your wheel and let you get on. It's not a good idea to hang about here. Where's the spare?"

"In the back somewhere."

As he swung out of the car, she saw the dark stain of blood on his trousers. Seeing her glance, he put his hand to the wound and gently eased the shredded cloth from the raw flesh.

"I'll have to get a dressing on this. I don't think it's very deep, but it hurts like hell." He moved away to the rear of the Rover.

Abby got out and looked at the back tire. Its walls were ripped, the tread hanging in shreds. Garland moved to join her. "There doesn't seem to be a spare." Then, pointing to the wheel: "And you're not going to get much farther on that. I'll have to find you another car. Plenty of them about. In the meantime I think we should push off from here. They're bound to follow us. We'll be safe enough at my place."

Abby's uncertainty showed in her face. "I don't know. I should be getting on."

"In that case we'll make a car the first priority. Incidentally, where were you heading?"

"A place called Waterhouse."

Garland reacted to the name. Abby said, "Do you know it?"

He nodded. "Yes. I know it." She sensed a caution in his voice, a wariness. "What did you want there?"

"I'm looking for my son. I heard there were some boys there about his age. He's eleven and a half."

Garland's easy manner returned. "I might be able to help you." He glanced back the way they had come. "I really do think we should get a move on. Those chaps back there are awfully keen to catch me. And seeing you helped me, they won't be too well disposed toward you." He put a hand to her elbow as if to steer her off along the path.

Abby stood her ground. "I don't know. I'm not sure. I don't want to get involved in your war."

"I'm afraid you already are. At least until I can get you out of the district. Now come on."

He took her arm more firmly, and still reluctant, Abby allowed herself to be led toward the trees. As they walked, he said, "By the way, my name is Jimmy Garland."

"Abby Grant."

"Can it be Abby?"

She nodded. His natural and relaxed charm made her feel more confident.

He said, "I know all this must be inconvenient for you. But you must admit it's exciting, isn't it?"

Abby stared at him. Then, shaking her head in wonder, she started to laugh. "You're really enjoying this, aren't you?"

His answer was perfectly serious. "Yes," he said. "Every minute of it."

It was another half hour before the hunters reached the Range Rover. They shuffled up in twos and threes. A ragged, weary group. Charles Knox prodded the ruined tire with the toe of his boot, then stared off toward the woods. He was a big man. Heavily bearded. The set of his body and the hard tone of his voice suggested a determined and stubborn character.

Trevor Bates looked every inch the clerk he had once been. Neatly dressed in a lightweight tweed suit. The only man in the group wearing a collar and tie. He stood beside Knox and followed his gaze. He said, "We'll never find him in there. He seems to know those woods like the inside of his hand."

Knox grunted. Then: "We'll find him. We'll keep pushing him, keep him on the move." He looked around at his men. They had begun to settle down, sitting on the grass and lighting cigarettes. They had little enthusiasm for continuing the pursuit. Knox said, "We'll keep going for another hour. Then we'll send half the men in to rest up and get some food. Then they can take over while we do the same. We're not letting up now. Even if it takes days. We'll keep him running. Keep him running." He called to the men. "All right. Come on, come on. We're not finished yet."

Grumbling quietly, they got up and trailed Knox and Bates toward the trees.

Garland halted Abby. He said, "Hang on a second, there's something I want to show you. I'll just check there's nobody about."

She watched him move away, impressed by the silence and ease with which he was able to move through the tangled undergrowth and close trees. She noticed that his wounded leg was quite stiff.

She lost sight of him for a moment and had a quick feeling of panic. She stood quite still, watching and listening for a sign of him. A minute passed. The woods that had seemed so pleasant with him at her side now looked dark and ominous. She was about to call out when he reappeared and beckoned her.

He helped her pick her way through a clump of young saplings and up to an iron fence that marked the edge of the woods. He pointed. Lying in a valley below them was a beautiful Elizabethan manor house. High yew hedges marked out courtyards and drives. To one side of the house were stables and outbuildings. Neglected lawns billowed with lush grass. On the driveway in front of the house were a number of vehicles. Cars and jeeps.

Garland said, "That's Waterhouse." There was a mocking note as he went on as though quoting from a guidebook. "Ancestral home and countryseat of the Waterhouse family. Now the property of the fourteenth earl, James, Lord Waterhouse . . . or, less formally, me."

Abby looked at him. "That's your house? And you really do have a title?"

"Yes. It's all meaningless, of course. I was the fourth son and never would have inherited. Then along came this plague thing. Now I'm the last of the line. Come on." He started to lead her back into the trees.

Abby said, "Aren't we going down there?"

"No. No, I actually live in somewhat more modest circumstances. That's what my little war is about. The gentlemen we had the brush with have taken over Waterhouse. I'm disputing their right to stay there."

They walked for some time, with Garland leading along a winding route into a densely overgrown area. He held back some bushes for Abby to pass and directed her attention to the ground.

"Careful here. There's a trip wire. It's rigged as an alarm."

She stepped carefully over it, and together they pushed through some tall grass that concealed an opening into the hollowed-out center of a huge clump of brambles. Behind the briers was the small opening to a cave. Abby followed Garland inside. She stood in total darkness, listening to sounds she could not identify. The scrape of metal on metal. A clink of glass. A hiss. Then there was the scratch of a match and a flare of light. Garland was holding a small butane lantern. Its mantle glowed, first yellow, then changing to a hard white light. The metal scraped again as he pushed the glass cover back down into position.

Abby looked around her. The walls of the cave were of dry rock. It was roughly rectangular in shape and had plenty of headroom for most of its spaces. The roof ran down sharply at the innermost point of the cave, and the area was too deep in shadows for Abby to see if the cave continued. Against one wall was a camp bed. There was a table with a store of canned provisions. A camping stove. In a corner were some rifles. Hunting bows with quivers of arrows. Fishing rods. Rabbit snares and nets.

"How long have you been living here?"

"About six weeks. My brothers and I used to use this when we were kids. It was our den. I don't think even our parents knew where it was."

Garland lowered himself onto the edge of the camp bed, keeping his injured leg stiffly straight.

Abby moved to him and dropped to her knees. "Let me have a look at that." She eased the cloth off the wound.

He said, "There are some dressings in that box. I'll get one." He made a move to stand. Abby said, "I'll get it."

She found what she wanted, then asked for clean water and a pan. He directed her to them. She lit the stove and put the water on to boil, then moved back to Garland.

"Tke your trousers off."

For the first time since they had met, Garland looked ill at ease. Abby laughed. "While you're being coy, you could bleed to death. Come on."

He unfastened his belt and then rested his weight on his hands while Abby pulled the trousers clear, easing them past the wound.

She brought the lamp across and set it on the floor beside them. Seeing the injury clearly made her wince. The shot had gouged a deep channel in the flesh. Much of the blood had congealed, and heavy bruising darkened the skin.

When the water was warmed, Abby cleaned and dried the wound. There was a tube of antiseptic powder included with the dressing, and she sprinkled it onto the raw flesh; then, working with gentle care, she bandaged the leg.

"How does it feel?"

"It aches. But it'll be all right if I keep moving and don't give it a chance to stiffen up." He crossed the cave and took a fresh pair of trousers from a pile of neatly folded clothes.

Abby said, "You look very pale. Why don't you lie down for a while?"

"I'm all right. Just a bit of reaction. The adrenaline has run down, that's all."

Firmly she took his arm and led him back to the camp bed. "Sit there. Now, if you'll tell me where things are, I'll get us something to eat."

Garland said, "Look, I'm sorry I got you into this. I promise I'll find a vehicle and get you on your way as soon as possible."

"I'm not going until I've had a chance to see if Peter is at the house. Do you have a can opener?"

He made to rise.

She said, "Just tell me where it is. You're not very good at letting people do things for you, are you?"

He smiled and settled back. "I'm just not very used to it." They talked as she worked, both finding themselves more and more at ease. The conversation was casual and relaxed. Abby realized that she had once again assumed responsibility for looking after someone. But this time it was different. She was enjoying it.

"Mr. Knox. Over here. I've found something." It was the boy who'd shot Garland. Knox threaded his way through the trees toward him. Bates followed. The boy was holding the limp body of a dead rabbit, loosening the wire snare from around its throat. He looked up as the two men joined him. "The rabbit's still warm. That means the snare must be fairly newly set." The hayfever-plagued boy wiped his streaming nose against his sleeve, looking up expectantly for approval or word of praise.

"What the hell has that got to do with anything?" Bates said snappily.

Knox was more thoughtful. "Any of our people trapping up here?"

"No," the boy said eagerly. "I've been on the trapping detail for two months. We never come up here. That's why I thought it was important."

"That was smart of you," Knox said. He paid the compliment the way he would pat a dog. It pleased the boy.

Bates still didn't understand. Knox explained.

"If it's not our snare, then it's got to be Garland's. And it would make sense if he set his traps reasonably close to where he hides out."

"You think we're near him, Mr. Knox?"

"It's likely. There's been no sign nor sound of him for a couple of hours. He's gone to earth somewhere. Could be close to here."

Knox looked up at the sky through the trees. "It'll be dark soon."

"We going to turn it in? Start again tomorrow?" Bates asked.

"No. We'll keep going. You, boy. You go back to the house. Fetch lanterns and flashlights. If he's hiding, we'll find him. If he's running, we'll keep him on the move. We've got to push him. Push him all the time. Wear him down."

Garland poured generous measures of brandy into the hip flask's fitted cups. Abby put their empty plates on the table and moved back to sit beside him. She took the drink and tasted it.

"That's very good."

"It's twenty-seven. Single year. I got it from the cellars at Waterhouse on one of my forays."

Abby took another approving sip of the brandy. "For a man living in a cave you seem to do quite well for yourself."

He said, "Not badly. But then, I've had plenty of practice. I've probably spent more nights sleeping rough than I have in proper beds."

"I don't understand."

Garland took cigarettes from his packet and, lighting two of them, passed one to Abby.

"I'm one of those expedition people," he said, inhaling deeply. "Started at university. Whenever some loony planned a trip in the name of science, I was always the first to

sign on. I'd done the Sahara and the Congo before I was
twenty. Then, like all good fourth sons and bad academics,
I went into the army. And that was splendid. There were
always bits of wars going on, and in between we'd organize
little walkabouts."

Abby listened with fascination. He talked about himself
with alightly mocking note, making little of any part he had
played on his expeditions.

"I spent some time in the Amazon, which was fascinating,
except that I don't like big spiders, so I didn't sleep for a
month. I did a polar walk, which was chilly. I did the Zaire
River, which was wet." He assumed a rather bad American
travelogue-movie accent. "Wherever white man had not
trod before, there was I." Then, more seriously: "But me
and my kind were running out of world."

"What do you mean?"

"Well, we'd climb some unconquered peak, get to the top
and find a television camera. We'd push our way through
darkest jungle, and there'd be a film crew shooting nature
pictures. There just wasn't enough empty world left."

Abby said, "You should have been born two hundred
years ago."

He turned to look at her, his face very earnest. "Oh, no.
No, now is the time to be alive. Now is the best time of all."

Abby's surprise was on her face and in her voice.

"Now? With things as they are?"

He nodded. No longer mocking, he said, "It's a time like
now I'm made for. I can use everything I've learned. All I've
trained for. I couldn't have dreamed up a better world for
me to live in. This is my time."

Abby felt herself stiffen slightly. Garland had shocked
her. He heard the disapproval in her voice.

"The millions and millions who died. Don't they mean
anything to you?"

He answered her quietly. Not looking at her. "If I'm
absolutely honest, no. I can respond to a tragedy on an
individual level, but not on this massive scale. The limit of
pain and suffering is what one person endures. That
suffering isn't magnified because hundreds of millions are

inflicted with it. And sorrow is like that, too. You can't mourn for a whole world."

He turned to look at her. She remained silent.

"I'm sorry. I've offended you."

"No," she said too quickly. Then, more thoughtfully: "Yes. Yes, I think you did. I suppose I've been seeing what happened in a totally conventional way. I'd not been able to put it in the same perspective as you."

"Mine might not be the right way. But it's a way of staying sane. In absolute truth, the world that ended wasn't one I very much liked. I was a misfit. And now I'm not. As I said, this is my time."

"And what will you do with your time?" She emphasized the last two words.

He answered without hesitation. "Take over my house again. Teach others to survive in this new environment. Lead them."

"Couldn't you just join them? Do you have to be the leader?"

"It's what I've been trained for."

He glanced at his watch. Then, grunting, he stood up. He flexed his knee, grimacing slightly at the ache from the stiffened muscles. He said, "It will be dark now. I can pick up that car. In the morning I'll get you close enough to the house to have a look at the kids. There are four of them about you son's age."

He picked up a rifle and limped toward the cave entrance. "I'll be back in a couple of hours. You get some rest."

Abby cleared away the remains of their meal, then settled on the camp bed and put her feet up. She thought about Garland and was still thinking about him when she fell asleep.

A hand touched her shoulder, shaking her gently. She wakened slowly, wanting to sleep on. She opened her eyes. Charles Knox was staring down at her.

Waterhouse's lofty entrance hall was paneled in oak.

Fading tapestries hung from brass rails. There were ancestral portraits and shields that carried armorial bearings. There were two suits of armor and a collection of ancient weapons mounted on the wall behind them. Unmoving, Abby stood at the foot of the impressively carved stairway.

Knox had left four men at the cave to wait for Garland's return. He had "suggested" Abby accompany them back to Waterhouse, but she didn't doubt that had she refused, he would have insisted. On the journey they had spoken very little. She answered some of Knox's questions, telling him only why she had come to the area. That he and his men remained polite and courteous did little to calm her fears.

Knox appeared at the top of the stairs. "Would you like to come up, Mrs. Grant?"

He waited on the broad landing until she reached him, then, leading the way down a wide corridor, halted at a bedroom door. He took a lighted candle from a side table and handed it to her. His voice hardly more than a whisper, he said, "The boys share this room. Have a look at them, but try not to wake them." He opened the door quietly, and Abby went inside.

Knox took a few paces away and leaned against the wall. He was tired. He let his eyes close, then a few seconds later reluctantly opened them again at the sound of the door being closed softly. There was no need for the question. He said, "I'm sorry, Mrs. Grant." He gave her a moment, then: "We have to talk. We'll be more comfortable in the study."

She followed him down the stairs and across the spacious hallway. In the study he turned up the flame on an oil lamp and indicated the armchair. When Abby had settled, he drew up a straight-backed chair and set it opposite her.

"Am I a prisoner here?"

Knox shook his head.

"Then I'd like to go."

Knox bent his head, softly massaging his eyes with thumb and forefinger. "I brought you here because I thought you might be able to help."

Stiffly Abby said, "I want to go."

"Just hear me out. Please. That young man Garland is going to get himself killed."

"Isn't that what you want?"

His voice had the despair and weariness of someone who had already explained a dozen times and failed to be understood. "No, no, no. What do you think we are here? Some sort of gang of bandits?"

Defensively she said, "You shot him. He's wounded."

"My people were trying to take him. They had guns, and they got excited. But that was the last thing I wanted. It's just that I can't allow him to go on terrorizing us."

Abby smiled derisively. "One man? Terrorizing?"

"Yes." His voice quickened and took an edge of anger. "He's acting like a character out of a *Boy's Own Paper* story. Adventure stuff. He's burned a barn. Driven off our stock. He's raided our food stores three or four times. Tonight, just before we got back, he took a car from the forecourt. And that despite the fact I had a man on guard. I tell you, he's got everybody running scared."

What he said was so clearly sincere, so evidently honest, that Abby felt her loyalty to Garland waver. She was on the defensive as she said, "All he wants is to get his house back. That's all."

Knox leaned forward in his chair. More vehement than before. "No, that's not all, Mrs. Grant. There are nearly thirty people here now. The beginnings of a good community. We can make this place self-supporting. We've laid claim to the place because it was essential to the survival of a lot of people. Any more that come are welcome to join us. But we can't allow one man to jeopardize our future."

She knew now exactly what he meant. His words, his ideas were things that she, Greg, Jenny, Ruth, all of them had said and thought many times. She couldn't help putting herself into Knox's position, seeing Waterhouse as their own hamlet. Would they let a Garland terrorize them? With less conviction Abby said, "Why not let Garland join you? Let him become the leader if he wants to. Or aren't you willing to give that up?"

Knox said, "You know the conditions he's made?" She shook her head, and he went on, "Everybody has to move out of this house. They can live in the farms and cottages. They'll pay their rent in food and services. They'll owe total allegiance to this house and its laws. He wants these people as his subjects. With the right to administer life and death."

He checked himself, aware his voice was rising in anger. To calm himself, he fumbled in his pockets and found his cigarette package. He took and lit one for himself before remembering to offer one to Abby. She shook her head.

"You said you thought I could help. How?"

Knox took a deep draw on his cigarette before he answered. "Talk to him. That's all. It's fairly obvious that he trusts you. Just talk to him. Make him see sense. Tell him we'll call a truce if he'll just discuss things with us. We don't want a war."

Abby thought for a moment and then nodded. "All right. I'll try. But how am I going to contact him again?"

Knox stood up. "Don't worry about that. I know Garland's character well enough by now. If he thinks we're holding you against your will, he'll be contacting us."

Abby slept deeply. Dreamlessly. Glaring sunlight already filled the room when she was wakened by the sound of angry voices and movement from the downstairs hall. She dressed quickly and hurried along the landing. From the top of the stairs she saw several armed men grouped around Knox. He looked dazed, still heavy with sleep, as he buttoned his shirt and tried to make sense of what the men, all talking at once, were saying. He finally brought them to silence with his raised voice. "All right, all right. Bates. You organize a search. Go right through the house. All the outbuildings."

Bates interjected, his voice quick with excitement, "We've already done that."

"Then do it again. And do it properly. Put the rest of the men around the house. And until we know what's going on, the women and children are to stay inside."

The men splintered away. Knox rubbed his hands across his face, then looked up as Abby started down the stairs, asking, "What's happened?"

"Looks like your friend has been busy. One of our girls is missing. Elizabeth. She went out early to collect the eggs and hasn't been seen since. We think Garland has taken her. You see what we're up against. He's crazy."

Garland adjusted the focus on the telescopic sight. The image sharpened. At five hundred yards the man was an easy target. He stood beside a sedan on the forecourt of the house. The angle of the cross hairs on the lens centered on his chest. Garland shifted the gun a fraction, then, holding it rock-steady, squeezed the trigger.

The window of the car blew to pieces, adding its sound to the roar of the rifle shot. The man seemed turned to stone. The shock held him in position for several seconds; then he flailed to the ground, scrambling and crawling to cover behind the car. The other men positioned around the forecourt had been quicker to seek positions of safety and were now nervously scanning the hillside to locate the spot from which the shot had been fired.

Hidden by the high gorse, Garland moved in a crouching run to a new position. Aiming carefully, he fired three rapid shots that chipped masonry from the wall above the heads of two men who had taken shelter behind the terrace balustrade. He heard the distant and confused shouts of alarm as he moved off again to take up another firing angle.

Kneeling on the floor, Knox raised his head a few inches to peer out of the window but jerked back down at the sound of more shots. Then, lifting his head again, he stared out at the hillside.

On hands and knees Bates shuffled across to join him. As though Garland might hear him, he kept his voice in a low whisper. "Can you see him?"

Knox made no answer. Abby watched both men from the angle of the stairs where she had been ordered for her own safety. Knox stared for a moment longer, then very decisively got to his feet and started toward the front door. "I'm going out there."

Bates grabbed at his arm. "You're out of your mind. He'll pick you off just like that!"

Knox shrugged the hand away. "If he was shooting to kill, he would have hit somebody before this." He moved to the door, paused, then, bracing himself, pulled it open and stepped outside.

Thinking he was unaware of the danger, somebody called to him, "Get down!" Knox ignored the warning and advanced slowly across the terrace and down the steps. His tension was evident in the stiffness of his movements. He crossed the forecourt onto the unkempt lawn, then down to the ha-ha, where he halted. He surveyed the hillside carefully. Nothing moved. Cupping his hands to his mouth, he called, "Garland!" He let the echo of his own voice trickle into silence before he called again. "Garland! You hear me?"

"Over here."

Knox swung to his right. Garland stood beside a large blue cedar not twenty yards away, the rifle held easily in the crook of his arm.

Garland said, "The girl is all right. I'll free her when you release Mrs. Grant."

Knox started to speak, then halted himself in a conscious effort not to gabble. He began again. "Mrs. Grant can leave any time she wants. Look, we must talk."

"I want to see her."

Knox found himself rushing his words again. "Things can't go on like this."

"Ask her to come out." The softness of his voice did nothing to diminish the note of command.

Knox turned and walked quickly back to the edge of the forecourt. He called sharply. "Mrs. Grant!"

Abby appeared at the front door, and he beckoned her to join him. As she came up to him, he said in an urgent whisper, "You can go to him if you want. But for God's sake, try and get him to come in and talk to us. No harm will come to him; I give you my word."

They walked together toward the tree that sheltered Garland. He stood beside it watching them approach. A gesture with the gun halted them both. He said, "Just you, Abby."

She gave Knox a brief nod, then moved on to stand beside Garland. He grinned at her. "Sorry I was so long." He nodded toward some dense shrubbery off to one side. "Cut down through there. Soon as you're out of sight, start running. I'll be right behind you."

Garland watched until she vanished behind a screen of rhododendron. Then he glanced at Knox. "I'll free the girl when we're safely clear from here." Then he turned and followed Abby.

His going was like a signal. The men from the house rushed down to cluster around Knox. A few of the more daring made to follow Garland. Knox halted them: "Let them go. Just let them go."

Bates said, "What about Betty? Will he let her go?"

Knox nodded. "He's given his word. That's one thing you can depend on."

The car was hidden in a deep gully some twenty yards off a bridle path. Garland pulled away the leafy branches he had used to camouflage it. He pulled open the driver's door and gestured for Abby to climb in. "There you are. There's about half a tank of petrol. It will get you well clear of here."

Abby didn't move. She said, "Have you got a cigarette?"

He did his trick of lighting them both, then handed one to her. As she took it, she said, "Knox told me you burned down a barn."

He nodded. "Mmmm. But that was months ago."

"But you did do it?"

Garland lowered himself onto the grass. It was evident from the way he positioned his leg that his wound was still giving him some discomfort. Abby sat beside him.

"It was before most of the settlers arrived. There were

plague victims in some of the cottages. I moved the bodies. The barn was the funeral pyre."

"Knox didn't tell me that."

Garland shrugged. "I wouldn't expect him to. I seem to get the credit—or blame—for anything that goes wrong around here."

"They also said you want to run everything. Be like some sort of feudal baron."

He turned to look at her. He was intensely serious now. "I'll tell you what I want. I want to see Waterhouse working again as a self-supporting estate. See the land worked. People living in the houses. It can be a society that provides for its strongest and its weakest members. It can be a more real life than any of us experienced before the plague. It seems to me that the people who've come through are desperately trying to re-create the world that died. They're just patching up. Well, that's not going to work. There has to be a different philosophy. A new . . . or rather, an old way of thinking."

"And the old way of thinking sets you up as lord of the manor?" Abby thought she added the right degree of mockery to her voice, but Garland missed it—or ignored it. He went on with such patent sincerity that she felt her question had been cheap.

"I honestly think I am better trained and equipped to administer the estate than any of them. It will need discipline and rules. Some sort of arbiter to settle the inevitable quarrels. All right, it might sound paternal, but it will always be benevolent. I'll put into that society as much as any other member of it. They'll have a voice in everything that is done. Give me a year, and I promise that I'll make that place work to the benefit of all who are there."

His enthusiasm had an intensity that was almost naïve. But there was no doubting his honesty. Abby was utterly convinced.

She said, "Then they haven't understood you. Please, you must talk to them. They think you just want to take over. Rule them. Like some sort of king."

Garland shook his head. "That's not true."

She reached out and touched his arm. "Then tell them what you plan. Tell them in just the way you told me. Make them understand. Look, Knox swore they would not harm you. He gave me his word. Let's take the car and go there now."

He stared down at the ground. Abby said, "Please."

He turned to her and grinned. "You're a regular little one-woman United Nations, aren't you? Come on then. Let's get it over with." As they started to get to their feet, he said, "First of all, I'd better go and release the girl."

Abby was eager that he shouldn't have time for second thoughts. She said quickly, "That can wait. I mean, she's all right, isn't she?"

He nodded. "She's fine. I've got her locked up in the folly."

"In that case Knox can send somebody to let her out. This is more important." She started toward the car.

Bates turned to the man beside him and said, "Tell Knox." He gave his attention back to the approaching car, watching down the barrel of his shotgun. When it halted, he stepped out of cover, keeping the gun at the ready. Abby climbed from the passenger seat.

She glanced across at Bates. In a soft voice she said, "It's all right. We've come to talk." Garland moved around to join her. They stood awkwardly, waiting for Bates to make a move. When he didn't, Abby took the initiative. "Where's Knox?"

Bates said, "In the house. Are you armed?" Abby shook her head and looked at Garland. "Come on." Together they started toward the front door. Bates followed them.

As they went up the steps, the door opened. Knox stared at them. Then, backing into the hall, he said, "Come in."

Garland stood aside, allowing Abby to enter first. He followed her a few paces forward until they were face to face with Knox. The two men eyed one another. Garland reached out his hand.

A man, until now hidden by the open front door, stepped swiftly into the open. Abby caught only the briefest glimpse of him as he rushed forward. He held a pistol raised above shoulder level. She began to shout a warning, but it was already too late. Garland started to turn, the movement deflecting the blow slightly onto the side of his neck. As his knees buckled, Knox moved forward and delivered a heavy-booted kick that caught him in the chest. The man with the pistol swung the weapon back for a second blow, but before he could strike, Abby hurled herself at him, grabbing for his wrist. As she grappled for the gun, Bates stepped in behind her and pulled her clear. Garland rolled onto his side and scrambled onto all fours. Before he could rise further, Knox aimed a kick that crunched under Garland's jaw. His head snapped back, and he toppled onto his side.

Abby struggled fiercely to free herself from Bates' embracing grasp, kicking and writhing. More men had entered the hall now, and other hands helped still her. Finally, gasping and helpless, she ceased fighting.

Knox ordered two of his men to tie Garland's wrists. Bates looked down at the barely conscious figure and grinned. "We've got the bastard then!"

Abby glared at Knox. Her voice trembled with rage. "You gave me your word!"

Knox glanced at her. He sounded almost casual. "He had to be stopped."

"But you promised."

Knox took a swift step that brought him directly in front of Abby. For a moment she thought he was going to hit her. Instead, he almost spat the words in her face. "Damn promises. We don't have room for those standards anymore. A man's word his bond. Contracts. Treaties. They don't apply. You do and say whatever is expedient. There aren't any Queensberry rules for survival!"

In the same loud voice she snapped back at him, "He wanted to help. That's why he came here. He wanted to help!"

"He was trying to destroy us!"

"That's not true."

Knox stepped away and turned to watch as two of the

men hauled Garland backward and set him in a chair. Unable to hold himself sitting upright, he began to crumple forward. One of the men grabbed at Garland's hair and pulled him straight. The other whipped the belt from around his waist, looped it around Garland's throat and tied the loose end to the chair back.

Knox said, "Just make sure he doesn't choke." He turned to Abby again. "Get out of here, Mrs. Grant. This is our business, and we'll handle it our way." He nodded to the boy who had wounded Garland in the hunt through the woods. "Ken, take her back to where we found her car."

The boy said, "Her wheel's shot up."

"That's her problem."

The boy crossed to Abby and took her arm. The fight had gone from her, and she allowed herself to be propelled toward the door. She halted and turned back to look at Garland. There was blood on the side of his face, and his head lolled on one side. His breathing was rasping against the tight grip of the belt around his throat. "What are you going to do to him?"

Knox said, "I told you to get out."

She turned then and ran from the house, helpless and sick with fear. She started to sob, head bowed and face covered with her hands. She made no resistance when the boy moved up beside her and steered her toward a Land Rover. He opened the passenger door and waited for her to climb in. When she made no move to do so, he gently insisted, half lifting her unresisting body and bundling her into the seat, where she lay slumped on her side, more of her on the floor than on the seat. Ken lifted her feet away from the sill of the door, then closed it without slamming.

The boy was embarrassed by Abby's sobbing. Frightened, too. He had never experienced emotion of such violence. He drove, sitting well away from her, afraid to speak in case she might turn her grief to anger and vent it on him. He tried not to look at her, keeping his distance in every sense.

They had covered several miles before Abby was able to calm herself. She made herself sit erectly and take deep, controlled breaths. Her hands were clenched tightly in her lap. She stared out the side window, keeping her face turned from the driver. They exchanged no word throughout the whole of the journey.

The boy halted the car beside Abby's Rover, keeping the engine running. She got out quickly, still not looking at the boy. She closed the door firmly, and almost immediately the vehicle started to pull away. It moved along about twenty yards, then halted and, with a slight grating of gears, reversed and turned to start forward the way it had come. It stopped beside Abby, and Ken jumped out and moved quickly around to the rear. He hauled out the spare wheel, letting it bounce onto the ground. Like a child with a hoop, he bowled it toward her. It fell on its side near Abby's feet. The boy looked guilty and nervous as he hurried back into the car. "You'll have to put it on yourself. Knox'll be expecting me back." He started the car forward before the door was closed.

The sound of the car had long gone before Abby roused herself and started to search among the tools for the jack and wheel brace.

Bates swung his hand in a full half circle, his clenched fist catching Garland just below the ear. His head twisted onto his opposite shoulder, then lolled forward again. He was barely conscious but alert enough still to feel the pain. Eyes closed, he waited for the next punch, his head aching thickly, his hearing muzzy. The leather belt pressed into his windpipe, and he tried to ease himself backward to reduce the pressure. At first the punches had the keen edge of new pain. Now, when they came, that edge was blunted by the numbness that enveloped him. Irrationally he thought, "They're not very good." But he found no pleasure in the realization. In his army career he had twice been sent on courses of interrogation techniques. Expert questioners concentrated on causing pain in the middle of the body. The testicles and the kidneys were where pain came quickly and lasted long. The head could take a lot of punishment. In a way he felt grateful for the lack of subtlety his captors were displaying.

"Where is she? Where have you got her?" Knox's voice sounded a long way off. Garland tried to speak, but the only sound that came was a strangled gurgle. Before he could turn the sound into words, Knox hit him full on the jaw. The force of the punch sent the chair teetering backward. It balanced for a moment, then slowly toppled. The wooden back splintered as it hit the ground. Garland didn't move.

Bates nudged him with his foot. He glanced at Knox. "The bugger is unconscious."

Knox looked angry. He said, "He'll tell us. By Christ, he'll tell us. Bring him round."

Abby pressed all her weight onto the brace. Gasping with the effort, she felt the wheel nut shift a fraction. She eased off for a moment, then pressed again. She sustained the pressure, feeling the nut begin to turn; then suddenly it was loose, and the brace turned easily, winding the nut from the thread. When it was clear, she gently shook it out of the socket beside the others she had already removed. She started to pull the wheel off, when she heard the car engine. She looked up in quick alarm. A small white sedan came around the bend. It was traveling quickly, and she had no time to obey her instinct and dash for cover. Her hand shifted on the wheel brace to grasp it like a weapon. The sedan drove right up beside her and halted before she recognized Greg and Jenny. Jenny was out first, rushing to embrace Abby. Greg stood back a little, listening to the two women answer questions with questions. When his chance came to speak, he began, "We got worried about you, so we—" But before he could finish, Abby interjected with such urgency that he was silenced.

"There's a man. They'll kill him, I'm sure of it, and it's my fault. We've got to do something. We must help him."

Garland said, "All right. That's enough." His voice was hardly more than a croak. The front of his clothes was wet, his hair still dripping from the water they had thrown over him. He had been twice beaten into unconsciousness and twice revived. If they beat him again, he knew he would have no strength left to play out his only chance. "That's enough," he said again.

Bates grinned at Knox, who nodded with satisfaction. Knox said, "It took you long enough. All right. Now, where is she?"

The words that came from Garland's swollen lips were indistinct. Blurred. Knox leaned closer to hear him. "What did you say? What?" he demanded.

"If I tell you, what happens to me?" Garland repeated.

Knox's answer came smoothly as though it had been long considered and prepared. "A car will take you out of the district. Anywhere you choose, as long as it's far away from here. If you ever come back, we'll killyou."

Garland recognized the lie in the voice. He knew the only reason he was still alive was that they wanted the girl back. He waited a moment, seeming to consider; then he nodded. "All right."

"Where have you got her?"

For Garland, this was the moment. If he failed now, he knew he had no more chances. It wasn't difficult to let defeat pervade his voice. He struck a note of total submission. "I'll take you to her."

It was Bates who snapped back, "Just tell us where she is. We'll get her."

Garland let no trace of argument shade his answer. "Even if I told you, you couldn't find the place." Then, for good measure: "For God's sake let's get it over with. I can't take any more of this."

It seemed like several seconds before Knox decided. "All right. Untie him and get him on his feet."

Garland felt the chill of excitement. They'd bought it. Now at least he had a chance. Once they were out of the house, he had a chance.

Garland moved slowly. Wincingly, Making it appear that walking was a considerable effort. He had once purposely stumbled and had lain facedown until Bates pulled him back onto his feet. Not all the pain was feigned. The wound in his thigh had stiffened his leg, and the beating still caused waves of dizziness. He realized that he would not have the strength to make a run for it. His only hope would lie in getting one of the shotguns. So far—and they had covered half the distance—his captors had offered him no opportunity of taking any action. They stayed a few yards behind, flanking him, shotguns at the ready.

Several of the men at Waterhouse had wanted to act as escorts, but Knox had refused them. Garland had realized that Knox wanted as few witnesses as possible to the killing. No consciences would be stirred by his murder if they believed he had died in attempting to escape.

Garland turned off the bridle path and into the woods. There had been a pathway here once, but lack of use and heavy overgrowth blurred its definition. "How much farther?" Knox sounded suspicious.

"Not far now." Garland convinced himself they would not take any action until they were sure the girl was safe. If he had any chance at all, he had to take it when they reached the folly. If one of them went to open the door, if the other should have an unguarded moment. The permutations of the action absorbed Garland.

He halted where the trees edged a broad clearing that was high with rank grass and weeds. At its center was the folly: a pagodalike structure that had been built a century before.

"She's in there." Garland felt the tension building inside him as he spoke. Whatever was going to happen was close now.

"She'd better be," Bates said. "She'd just better be. Keep walking."

He felt a moment of relief. They weren't going to do anything until they checked the girl was safe.

They moved forward, the men with guns eager now and forgetting some of their caution. Garland deliberately slowed his pace, and the two men drew level with him, their attention on the solid door of the pagoda.

Bates moved slightly ahead. Garland glanced toward

Knox. He was about four yards off to the right, his gun pointing at the ground. "Not yet," Garland thought. "Not yet." With each step he edged a little closer to Knox, closing the space between them. Knox remained unaware of the reducing distance.

Nearing the door, Bates stopped and called loudly, "Elizabeth?" Wood pigeons in the nearby treetops clapped away in alarm. He shouted again, and still there was no answer. He turned to look accusingly at Garland. "If she's not there. If you're trying something on. . . ."

Feeling a surge of alarm, Garland said quickly, "She's there. She couldn't have got out."

Knox was wary again now. Watching Garland, he said to Bates, "Go and take a look."

The man moved forward and up to the door. He seemed to listen at it for a moment, then cautiously pushed it with his hand. It opened creakingly. Bates said, "It's not locked."

Garland was puzzled. He had slotted a strong stick through the hasp. There was no way it could have been removed from inside the pagoda. He made to move forward as if to check the door for himself but was stopped by a sharp command from Knox.

They watched Bates step into the dark doorway and vanish from sight. There was silence. Then, with a clatter and a suddenness that startled them both, Bates came hurtling backward through the door and fell sprawling among the nettles. Before he could get to his feet, a man appeared at the door. He was holding Bates' shotgun and instantly leveled it at Knox.

Greg said, "Put the gun down," and when Knox was slow to comply, he nodded to Garland. "Take it from him."

Knox looked too dazed to offer any resistance. He stared blankly at Greg. He said, "Who the hell are you?"

Greg didn't answer. Instead, he glanced over his shoulder and said, "All right. You can come out now."

The hunched frightened figure of a girl came out of the darkness. Knox said, "Are you all right, Elizabeth?" She nodded.

Greg allowed her to pass and said gently, "Go and stand with your friends." She hurried across to Knox. As she reached him, the attention of them all was taken by the sound of a car engine starting up. Turning toward the sound, they saw the Range Rover appear from the sparse trees on the left of the clearing. As it lurched across the uneven ground, Greg beckoned to Garland, and the two men ran to meet it.

Abby was at the wheel, Jenny beside her. With the vehicle still moving, Greg pulled himself onto the rear platform, then helped Garland up beside him. Abby swung the wheel in a tight circle and headed back to the trees, making the Rover bounce violently as it picked up speed.

Rubbing his hands against the nettle stings, Bates crossed to stand beside Knox. His voice held a whine of apology. "He was hiding behind the door. I didn't have a chance. He jumped me." Knox stayed silent. Bates turned on Elizabeth, determined to free himself of any blame. "You should have warned me. You knew he was there. You should have shouted or something when I came in."

Elizabeth looked at the ground. "I was afraid."

With growing aggression in his voice, Bates appealed to Knox. "If she'd said something, I could have been ready for him. She should have—" Knox cut him short as he turned and started to walk swiftly back the way they had come, his gait stiff with the rage that still gripped him. Elizabeth and Bates followed, staying some little distance behind.

"Abby remembered you said you were holding the girl at the folly," Greg said. "We found the place on the map and went down there. I thought we might be able to use the girl to bargain for your release. Then Jenny spotted you coming, so we had to do something quickly."

Garland nodded. "I'm grateful. I had some vague sort of idea that I might get hold of one of their guns, but they stayed very wary. I don't think I would have got away with it."

Abby halted the Rover a few yards behind the white

sedan. All four of them scrambled out and stood in a group between the two vehicles. There seemed suddenly nothing more to be said. Before any of them was able to feel uneasy in the silence, Jenny said, "I don't think it's a good idea to stay around here. I'll go with Greg in the Ford. Will you follow us?"

Abby nodded, eager now to be away from the danger. "I'm sure that's best. Let's get started."

Greg and Jenny moved to the car. He called from the driver's seat, "Have you got enough petrol?"

Abby reached into the Rover and switched on the ignition. The fuel-gauge needle swung over to more than quarter full. "We'll need some before we get home, but we're all right for the moment."

Greg gave a thumb-up sign and started the engine. The rear wheels slithered briefly on the damp grass, then, gaining traction, propelled the car onto the road. He moved through the gears sharply, picking up speed, and quickly drove around the bend out of sight.

Abby turned to Garland. "Will you drive?" In the pause before he answered, in that tiny moment of time, Abby knew. He wasn't coming with her.

They spoke in the wrong order. Abby said, "But you can't stay here!" as he began to say, "I can't leave."

Garland said, "I can't go. Nothing is settled yet."

"But they'll kill you. You know that now. There'll be no talking anymore. They'll go all out to kill you."

He reached both hands forward and touched her shoulders. She wanted words. She wanted tears. Wanted anything that would make a bond between them that could not be broken, an emotional chain that would bind them and with which she could make him go with her. But no words came. No tears. Only the total realization that her first instinct had been correct. He was staying.

Garland said, "Waterhouse is still my responsibility. It always has been."

Her words were formal-sounding. Sharp-keyed. Polite. "Shall I see you again?"

"Yes." He kissed her forehead, his hands still on her shoulders, but now tightly gripping her. She stayed rather stiff, not responding to his touch. Then, quickly, his lips and hands left her, and he walked toward the trees.

Pointedly not looking at him, Abby climbed into the car and started it forward. The tears did not come until many hours later, when she was alone and in her bed.

12

THE weeds brought the scavenging to a halt. The foraging ended with hundreds of items on the Shopping List for Survival still unfound.

The speed of growth astonished them. It started as a barely detectable haze of green that shaded the fine tilth. In less than a week the pasture land that had been so painstakingly plowed and rototilled was burgeoning with strongly growing weeds and grasses. It took close examination to find the seedlings of the crops they had planted.

Bill Faber fitted the Rototiller blades to the tractor, intending to churn up the intrusive growth before it took too firm a hold. It was only then they realized that, in their eagerness to utilize the soil, they had planted the rows of seed too close together. There was no room for the tractor to work between them.

The following day the women began to clear the weeds with hoes and trowels. By evening there was very little clear ground to show for their backbreaking labor. All other projects were set aside, and the entire group moved onto the land. It took them three weeks, beginning at dawn and ending only when it was too dark to distinguish weed from crop. As each day passed, they felt the aches in their bodies numbed by weariness. There was little conversation at their evening meals, and when the food was finished, they went quickly and gratefully to their beds.

Finally, the work seemed done. The neat close rows of seedlings were as clean and defined as lines ruled on notepaper. Abby arranged a schedule of work that ensured that two people would work each day at hoeing the ground. The untended fields around their cultivated section blossomed with high grasses and thistles. The briers in hedgerows snaked out their tendrils and established new bushes. In the orchards sucker shoots sprang from the roots of the trees, sapping the strength of the fruiting branches. Undisturbed, seed from ash and elder germinated and rooted. In once heavily grazed pastureland great colonies of nettle and thistle were quickly established. Drainage ditches maintained so carefully for centuries thickened and filled with debris and waterweed, clogging and damming.

The rich compost of rotting leaves from that last autumn layered the roadways. It nurtured forests of seedlings that rooted through the cracks in the surface, widening, deepening, crumbling them. From the roadside verges the creeping grasses edged forward to narrow the tracks.

Elaine Corman noticed it first. With Jenny she was on what had become known as the weeding detail. Rubber-gloved and kneeling on a folded sack, she painstakingly forked out fresh weeds that were establishing themselves among the rows of peas. She saw there was a section several yards in length where the tender green tips of the shooting vines had been lopped away. She called Jenny to show her. They examined the other rows. A good many of the plants had suffered in the same way.

"Rabbits," Elaine said stiffly. "That's what's done that. Rabbits. They can be little devils, they can."

Jenny went back to the house with the news, and everybody trooped out to look.

"I suppose it could be mice," Philip said, as though trying to be fair.

Tom Price shook his head. "No. It's rabbits all right. Mice

will take the seed, but they don't give no trouble once the plant is through."

"Bloody things!" Greg snarled, staring out at the hedges that bounded the field. "God knows they've got enough growth to feed on without starting on our stuff."

Bill Faber came up with the solution, and they spent the next days fashioning cloches of close-meshed chicken wire. The peas were saved from further attack.

The small plot behind one of the houses had been set aside to raise seedlings for transplanting. The garden's original owner had evidently been an enthusiast. The soil was rich and easily worked. No long-term weeds had been allowed to establish here. The seeds of cabbage, cauliflower, onions, sprouts and salad greens made an early showing. After much reference to the gardening manuals they had collected, Philip judged that the crop would be ready for planting out within a week. Fresh ground was worked and arcs of wire netting prepared, but before the plants could be forked out, the rabbits penetrated the garden and destroyed hundreds of the seedlings.

They organized a shoot with the intention of thinning down the infestation before the new generation of rabbits could reproduce. In two days of shooting they had expended more than one hundred cartridges and killed fourteen rabbits. Greg halted the war when he recognized the high cost in ammunition set against the destruction rate. They ate rabbit that week until there was no new way to disguise it and until they were sickened by the taste of the flesh.

It was after this that Tom Price revealed an unboasted talent. He spent a few hours in the house they had adapted as a workshop, refusing to tell anyone what he was doing. That evening he set out at dusk. The others were in bed before he returned and not yet risen when he left the house before first light. They were breakfasting when he came back with eight rabbits, gutted and strung to a long stick. Hanging from his belt were a dozen of his homemade wire snares. Though no one relished the prospect of more rabbit meat, Price was duly praised and applauded. He accepted their congratulations with uncharacteristic modesty. When finally the praise exhausted itself and conversation turned to other things, Price's brief modesty submerged, and he launched into a story of his past when he was head gamekeeper to Lord Glamorgan, in charge of several thousand acres and with more than twenty other keepers under him.

"There's not much about nature I don't know," he admitted to his reluctant audience. "Living near the land, see. Knowing how the birds and animals live, knowing how they think. And never short of birds when his Lordship had a big shooting party. Pheasants, partridge, grouse. Knock down hundreds of birds in one day, they would. Me directing the beaters, see."

"I didn't know there were many grouse in Wales," Philip said slyly.

Price continued unchecked. "You're right. Nearly extinct they were until I started breeding them again."

In the months that followed he regaled and bored them with his imagined career, constantly changing the facts and names. It became increasingly hard for him to find a listener, but even this seldom silenced him. He did, however, continue to make good catches with his snares, and the suplus meat was put into brine and stored.

The domestic animals—the dogs and cats that had survived and become semiwild—all seemed to throw large litters that spring. Foxes, too, increased in numbers, and the young survived on the abundance of fresh meat that the parent animals were able to catch. The birds, too, though terribly depleted in numbers by that terrible winter, seemed to proliferate. Pigeons and ringdoves were seen in great flights. Disturb them at roosting time by walking into the woods, and the clap of their wings was like a roar of thunderous applause. The catlike mewing of the ringdoves and the throaty call of the wood pigeons dominated the birdsong that filled the days.

There was little respite from the grindingly hard work of farming. The days drifted unnoticed into July. Since planting time there had been only two forays out of the village, made on both occasions by Greg and Philip. They badly needed the means for preserving their steadily growing surplus of food: kilner jars, salt, potassium nitrate, insinglass, stoneware crocks and barrels. They had discussed the possibility of running deepfreezers from portable generators but ultimately decided against them because of the heavy use of gasoline and the risk of breakdown and subsequent spoilage.

The two journeys were more difficult than those made earlier in the spring. There seemed to be more barriers of fallen timber on the roads, and there were always deeply flooded sections on low-lying ground. The motorways had stayed fairly clear but already showed the marks of neglect: earth slips on the high-banked cuts, thistles pushing up through the tarmac sections.

Finding the goods they wanted took longer than they expected. Many buildings bore signs of earlier looting, and no place seemed free of the musty smell of damp and decay. The July sun did nothing to take the chill from the deserted houses and shops. Speckled black mold crawled across plaster walls. Growths of fungus had been established, and wallpaper peeled away.

With a mask soaked in disinfectant Greg searched one house and found a dank carpet sprouting green with shooting grass. The spread of timber rots, dry and wet, seemed to be accelerating.

After much searching they found the salt and sugar they needed. The bags had solidified into concretelike lumps, as had the saltpeter. In a storeroom behind a hardware shop they located the storage jars. The water-soaked cardboard cartons broke in their hands as they lifted them.

On their second trip the shopping list was more specialized and the search more demanding. By late afternoon they had not found all they wanted. Philip suggested that they use the remaining hours of daylight to go into territory that they had not yet covered and, if necessary, spend the night away from home to continue the search the next day. With the maps Greg plotted a large circling route that would ultimately bring them back to the far side of their own settlement.

The road took them through silent villages, along main streets lined with flat-tired, rusting cars. In almost all the villages there were buildings that had been destroyed or damaged by fire at the time of the Death: caved-in roofs and charred timbers, scorched and sooted walls. Once carefully tended roadside gardens were high with growth that almost hid ground-floor windows. Among the tangle, rosebushes had battled upward and bloomed, determinedly competing.

They drove beside a high-banked section of electrified railway line. A seven-carriage commuter train stood waiting in the middle of nowhere. As far as Greg could remember, the first station was some twenty miles up the line. He wondered how long the passengers had waited before deciding that their journey had ended. It was as though Philip read his thoughts. He said, "I was on a train once when there was a power failure. We all sat there for hours waiting for them to put it right. It never occurred to any of us to get out and walk. I suppose we always expected that any minute they'd put things right."

Greg nodded. "And somehow they always did. A washer on a tap or a race riot. There was always someone to fix it."

Greg slowed the car as the road dipped steeply to run beneath a railway bridge, then to rise again on the other side. The hollow was filled with still, scummy water. At the center of the flood and just below the surface they could discern the vague outline of a car's roof.

"We're not going that way, that's for sure." Greg reversed and started back the way they had come. "I'm glad we didn't hit that in the dark."

Their detour took them through a small industrial estate on the outskirts of a town. Blocks of low modern buildings built in brick and housing small engineering factories, builders' merchants, discount warehouses and the like.

"That might be worth a look." Philip pointed to an

arrowed sign that directed traffic to "Rayburn Cash &
Carry Grocery (Wholesale Only)." Greg nodded and swung
onto the concrete slip road that led up to a broad tarmac
parking lot. The place had the look of an abandoned
dodgem track. Dozens of wheeled wire trolleys were
scattered around the area. Near the entrance was a litter of
torn cartons, broken glass and split bags. There were
battered but unopened food cans scattered everywhere.
Salt, flour and milk powder had been washed out of broken
bags by the rain and stained the black tarmac surface.

"What a waste." Greg picked up a dented tin. The label
came off in his hand. He glanced at it. "Italian Peeled
Tomatoes." There was an illustration of unnaturally red,
plum-shaped fruits. "I used to like these." He smoothed the
paper out on the palm of his hand and looked at it
thoughtfully. "How long will it be before anybody has
enough surplus to put it in tins and send it thousands of
miles?"

Philip shrugged. "Not in our lifetimes." Greg crumpled
the label and tossed it aside. They moved on around the
angle of the corner. Two large sliding wooden doors stood
partly open. Scawled across one of them in dribbled black
paint was: "Keep Out. This food store the property of the
National Unity Force." On the other door it announced,
"Looters will be shot."

"National Unity Force—wasn't that the lot that Pricey got
himself mixed up with?" Philip asked.

"I think so." Greg tried to remember. "It was run by a
man called Hornley. . . . No. Wormley. Arthur Wormley.
Abby ran across him once."

Greg moved on toward the door. Philip hesitated.
"Listen. Do you think we should go in?"

"Why not? They don't have any right to go around
claiming exclusive access to places. Anything that's left is
common property."

Greg pushed through the narrow gap between the doors
and stepped into the dark interior. Philip hesitated for a
moment, then made to follow. As he reached the opening,

Greg came barging out, pushing him aside. He was retching violently and brushing at his face with both hands like a man who had walked into a wall of cobwebs.

"What the hell's the matter?"

Greg couldn't answer as the bile filled his mouth. He spat it out and gulped for air.

Philip peered cautiously into the door. It took him a second to accustom his eyes to the light. Then he saw it. The hanging body of a man. The rope around his throat was lashed to a high beam. The body was swaying slightly and slowly turning, set in motion by Greg's collision with it. As it spun to face him, Philip felt his stomach clench in sickened disgust. The face was badly decomposed. There was a piece of roughly torn cardboard pinned across the chest. Boldly lettered, it proclaimed: LOOTER.

Philip said, "Let's get away from here."

Greg nodded. He shuddered and rubbed his face again. "I walked right into it."

They drove away quickly, not speaking until they were some miles along the road. Then Philip said, "Christ! What sort of people are they? They kill a man and just leave him hanging there."

"It's a damn sight more effective than any 'Keep Out' notice. I still don't think they have any right to keep stockpiles to themselves."

"I agree. But if that's the way they're going to carry on, who's going to argue with them? Not me for a start."

Greg said, "There might be a time when you have to. Argue with them, I mean."

Philip looked at him. "What are you talking about?"

He didn't answer for a moment. He wasn't entirely sure what he was talking about. He wanted to consider. In the past they had talked about protecting themselves against possible attack from marauding bands. Any strategy they had discussed had been based on the idea that any such attack would be in the nature of a swift raid. A hit-and-run operation to steal food or materials. The prospect of being placed under sustained pressure or of being designated as part of a political and military area had not been envisaged.

Greg spoke slowly, thinking his way through the words. "What if this National Unity Force have just drawn a big circle around their base? A sort of arbitrary line? Then they claim that everything within that circle is under their control. So what happens if our place is inside the line?"

There was swift anger in Philip's reply. Indignation and self-righteousness. "Well, they can't do that. We've built that place up. Nobody can just walk in and tell us what to do. That's our place!"

"Right. Right. I agree," Greg said, trying to calm him. "But in the present situation, where does any kind of ownership begin or end? Look, just for example, the big orchard. What is it? About two miles from the house? Now we haven't done anything about it. But it's near us. Now, if there's a lot of fruit there and somebody else comes along and picks it, what are we going to do? Just sit back and let them take it?"

"No! Certainly not." Philip had no doubts. "We're the nearest group to the orchard. It's ours. We can't have people just wandering in and helping themselves." Then, moderating slightly, becoming more generous, he went on, "If we've got plenty, all we need, then fine, we can give some away. But they can't just come and take it."

Greg said, "I read a book. Long time ago. It was called *African Genesis*, I think. Anyway, it dealt with territorial rights. As far as I can remember, it was saying that all creatures set boundaries to the area they live in. Then, when another animal tries to cross that boundary, they fight. It looks like we might be doing the same thing sooner or later."

"I damn well would fight, too! I mean, it's not as if anybody is going to be short of space. God knows, if you divided up the country between those of us who are left, we'd each have thousands of acres all to ourselves."

"It's not just land, though, is it? It's the resources on the land. Everything is running out a lot faster than I—than any of us—ever thought. The hardware will go on for a long time, I suppose, but food is already getting tougher to find. Petrol is going to be a problem soon. Clothes? Well, a lot of stuff seems to be rotting and decaying. Give it a couple more years, and I reckon we're going to be hard pressed to just go out and pick up whatever we want."

"So what do we do?" Philip demanded. "Just let people walk in and order us about? Let them help themselves to our stocks?"

Greg shrugged. "I don't know. It's just that I can see a case for unifying. Maybe one of these days we're going to run short of something and need outside help."

"Then if we do, we trade for it. Potatoes for corn. Fruit for petrol. But we're not going to work our arses off and throw everything into some big communal pot so that every idle bugger who wants can come and dip in."

Greg started to laugh.

Philip sounded angry. "What's so funny?"

"No, not funny. It's just that after all that's happened we seem to be exactly where we were politically when all this started. The haves and have-nots. And it's still not settled."

"It's settled for me. I'll share with the people who work alongside me, and that's it. So where do you stand?"

Shaking his head, Greg said, "I don't know. All my life I've been so busy seeing the other man's point of view, I've never had a real opinion of my own. You know something: I never in my life went to vote, because everybody talked such damned good sense. When a pro group demanded that we stand up and be counted, I stood up. And when the anti group asked the same thing, I stood up again."

After that they traveled in silence, Greg feeling Philip's disapproval. The journey was uneventful. As sunset neared, they drove onto the forecourt of a garage, hoping to fill up with gasoline. The casing on the pumps had been lifted off, and there were crank handles still slotted in position. The filler pipes had been left to trail on the ground. They quickly established that the tanks were dry and refilled the Rover from the drums they carried with them.

"It'll be dark in another half hour," Greg said. "Start keeping an eye out for a good place to spend the night."

Road signs, half hidden in the spreading hedges, warned

of a steep hill and zigzag bends. In the interest of gasoline economy it had become a habit to switch off the engine on hills and let the car coast. They ran silently down the twisting road, using the whole width of the two lanes to negotiate the sharp bends. They began to slow as the road leveled out. Greg reached forward for the starter as they began to turn the last tight curve.

Greg slammed on the brakes. Philip was thrown forward and his head cracked against the windshield. The rear of the car slued around, and they jerked to a halt.

Lining each side of the road were several huge vans. There were two gasoline tankers and a jeep. Set on the crest of the road was a table around which were placed brightly colored folding chairs. Beyond was a large log fire with molten tarmac trickling away from its base.

The car's silent approach had taken the people totally by surprise. Those seated at the table jumped from their chairs. The group around the fire ran toward the trucks. But the confusion was brief. Before Philip had recovered from his dazed state, three or four armed men were advancing toward them.

Greg got out quickly, still shocked enough to be angry rather than fearful.

"That's a silly bloody place to park. I very nearly went right through you!"

More men were coming forward now to back up the leaders. Beyond them Greg could see a group of women clustered behind one of the big vans. Philip climbed out, looking frightened and shaken, a flaming-red bump already growing in the center of his forehead. He felt unsteady and clung onto the open door.

An older man pushed through the line that stood facing Greg. He glanced at Philip with a measure of concern.

"You all right?"

Philip nodded and, in a voice that invited pity, said, "I banged my head."

The man turned to Greg.

"Are you armed?"

"We have weapons in the back of the Rover."

"Have you any sickness?"

Greg shook his head. "We're all right." Then, with his anger gone, he went on lamely, "It's a damn silly place to park."

The older man said, "Yes, you're right. I'm sorry. One gets so used to seeing nothing and nobody, you don't think about it. Look, we'll be eating soon. You're very welcome to join us. But if you don't want to, we'll clear a way and you can go on through." He looked at Philip again. "We might have something to take the sting out of that bruise."

There was a moment of hesitation; then Greg said, "Thanks. We were just about to stop for the night anyway."

The tension immediately eased and guns were lowered.

The man introduced himself as they moved to the table and chairs.

"Frank Berry." He offered his hand. He pointed and gave the names of some of the others, then gestured for Philip and Greg to sit at the table.

Berry said, "You settled around here or on the move?"

Greg explained the purpose of their trip, then asked, "What about you?"

"We're salvaging." He pointed toward the vans. "You know, picking up a bit of this, a bit of that. At the same time we're having a good look around. Finding out where the communities are setting up and letting them know we're in business."

Philip let the surprise show in his voice.

"Business?"

Berry nodded. "Yes. We're doing a little trading. Not much demand yet, though. There's too much of everything left. Give it another year or so, though, and the shortages are going to show up. That's when we'll really begin to get going in a big way."

The women who had been at the cooking fire began to serve dishes of hot stew. Bottles of wine were brought to the table. As they ate, Berry told them that he and his group had established a base just south of Birmingham. They were more than seventy adults. A quarter of them worked the land while the remainder split into teams and scoured the country—"salvaging" as he called it.

"Before the Death I had a mail-order business," Berry said. "Something like five thousand items in my catalogue. So, when things started to sort themselves out a bit, I thought I'd better stick to what I knew. Couldn't do any physical grafting." He tapped his chest. "Bit of a shaky ticker. So I started collecting things. But careful, though. Picking and choosing. The stuff that people are really going to want. Began with petrol. We've got thirty-two tankers full. That's going to be worth a packet in a while." He pushed his empty plate away from him and settled back in his chair. He was a very confident, satisfied man. His eagerness to tell his story suggested that he had become short of audiences. He was enjoying some mild boasting.

Philip asked, "What do you take in exchange? I mean, if you've got everything, what do people pay you?"

Barry became expansive. "Anything. We'll take anything just so long as I think I can find a demand for it somewhere else. And if they haven't got goods to trade, then I'll take gold."

Philip and Gregg spoke the word aloud at the same instant. "Gold?"

Greg added, "What good is that?"

"None at all. Not now. It's an investment for the future. Fifteen, twenty years from now—when the barter system begins to break down, and we need some sort of symbol of wealth—that's when it will count. Gold has had its ups and downs in the past, but it always comes good in the end."

Philip said, "But there must be thousands of tons of it about. If it was shared out among the population that's left, everyone would have loads of it. It's worthless."

Berry grinned at Philip. "Have you got any?"

"No."

"Have you?" he asked Greg.

"No."

"Exactly. Then let me give you a tip. Get some by you. Keep it on your list whenever you go out foraging; then keep it by you. It doesn't take up much room, and it doesn't eat anything. I tell you something interesting. The people who lived through, the wealthy ones, I mean, they left their cash, their paintings, their rare books; but I'll give you a shade of odds that if they had gold, they tucked it away somewhere safe so they could always go back for it. Gold is like that. You just don't part with it."

When the meal was finished, Berry showed them the insides of the vans. They contained an incredible quantity of goods. He walked them around with a proud proprietorial air.

Greg said, "You're a long way from your base. Are things getting so short you have to come this far to find them?"

"No, no. The main reason is to have a good look around. See what's happening. Find out where people are and let them know where we are. What I plan is to make the trip down south about twice a year. Call in on everybody. See what they need."

"You could run into some trouble around here," Philip said. "There's a group calling themselves the National Unity Force. They've laid claim on most of the stuff left in the area."

"That's worth knowing. Thanks for the tip." Berry seemed interested but unconcerned. "We've come across that sort of thing before. If we get warned off, we just move on. We're not looking for a fight."

Later they sat around the fire and shared the bottle of whiskey that passed around. There was a good deal of talking, and the evening went by quickly. The women tended to stay grouped together, but when Berry announced it was time to turn in, they paired off with the men. A pretty girl of about sixteen waited until Berry said goodnight to Greg and Philip, then walked with him across to one of the vans.

In the morning Greg was wakened by the sound of engines being revved. He started to struggle out of his sleeping bag, stiff from lying across the front seats of the Rover. The driver's door opened, and Berry peered in.

"Morning. We'll be on our way in a few minutes. Just wanted to give you these."

He handed Greg a dozen or so sheets of paper. Each showed the same map and set of directions, printed in smudgy purple duplicating ink.

"That'll show you how to find me if you get pushed for anything. And there's a few spare copies to hand out if you run across anybody."

Greg scrambled out of the car. The whiskey of the previous evening had left a band of pain across his forehead.

Very businesslike, Berry was unfolding and spreading a map across the bonnet of the Rover.

"If you'd like to mark your settlement on here, I'll make sure we call on you next trip down."

Greg tried to focus on the map. It took him some moments to locate the settlement. He hesitated before indicating it, wondering if it was wise to advertise their position. Deciding, he pointed to the spot.

"We're there." There was no point in making a secret of it, he concluded.

Berry circled the spot with a felt-tipped pen. "Good. Good. That's fine." He shook Greg's hand heartily. "Good luck. All being well, we'll see you next year. And remember what I said. Get some gold by you." He gave a nod and moved away, still folding the map.

Philip climbed out of the back of the Rover and stood beside Greg to watch the convoy start away. The vans' exhaust was clouding the clear, bright air.

When they were out of sight, Greg said: "We might as well get going, too."

They made a few stops on the way back and reached the settlement late in the afternoon. Philip gave a long blast on the horn, but no one came out to greet them.

They unloaded some of the boxes and carried them into the living room. The fire was unlit; the table set with plates of half-eaten food, cold and greasy. Greg felt a nudge of fear. "Where the hell are they all?"

Philip called loudly. There was no answer. The men walked out of the back of the house and stared across the fields. They could see no one.

"Well, they can't be too far away," Greg said uncertainly. "We'll take the Rover and look for them."

They moved through the side gate and onto the road. Elaine Corman was walking toward them. She wore no makeup, and her hair was disheveled. She had been crying.

"What's happened?"

"The little one's gone. Claire. We can't find her nowhere."

13

AFTER three days of haphazard searching, Bill Faber organized them into groups and set out a more methodical pattern for the hunt. Elaine stayed at the house and provided food whenever a party came in for a break. At the end of a week Abby called off the search. Only Elaine made any complaint. The rest of them had known for some days that they would never find Claire.

The quiet, withdrawn child had never made a strong emotional contact with any of them. She had been too shy and unsmiling. None of them had spent much time with her, and she had seemly glumly content to pass the time in her own private world. Nonetheless, her going marked them all. In varying degrees they felt guilt, though little grief. Greg remembered the same guilt from his childhood, when he had let a pet kitten suffer through his neglect. Elaine conformed to all the popular conventions and wore the very special face that tragedy demanded. But she, perhaps more than any of them, was touched by their loss. For it was *their* loss. One of the group, the family, had gone. It was the mystery of her going that affected them most powerfully. She had vanished soundlessly, disappeared without trace. It was if she had been spirited away, taken by some supernatural force. It frightened them, and in their fear they came closer together.

They lifted the first of the potatoes in mid-September. Greg stuck the fork deep into the ground, then levered it back. The wet earth gave easily, and the root came up, spilling soil. There were five or six good-sized potatoes and several smaller ones. The big ones were all pitted with holes and scarred with slimy-looking gouges. There were small glistening black slugs feasting on the flesh.

They dug several more plants, all of them similarly afflicted. They moved to another part of the field, but virtually every root harbored its family of slugs.

Abby researched the gardening reference books. The closest she could come to a solution was that they had planted in grassland that had been plowed for the first time.

They salvaged what they could. The undamaged potatoes were set aside as seed; the others were cleaned and put in brine. They continued until there were no more airtight containers left. The work took two weeks, and at the end of that time they had less than two hundredweight of seed and a modest quantity for eating. The yield had been less than they had sown.

In October Malcolm Christopher and Peter appeared at the settlement. Christopher explained that he considered their continued isolation would be bad for the boy, and with winter coming quickly, they were "looking around" for a group to join up with. They stayed two days before deciding; then Christopher asked if they could move in permanently. The meeting to discuss the request was a formality quickly dismissed. The following day the men set off with tractor and low loader to collect the newcomers' belongings. In the neat garden beside the cottage there was a good crop of potatoes. Faber was eager to stay and lift the crop, but Christopher said he would prefer to wait until they had a few days of dry weather before digging them. They loaded preserved foods and clothes, the carefully saved seeds, the tools, guns, cartridges, lamps and paraffin and finally the two hives of bees and the equipment that went with them. When they were finished, Christopher locked the door and put the key under a flower pot on the porch. "That's where it was when we took over the place," he said. They reached the village before dark. The goods were unloaded and put into the communal store. Now they belonged to the group, as did their previous owners.

Christopher's experience as a rose grower immediately qualified him to take over the planning of the small holding. He started by walking around the ground, making notes on scraps of paper. He listed what they needed. Plotted new sites for the following year's planting. Watching him, Abby felt the same sense of relief as when, with illness in the house, the doctor arrived. The illness wasn't cured, but at least it was in good hands.

The end of the month stayed dry, and when Christopher was satisfied the time was right, they again set out for the cottage to harvest the potatoes.

The front door was still locked, but the window beside it was shattered. Inside, the rooms had been ransacked in a search that had been needlessly destructive. The garden, too, had been laid waste, the crop of potatoes carelessly dug and collected. They were able to identify from footprints that several people had worked in the garden.

"Thieving bastards!" Faber snapped. "Bastards!" He stared at the freshly turned earth.

Greg shrugged. "I don't know. We probably would have done the same, wouldn't we? An abandoned cottage and a garden full of spuds. We'd have dug them."

Christopher knelt and scooped his fingers through the loose soil, unearthing a large tuber. "They didn't do a very good job. Careless. Let's fork over the ground, see what they've left."

By the time they finished they had collected a sack and a half of good clean potatoes. As they drove away, Christopher looked thoughtful.

"I wonder what they would have done if Peter and I had still been there?"

"Probably just gone on their way," Greg said.

"I don't think so. Seven of them. Perhaps more. Remember, there were no garden tools left at the cottage, so presumably they were carrying some. That makes me think they were out looking for crops."

"I still say we might have done the same."

"And would you have made the same mess inside the cottage? They had no call to do that. No, I think they would have taken what they wanted even if we had been there. Then I would have tried to stop them, and God knows what would have come out of that."

They didn't talk about it again until they had finished supper that night. Abby said, "It's been on my mind for a while that we ought to do something about defense. The least we should do is make one of the buildings a central storehouse. Board up the windows, strengthen the doors. Put good locks on."

"That makes good sense," Philip said. "And perhaps we should arrange the work so that there is always somebody at the house. Most of the time we're out in the fields. Strangers could walk in here and clean us out and be gone before we even knew it. We could fix a bell or something. A warning signal."

The next day they began to set up a modest range of defensive measures. The aim was not to fortify, but simply to be in a position to discourage raiders. Guns and ammunition were cached away from the houses. If the warning bell sounded, the men would collect them and move to planned positions.

Tom Price found a schoolboy enthusiasm in the preparations. He had long abandoned his fantasy of wise old countryman and gamekeeper and allowed his slovenly and slothful character to repossess him. The military overtones of the new project straightened his back and sharpened his speech. It became his habit to call everybody Captain and to acknowledge the end of almost all conversations with a casual salute. He reminisced about his past campaigns, his heroism and the medals that recognized it. He endlessly suggested new defense measures that ranged from minefields to armored cars. He sited positions for machine guns and mortars. One of his ideas, although much modified, was adopted. Two hundred yards beyond the houses at each end of the village they dug ditches in the road. Three feet wide and three feet deep. They put up notices warning of the ditch and advising travelers to "Sound Horn for Admission." At each trench two heavy boards were hidden in the hedge to provide a bridge into the village. After the first heavy rains the ditches filled with water and became known as the moats. It was satisfying to feel that no marauder could drive in and take them by surprise.

The last major job they tackled before winter set in was the construction of a large greenhouse. Malcolm Christopher found the one he wanted at a garden center. It was carefully dismantled and then rebuilt near the houses. Using a wood-burning stove, Greg fashioned a heating system. Its completion gave the promise of earlier and more prolific crops.

Despite modest success with some root crops and winter greens, the cold months severely depleted the food stocks. Ten appetites, made hearty by the outdoor work, ate deeply into the stores. They began to feel the shortages. The carefully stored flour had become fusty and added a stale taste to the flat bread they baked. Instant coffee became a luxury in which they seldom indulged. They made tea only once a day. The stock pot provided the meals for most days, being constantly topped up with rabbit meat and whatever vegetables were ready. The canned foods were carefully preserved for what Abby called "an emergency."

The stock of paraffin ran down quickly as the daylight hours shortened and the lamps were needed earlier. Candle drippings were remolded around braided string, but even this economy did little to preserve the dwindling supply. To conserve what they had, lights-out time was set for eight o'clock.

From late November, winter again held them in siege. There was little they could do on the land, and the daily work was limited to collecting fuel and hunting. Abby

remembered her realization of the previous winter: that the
effort expended in collecting food and wood exceeded the
energy it provided. She calculated that they would just
about get through to spring on their reserves. Then, with
the new crops coming, they would not go hungry. Projecting ahead to the next winter and the ones beyond that, she
saw their difficulties growing, not, as the others predicted,
lessening. The irreplaceable manufactured items were
running out. If their next foraging expeditions were
successful, they might be able to restock some items, but
there was a very foreseeable limit. The manufactured
abundance of their old world was running out.

The harsh weather kept them inside for much of the
time, and this close contact caused chafing. Quarrels were
snappy rather than violent. Tempers smoldered rather
than flared. Aware of the danger in the tensions, Abby
opened up another room. It doubled the cost of lighting
and fuel, but disputing parties had a chance to separate.

Shortly before Christmas Jenny and Ruth had a savage
row, each accusing the other of evading her share of work.
It ended with, first, sobbing, then tight-lipped refusal from
both to settle the quarrel. Ruth tried to gather allies to her
cause while Jenny went off to her room. Much later that
night, when the house was sleeping, Jenny went to Greg's
room and climbed into bed beside him.

They didn't touch or speak for some minutes; then Greg
asked, "Are you sure?"

"Do you want me?"

"Yes."

They made love with a desperation so great that it
satisfied neither of them, but it seemed not to matter.
Through the night they clung to each other with fierce
need.

As it started to get light, Jenny said, "Can I stay? I mean,
be with you all the time?"

She felt his head nodding. His voice, muffled on her
shoulder, said, "I want that. You're my wife now."

They told Abby first. Her pleasure and approval were

echoed by the others when they were told the news. Ruth was quickest to show her pleasure and ended their dispute with a kiss and embrace.

They had set aside a date on their uncertain calender to celebrate Christmas. They used the day to mark the "joining" of Greg and Jenny. Joining was Jenny's choice of word, as "marriage" seemed inappropriate. On that day they were a complete family. They forgot their differences. They did no work. Abby broke out from the stores the few special things that had been set aside. They ate, drank, smoked, joked, laughed and made speeches, all to excess. When bedtime came, Greg and Jenny were escorted to their room and showered with confetti and ribaldry.

The party broke up slowly, and finally, Abby was left alone by the fire. She felt guilty about the extravagance of the day but consoled herself with the thought that it had provided the therapy they all needed. "The pagan feast days were probably held for the same sort of reason," she thought, and resolved that they would have more special days in future. She finished her whiskey and went upstairs. She could not sleep and lay on her back, her legs drawn up. She wondered vaguely if Greg and Jenny were making love. Then she remembered her own lovers and especially David. She jerked out of the half-awake world into the almost shocked realization she was masturbating. She pushed her nightdress down quickly and turned on her side. It was so long since desire had stirred her that its wakening alarmed her. Now she ached with her need. She tried to imagine her husband beside her, but the only face she saw in the darkness was Jimmy Garland's.

The raid came in February after a week of day- and night-long frosts. Only Elaine Corman and Peter were in the house. Two jeeps came in very fast, the water-filled moats, frozen solid, providing no deterrent. The four men from the first jeep crowded into the house. They wore sheepskin coats with red armbands on the sleeves. There were gun belts around their waists, and they brandished their pistols as they entered. Elaine was so frightened that her legs trembled and wouldn't support her. She crumpled back inelegantly into a chair. Peter tried to run for the door but was caught by the collar and heaved back into the room. The two men and a woman from the second jeep had by now circled the building and looked around. The woman reported that she could see nobody about.

A small wiry man who seemed almost buried in his heavy coat was obviously their leader. "How many of you living here?" he demanded of Elaine.

"Ten," she tried to say, but it was only at the second attempt any sound came from her throat. "Ten."

"None of you, nor this place, is registered with the National Unity Force."

"I don't know nothing about that," Elaine said with an almost apologetic smile. "Abby looks after all that sort of thing."

"This village and the lands around it come under our protection." From the way he said the words it was obvious they were learned by rote. Sentences calculated to give an air of authority and legality to his actions.

"By order of the Council Elect, all citizens within the zone will contribute goods or foodstuffs to the Community Support Center. Level of contribution will be assessed on a per capita basis. This has been set at —"

The woman cut him short, interjecting, "Oh, for God's sake, Charlie, you don't have to go through all that." She turned to Elaine. "Where are your stores?"

Peter said, "Don't tell her."

Without hesitation Elaine said, "The next house. But it's all locked up. Abby's got the key. She shouldn't be long if you'd like to wait." She gave another sickly smile and wondered if she should offer them a cup of tea.

The woman and one of the men remained. The rest of them went back out to the roadway. A minute later the sound of hammering echoed into the room as the raiders worked on the door of the storehouse.

The woman took a note pad and pencil from her pocket and started to scribble. Finished, she ripped out the page and handed it to Elaine.

"That's a receipt for what we take. Just to make it official."

The note read: "Received: Goods. N.U.F. Defence levy."

Outside, the men prized the hasp off the storeroom door and piled inside. They quickly selected what they wanted and formed a chain to pass it out to the jeeps.

"I want the names of all the people living here. For our records." She poised her pencil.

"My name is Elaine Muriel Corman." The woman started to write. Her hands fascinated Elaine. The skin was soft; the nails were carefully shaped and coated with a dark-red polish. "Takes care of herself," Elaine thought. The glistening mink jacket over the bright ski clothes confirmed her opinion. She continued listing the names.

"There's Ruth. I don't know her second name. Then there's Greg Prestou."

The woman looked up in surprise. "Greg?" she said. "Is he here?"

A voice from outside called, "Come on. We're ready to move."

"I'll finish the list another time." She moved toward the door. She smiled. "Give Greg my love. Tell him Sarah was here. Sarah Boyer." Then she was gone.

Peter ran outside and started to clang the alarm bell, its note mixing with the roar of the engines as the jeeps raced out of the hamlet.

14

THE north winds kept the spring at bay. Because of its slow arrival, and with stocks depleted by the raid, the last months of winter were hard and hungry. The foraging expeditions yielded little, the ground having been picked clean.

Hearing Sarah's name again reminded Greg of the quarry and Vic's hoard. The roads had deteriorated still further and were mostly covered with a thick mire of rotting leaves. They had difficulty in locating the quarry and, when they did find it, were disappointed to find the sheds empty. As they were leaving, Bill Faber pointed to something about fifty yards from the main hut. Greg didn't need to go near the bundle of rotting rags and flesh to know it was Vic.

The spring planting went well, though the tractor work bit heavily into their dwindling supply of gasoline. Seedlings transplanted from the greenhouse gave them early crops.

The boar and two sows that Bill Faber had brought produced two litters. From the fourteen that were born eight survived.

With Philip's help, Greg constructed a wind-powered

generator that gave them welcome, if uncertain, lighting in the two downstairs rooms.

The alarm bell stayed silent until August. When it sounded, they snatched up their rifles and ran in from the fields at top speed, to find two eighteen-year-old boys standing astride bicycles on the far side of one of the now-drained moats.

The boys stood with their hands raised until Greg was satisfied they were unarmed. The tension eased, they were invited in. They introduced themselves as Donald and Hugh and said they came from a settlement of twenty-five people living thirty-odd miles to the west. They wanted to trade. Hugh produced a grubby postcard that listed the things they had for barter.

Abby, Greg and Christopher went into the other room to study the list. The others crowded around the boys, eager for news from the outside.

"What sort of winter did you have?" Ruth asked.

"Not very good." It was Donald who answered. "We were on short rations most of the time. Couple of our people died. Pneumonia, the governor reckoned. Mind, they were quite old. Both of them in their fifties."

Hugh took over. "You seen anything of the National Unity Force?"

Nodding, Philip recounted the story of the raid.

Hugh was sympathetic. "Us too," he said. "Knocked us for a lot of stuff, they did. They governor was bloody livid. We was all set to go and get it back. We got all the guns and ammunition we could lay our hands on, and off we went like a bleeding expeditionary force. All fighting mad, we were. It took us three days' walking to get near their place, and we'd cooled down a bit. Just as well, too, or we'd have gone charging in, and they'd have done us up proper. As it was, me and Don and the governor done a little recce in the dark. Good Christ, you should see what they've got up there!"

"A tank!" Donald exclaimed. "Would you believe it? A tank! And they've got barbed wire and watchtowers. And the hardware! Mountains of stuff. All sorts of things.

There's a big line of petrol tankers. If they're full, they should be able to keep going for years. Loads of all sorts of gear. . . ."

"Many people?" Bill asked.

Hugh shrugged. "Couldn't tell properly. Quite a few, though. There was a lot of caravans and quite a few prefabricated buildings. It could easy be over a hundred living there. Enough to scare us off, anyway. No sense in going up against those sort of odds, so we turned it in and went back home."

"If they try ripping us off again, they won't get away with it so easy," Donald said defiantly. "We'll be ready for them next time."

"Same here," Philip said. "We won't get caught by surprise again."

Abby came back in. "You've got chickens," she said casually. "We might be able to use a cockerel and a few hens. There's nothing else on the list we need too badly. What we're really after is a lamb."

The boys looked at one another. His voice filled with trading guile, Hugh said, "We've got two ewes. They both had twins this spring. Mind, we'd want a hell of a lot to part with one of them."

Abby said, "Pity." Then: "What about pigs? Do you have any pigs?"

"No."

"We have," she said. "Just finished weaning. Mind, we'd want a hell of a lot to part with one of them." She smiled.

Hugh grinned back at her. "I think we might do business," he said.

Jenny had her baby daughter in the autumn. Ruth's son was born the next spring. She had not gone through the formal announcement of "joining," but instead enjoyed an easy and happy relationship with both Bill Faber and Malcolm Christopher. For the men there was no jealousy or dispute in the arrangement, and both found pleasure in the responsibilities of fatherhood.

By the fourth year trading by barter had become a regular happening in spring and in autumn. There were three communities within cycling or long-walk range. The largest of them supported no more than thirty adults. The twice-yearly market days became times of holiday and celebration. When they met and when the trading was finished, they would eat and drink and talk. Discussion frequently ranged around the idea of two or more communities coming together to form bigger and stronger units. The principle, though fully agreed, was never acted upon. None of them seemed eager to leave the homes they had established. Their individual identities were already deeply etched in the soil of their own small holdings.

Elaine Corman died at the beginning of the fifth year of what they believed was cancer. She suffered great pain which, for all her stoicism, could not be borne in silence. Without break Abby stayed beside her for two days and nights. She screamed with agony until neither could endure it. When she sank into a coma, Abby pressed the pillow over the gasping mouth, wishing she had had the courage to do it earlier.

She went downstairs and told them that Elaine had died in her sleep. Then she packed some food and walked out of the house. She did not return for six days. When she did, she told no one where she had been.

Some roads had almost vanished, and passage along many was all but impossible. Weeds and saplings and brier buried the land and what stood on it. Only the small pockets of cultivated ground around the communities remained. Like islands in a rising green sea. The survivors found the limits of their worlds at the edges of their small holdings. They ate, and they worked. And they worked to eat. The demands of maintaining that cycle allowed them little else. They had survived for half a decade and had provided for themselves the means to go on surviving. Life was immediate. Each day was concerned only with the weather and the crops and the health of their animals. The farthest future was the next winter or the next spring. They made no projections beyond the six months to come. Outside of their farming they had learned very few crafts and skills. They still relied on their stores for footwear and clothing. They still adapted things from the past to fit their current needs.

BOOK THREE

EXODUS

BOOK THREE

15

ABBY prepared with great thoroughness. In the evenings she spent much time alone, researching and planning. Ready, her facts assembled, she waited until she judged the time was right.

She chose the evening of a day that had been particularly hard. A tree, blown down by the October gales, had fallen across the roof of the house they used as a grain store. Cutting away the branches had taken most of the day, and it was growing dark before they could patch the gaping hole in the timbers and tiles. A sky clouding with the threat of rain forced them to move the grain to new premises. It was late when they finished, and they came in to their evening meal exhausted. They ate in silence, too tired to talk.

Tom Price finished first. He got up and started to shuffle from the room. Abby halted him.

"Tom, would you get a bottle of whiskey from the big cupboard?" She crossed and gave him her keys. The others at the table stared at Abby. A bottle of whiskey was an event.

"Something up?" Greg asked.

Abby nodded, then, turning to Ruth and Jenny, said, "When you've put the kids to bed, will you come back down?" The young women were intrigued.

"You want us all here, Abby?" Bill Faber inquired.

"If you don't mind. I think it's important." To avoid any more questions, she went into the other room. She stayed there until Philip peered around the door and, rather nervously, said, "We're all here, Abby."

She followed him into the living room. The fire was burning well, and the generator, powered by the high winds, was giving a steady light. Tom handed her a well-filled whiskey glass, then settled back with the others to stare at her.

She felt vaguely uncomfortable now and wished she had prepared a more ordered statement instead of depending on a series of mentally headlined notes. The faces watching her were serious and intent. She wanted to relax herself and her listeners. She smiled and raised her glass. "Cheers."

The others acknowledged the toast and sipped their drinks.

"I'm sorry. It's turning out to be a bit like a shareholders' meeting. I didn't mean it to be quite so formal. Well, I'll get on with it anyway." Her effort to bring a more casual note to the event failed. They were expecting something important.

"All right then. I'm not going to go over all the things we've done. None of us needs reminding how hard it's been. When we began, we had only one aim, and that was to stay alive. To do that we had to have food, warmth and shelter. Well, we've got all three. Right now, at this moment, our situation is that we're coming into winter with enough supplies to see us through until spring. That's assuming that everything continues to go well and that we don't have any kind of disaster. I'm not purposely trying to look on the black side, but there is always a risk. It could be a fire. A flood. Looters. Almost anything. And if it did happen, we couldn't expect much help from the other communities. If they had to share with us, they'd put themselves at risk. But as I say, that's looking on the blackest side. With luck we'll get through. By March we'll have to start slogging away again on those fields to prepare for the winter after. If we're not growing it, we're harvesting and preserving it. There's no letup. What we've got now is, if we're lucky, what we will have for the rest of our lives."

She paused and took a drink. She had been standing with her back to the fire and only now became aware of its uncomfortable heat on her legs. She moved aside and sat on the arm of a chair.

Bill Faber looked as though he were about to speak. Abby said, "Bill, I know you want to say something, but do you mind if I finish first. I want to say it through while it's clear in my mind."

"I'm sorry. I didn't mean to interrupt. You go ahead."

"Thanks. I'll try and get to the point. What I'm trying to say is that we're making very little progress. Outside of the food we grow we've created nothing. We're still like castaways using things washed up from the wreck. The tools we use. The clothes we wear. Everything. Even the bottles and barrels and jars we preserve our food in. We've made nothing."

Greg couldn't restrain himself. Quickly, defensively, he said, "We haven't needed to!"

Abby answered with equal speed. "And thank God for it! Because apart from the fact we don't have the skills, there's never been the time. And there never will be." She had to pause for a moment to stop herself wandering from her main theme by dealing with Greg's interjection.

She began again. "It seems to me that our biggest battle is against the weather, our climate. We are into a cycle where we have to work constantly against the winter. I don't see any way of avoiding that. If we could enlarge our own community or if we joined with another, it wouldn't change things very much. As we get older, the work is going to become that much harder. Very few children of under seven or eight survived the Death, and that makes a huge generation gap. There'll be no youngsters coming on to take over from us. It will be fifteen or sixteen years before the post-Death generation is old enough to do any intensive physical work."

She paused and then launched into the only part of her

speech that she had actually rehearsed. "I don't think it's enough to simply live until we die. We have to give the living a quality. For ourselves and for the children. I don't think we can do that if we continue as we are and stay here. Now I know that what I'm going to suggest will sound impossible. But I've spent a lot of time thinking about it, and it can be done. I want to cross into Europe and move down to the Mediterranean. Probably Italy."

Abby counted off the seconds of silence. She reached six before Malcolm Christopher said, "Jesus Christ!"

The silence broken, Abby expected everyone to speak at once. Instead, they remained very quiet. She gave a nervous laugh. "Isn't this the moment when, traditionally, I'm supposed to say, 'Any questions?'" Still nobody spoke. "Well, for God's sake, somebody say something!"

Bill Faber stood up. "Question: Do you think I could have another drink?"

The tension eased, and the comments began. Tom Price filled the glasses while Abby listened to an assortment of remarks that reflected the surprise and bewilderment of her audience. She was pleased and relieved that nobody immediately condemned the idea as stupid or impossible. Neither was there any approval, but she had not expected that.

When they'd settled again, Greg said, "It would be a hell of a journey. Could take a long time. Hell of a journey."

"If we did get there, what would we do then?" It was Ruth this time.

"Start with a place of our own. Or, if we were lucky, join up with an established group. Listen, I don't expect it to be any land of milk and honey. We'll still have to work, and work hard, but we won't have to contend with six months of winter every year."

Malcolm Christopher said, "The Mediterranean is where it all started, I suppose. Egypt had a fairly intensive agricultural system. Then Greece and Rome. We tend to think of them only for their cultures. Their buildings, writings, political systems, philosophies. But all those things came later. Cultivation on a large scale, food production, was the real beginning. When a population has full bellies, it can take time out to build a Parthenon or a Colosseum. It's a fair measure of man's priorities to remember that when he discovered how to work in metal, the second thing he made were tools to work the land."

Philip asked the inevitable question. "What were the first things?"

"Weapons for hunting and defense." Malcolm became apologetic. "Listen, I'm sorry. I didn't mean to launch into a history lesson. What I set out to say was that I go along with Abby's logic. I think we could have an easier life simply by being in a better climate. But the idea of a journey like that frightens the hell out of me."

Abby said quickly, "Look, I'm not asking anybody to make a decision right now. I agree it's an enormous step to take. It might even be impossible. I just want us all to think about it and talk about it. It's not something we're going to rush into."

"When would we leave?" Greg asked softly.

Abby shrugged. Her voice was unconvincingly casual. "I don't know. I hadn't thought much about timings."

"Oh, come on, Abby." Greg grinned at her. "I know you well enough by now. You don't come up with an idea like this until you've thought the whole thing through. When would we go?"

"Spring."

They would make the journey. Abby became certain of it in the next few days. None of them committed themselves to the idea, but neither did they reject it. There was a new sense of excitement among them. Mealtime conversations became animated and noisy. In the evenings they stayed much longer beside the fire, preferring to talk rather than go to their beds. The big atlas was constantly in demand to calculate routes and distances. Opinions changed frequently and erratically. But slowly practical ideas began to emerge. When any one of them pointed out a major problem, the others set about ways of solving it.

Abby allowed them time to get the feel of the idea before

advancing the scheme a step further. "Just as a sort of exercise—and of course it wouldn't commit us—why don't we break down the whole journey into sections? For instance, we could all make out lists of what we need to take then compare them. Then we could do a study on how we travel. Then we need to come up with some ideas of how we handle the Channel crossing. I've had a bit of experience with sailboats, but I'm in no way an expert sailor. If we really get down to details and plan this thing like a military operation, then at least we can look at the whole scheme and decide if it's practical."

They entered the second stage with enthusiasm. Lists were written, discussed and rewritten. Ways of travel on land and sea were debated. So absorbing and time-consuming was their interest that they welcomed weather bad enough to keep them indoors.

Late one evening Abby was alone beside the dying embers of the fire. Greg, who had gone to bed an hour earlier, came back into the room.

"Can we talk for a minute?"

Abby nodded.

"Jenny and I have decided. We want to go. I think we're both so hooked on the idea that even if everybody else wanted to stay here, we'd go anyway."

Abby smiled. She let her eyes close and sighed with relief. "Thank you, Greg. I've been waiting for that. I needed someone to commit themselves. I'm glad it's you and Jenny."

"Tell you the truth, it was Jenny who really settled it. You know me: I'm not exactly decisive. But seeing the three of us started out together, it seems to make sense that we go on."

"We will. We will go on." If she'd allowed herself, Abby would have cried then. Instead, she said, "If we put it to the vote now, how do you think it would go?"

Greg considered. He said slowly, "I think Malcolm would be with us. Bill Faber I'm not sure about. He's pretty settled. But I think both their votes would depend on Ruth. If she goes, then they'll go, too."

"Ask Jenny if she'll talk to Ruth. See if she can't do a little gentle sales talk."

"All right. As for the rest of them: well, I don't know. Tom Price is anybody's guess. Philip is more of a problem. He gets over to see that girl at Little Barton as often as he can. If he could get her to come with him, I'm certain he'd be all for it."

They talked until the room grew cold. Abby shivered and stood up. "I think we'll call it a night."

Greg hesitated. When he spoke, he sounded uneasy. "There's one more thing. Jenny suggested it. And I don't want you to think we're interfering, but . . . well, listen, would you like me to go off and see if I can find Jimmy Garland? Tell him that we're thinking of moving out?"

Abby turned and looked at the remains of the fire. She shivered again.

Thinking he had offended her, Greg said quickly, "I'm sorry. I didn't mean to interfere. I just thought . . . well, that you might want him to know."

"I appreciate it. But there's no point. You remember I went away after Elaine died? That's where I went."

"Did you see him?"

She shook her head. "They showed me where he was buried. They made me go and see the grave. I didn't want to, but they made me. Knox seemed to get some satisfaction out of making me see it. A sort of revenge, I suppose."

"Oh, God. Abby, I'm sorry," Greg said, feeling the words deeply.

"It's all right now. I don't know why I didn't say anything before." She went on in a conversational tone, not allowing emotion to shade her words. "They didn't catch him, you know. After we left, he went on giving them trouble for about a week or ten days. Then he stopped. They didn't see or hear anything of him. It was by pure chance they found him. Apparently he'd not been dead long. The wound on his leg had turned gangrenous."

They were both silent. Then, starting for the door, she said, "I'm tired now. I'm going to bed."

16

RUTH remained indecisive. Her uncertainty led to angry arguments and frustration. So far the project had been mostly academic, all the planning and discussions directed to deciding if the scheme was practical. When Abby attempted to advance the plan into reality, they shrank away from it. She felt helpless as she watched the enthusiasm begin to wane. She, Jenny and Greg remained doggedly convinced, but despite their efforts to revitalize the discussion, the others drifted back into their routine way of life. The excitement had gone, and there seemed no way to regenerate it. It was Ruth who finally settled the matter by announcing she was three months pregnant. Now they would have to stay. They began to concentrate on the plans for the next planting. The future had shrunk again. Spring was its limit.

The gunfire came from a long way off, the sound carried by the cold northern wind. Greg and Philip, who were cutting logs, stopped sawing and listened. There were several more shots.

"They're not shotguns. That's rifle fire."

Philip nodded agreement, then asked, "How far off do you reckon?"

"Hard to say."

They stayed silent for a few minutes, straining to hear, but there was no more shooting, and they went back to work.

Bill Faber wakened swiftly. He lay still, waiting for the sound to come again. Then he heard it quite clearly. It was the creak of a gate. Quickly, silently, he climbed out of bed and crossed the darkened room to the window. In the blackness of the night he could see nothing. There was a scuffling sound, then, unmistakably, a voice, muffled and hardly louder than a whisper.

He moved rapidly out of his room and across the hall. He shook Greg's shoulder, rousing him out of a deep sleep.

"Greg, there's somebody outside. I'm going to wake the others."

He was gone before Greg could ask any questions.

By the time Greg got downstairs Philip and Malcolm were loading shotguns. Bill stood near the back door and made a sign for Greg to stay silent. He listened intently for a moment and then, his voice urgent and low, said, "They're on this side of the house."

Greg took the gun Philip handed him and went to the window. "Can't see a damned thing."

There was a sudden alarmed cackle and squeaking from the chicken house.

Bill Faber threw open the back door and ran a few paces outside. Pointing his gun at the sky, he fired a single shot. As fast as an echo there was an answering shot. He saw the brief muzzle glare and heard the kitchen window behind him shatter. Two more shots came from his right, and he swung and emptied the second barrel in that direction. Then Greg and Philip were beside him.

There was the sound of hurried movement from the end of the garden. Philip fired toward it. The answering fire came from the left this time. Several rapid shots from an automatic rifle, whining and ricocheting off the wall, above their heads.

"Get back inside!" Greg yelled. The three of them bolted

for the door. Philip slammed it shut. The women were cowering together at the foot of the stairs. Tom Price was trying to light a candle in the living room.

"Put that out, you silly bugger!" Bill screamed at him.

From the front door Malcolm yelled, "This side. They're on the road!" Philip ran to join him.

Greg began to shout orders. "Tom, get upstairs. Take a back window and keep firing. Doesn't matter if you can't see anything. Just keep shooting. Bill, you do the same at the front of the house. Abby and the rest of you, start passing out ammunition. Keep low and away from the windows."

They kept up the barrage for almost five minutes, firing as fast as they could load. In the roar of the gunfire, it was impossible to tell if their shots were being returned.

"All right, hold it now," Greg called and, when the shooting continued, said, "Pass the word to stop firing."

They waited in the darkness for a long time, listening for any telltale sound. After an hour Greg told them to take it in turns to go off and get dressed.

When the darkness began to ease from the sky, Greg inched the back door open. He turned to Bill. "I'm going down to the far wall. You stay here and cover me." He stepped outside.

Moving slowly, he made his way down the path. There was a stealthy rustling sound in the fruit bushes ahead of him. He jerked his gun up ready to fire, then lowered it as a chicken stalked into sight.

Even in the half-light he could see the hen-house door was open. Crossing to it, he peered in. The birds were clustered together in a distant corner. There were broken eggs on the floor.

The gate to the pigpen was open, and the sty was empty.

Greg moved on, then turned back toward the house. He beckoned the others to join him.

"They've gone. We'd better see what the damage is."

By the time it was full light they knew the worst. The greenhouse had suffered badly, with more than half its glass shattered by the gunfire. What was most galling was the realization that it had probably been their own shots that had caused the damage.

All but one of the pigs were found, grubbing among the Jerusalem artichokes, and when the chickens were finally rounded up, there were six missing. The door of the storehouse bore signs of attempted entry, but the lock had remained secure.

They found empty shell cases littered around the garden and on the roadway. These and the chipped brickwork of the house bore evidence of the heavy fire that had been directed at them. As to the identity of the raiders, there was no clue at all.

"Just a gang on the move, I suppose," Abby said. "They took a chance on picking up some supplies."

Greg was less certain. "They seemed too well armed. They weren't hunting guns they were using. Still, I don't think they'll be back in a hurry. They know now we're not a pushover."

They spent the morning replacing broken windows, taking glass from other houses, overcoming the lack of putty by fixing it with wooden laths.

At eleven that morning they were startled by a long blast on a car horn. A convoy of four vehicles had halted at the moat. The dozen men from the cars wore army camouflage jackets and carried automatic rifles. Some had bandoliers of ammunition slung across their shoulders. The men were dirty and unshaven, their uniforms grubby.

Several of them had already stepped across the moat and were walking toward the houses when Greg, Bill and Malcolm reached them.

"Who are you and what do you want?" Greg demanded.

A tall gaunt man pushed forward. He looked tired. The gray stubble on his chin seemed to emphasize the dark rings around his eyes. When he spoke, his voice had a crack of authority in it and a tone that more than hinted he would put up with no nonsense.

"My name is Scott. I'm in charge of this detail. My men need some food and a chance to clean up. Don't give us any trouble, and we'll be on our way out of here in an hour."

Scott advanced. Greg raised his gun slightly and said, quickly, "Now just wait a minute."

However tired the men might have been, they were alert enough to respond quickly to the implied resistance. Rifles swung up and leveled at the three men strung across the road.

Scott flapped his hand in a calming gesture. His voice was weary. "Don't be silly. We're doing what we can to protect people like you. Now, let's get some food organized, and we'll be on our way."

He beckoned to his men, and they moved past Greg and the others, leaving them feeling both helpless and foolish.

The women made food and hot drinks while the detail took it in turns to wash and shave or simply relax in front of the fire.

Scott settled in a chair at the table. He rubbed his eyes and yawned widely. "Jesus, I'm tired."

Abby stood beside him. "What's going on exactly?"

He yawned again. "There are a few groups of NUF people in the area. We're trying to push them out before they can reform."

Surprised, Abby said, "I thought *you* were the National Unity Force!"

He shook his head. "No. For the want of a better name, we've been calling ourselves the Liberation Front. But we're not any kind of permanent military or political body. We're made up of men from several communities. All north and west of here. The Unity Force was giving us all such a hard time, we finally had to get together and fight back."

Greg joined the conversation. "We were attacked last night."

Scott nodded. "We heard firing. They get anything?"

"Some stock. It could have been worse."

Jenny brought a plate and set it in front of Scott. He began to eat without enthusiasm. "You had much trouble with the NUF?" he asked, through a mouthful of food.

"Not really," Abby said. "They've only been here once."

"You're lucky. They've been concentrating on our side of the country for the last few years. I tell you, we've had some bad times because of them. They talk all that political shit and then steal half your crop. So we finally decided to hit back."

"Did you attack their place? Their headquarters?" Greg asked.

"Christ, no! They'd slaughter us. Have you seen that place? They've got a tank up there!"

"So we've heard."

Scott scooped some more food into his mouth. After he swallowed, he said, "No. What we did was shoot up some of their patrols. Then they sent out a pretty big force. Fifty strong. They didn't expect any kind of unified attack, and we really took them to pieces. Then we got our main strength between them and their headquarters and cut them off. Now they're scattered all over the place trying to get back. We'll get a few more of them before we go home."

Scott finished his meal and roused his men. He thanked them for the food and started out of the house. Greg and Abby walked with him.

"You think the NUF will be finished after this?" Abby asked.

"No. No, not a chance. They're too strong. But it will be a long time before they come into our area again. My guess is they'll begin to work over different territory. Perhaps this direction. Take a tip: Get organized now. You might have to fight a war of your own before too long."

Three weeks later Philip set off to cycle to Little Barton. In the past he had usually stayed away for two or three nights, so they were surprised when he returned the following evening. He seemed both frightened and excited as he told them his news.

"They've had a visit from the NUF. Wormley himself, apparently. Made a big speech. They don't know what they're going to do. I said they'll have to fight. That we should all join together." Philip was gabbling in his eagerness to explain.

Malcolm said, "Slow down a bit, Phil. What is it Wormley is supposed to have said?"

Philip made an effort to calm himself. "Well, something about a threat to everybody's freedom, and that the Liberation Front were planning to annex the whole of this area."

"That's a lot of rubbish," Bill Faber interjected.

"I'm only telling you what I heard," Philip said defensively. "Anyway, the thing is, they're taking names of all the men in the area. Anybody over fourteen. In the spring they're all going to be conscripted into a force to attack the Liberation Front."

There was a general babble of comment. Greg's voice came out of it loudest. "How's he going to make it work?! I mean, how's he going to make the men go off and fight? It can't be done!"

Philip took their attention again. "Wormley said the provisional government had made conscription official. Men would have to report for duty when called on; otherwise they'll be listed as deserters. Any community that harbors or shelters deserters will be made to forfeit stores." Philip spoke carefully, trying to quote exactly what he had been told of Wormley's speech. "He said that any community that did not cooperate fully would be considered hostile and would suffer the consequences. Something like that, anyway."

Again it was a night when they went late to bed. Of all the many ideas they discussed to avoid involvement with the NUF, none proved satisfactory. After much noisy talk, only two alternatives seemed open: to fight with the NUF or against it. When the argument was at its loudest, Ruth started to cry. Her sobbing silenced them. Abby went to her.

"What is it, Ruth?"

Her words sounded jerky as she snuffled through them. "I don't want to stay here. We should have done what you

said and moved away. I don't want to stay here anymore."
She broke down into even louder sobs. Jenny moved to
comfort her.

Abby saw Greg looking at her. She gave him the merest
hint of a nod.

17

THEY killed and cured two of the pigs. The rest, along with the other livestock, were traded for gasoline and preserved foods. Their hardware and surplus stocks of clothes were not in demand, and they got little for them.

By the end of February they had assembled most of the things they had listed. Greg had checked and rechecked the Rover, and it was running perfectly. He put new tires on the trailer that would carry their goods and precious gasoline.

They had a total of slightly less than thirty gallons, and there had been long discussions on how it should be used. At first, the plan had been to use enough vehicles to carry them and all their belongings, but this would have used up the fuel very quickly.

Abby insisted that they keep enough in hand to power a boat across the Channel and, ideally, keep still more in reserve for trading once they reached France.

Another alternative was to travel like refugees, pushing handcart and prams, but this would have made the journey long and slow, particularly with a pregnant woman and two small children.

Finally, they decided that the Rover would tow the trailer and carry as many as possible. The others would cycle. In that way, the gasoline would be used most economically and the heavy load easily transported.

They allowed themselves a month for preparation but were ready a fortnight before the date set for departure.

They filled in a day or two with unnecessary jobs, then Abby said, "We're ready. Why don't we just go? Tomorrow morning."

The sudden advance to their departure alarmed them. The move became a reality.

Despite their concern over the change of plan, only Philip had a valid reason for wanting to delay the start. "I promised I'd go over and see Mary. I mean, I told her the date we were going, and she promised to decide. I've got to see her."

Abby said, "That's all right. Take one of the maps. Greg will show you roughly where we'll stop for the first few nights. You can easily catch up with us."

Philip looked relieved. "I'll go now then," he said. Then: "If she agrees, can she come with us?"

Without reference to the othes, Abby said, "Yes, of course. Tell her we want her to come."

"It's another mouth to feed, isn't it?" Tom Price said grumpily, but they all ignored him.

Their last meal in the house was a very silent affair. The room seemed already deserted. Cold and alien. Abby made an attempt at cheerfulness. "We should have a bottle of something, make a farewell toast."

"It's packed on the trailer," Greg said.

"Could you find it without too much trouble?"

"I suppose so," he said with no enthusiasm.

Malcolm said, "Don't bother on my account. I'm turning in early anyway."

"I am, too," Bill said.

Nobody else seemed to care one way or the other. Abby

shrugged and raised her cup of hot honey water. "To the future."

They cleared the plates, Abby welcoming the activity and clatter in the mournful room. When the table was tidy, they sat uneasily around the fire. No one settled back. They perched on the edges of chairs like visitors in a strange house.

Malcolm crossed to the window and stared up at the sky. "Could rain."

Nobody debated his forecast. He came back to the fire and drummed his fingers on the chimneypiece.

There were a few attempts at conversation, but none of them developed beyond polite exchanges, and it came as a relief when Ruth stood up and said, "Well, I'm off. Big day tomorrow. Good night."

Within twenty minutes only Abby and Greg were left.

"They're not exactly bubbling with excitement, are they?" Abby said.

"Not exactly. But I know how they feel. It's real now. It's actually going to happen. I think they're scared. I am, too."

"It's a bit late in the day, but I suppose we are doing the right thing?"

Greg grinned. "Of course we are. And you know it. I think the others do, too. But we've all become so routined that any break in the pattern throws us. We've sort of dug ourselves a hole here. However bad it is and however much worse it may become, at least it's a hole we know. Climbing out of it isn't easy."

"I suppose." She was silent for a moment and then, for no reason she could think of, said, "I wonder whatever happened to little Claire?"

Greg made a movement with his shoulders that deflected the question. Then, quickly, he said, "Listen, do you want me to get a bottle from the trailer? It's no trouble."

Abby stood up. "No, thanks. I think I've run out of party spirit. Come on. We might as well turn in, too. I don't think anybody's going to sleep all that well, though."

Greg said, "I'll just have a last look around." As Abby moved to pass him, he put his hand on her arm. She looked up at him, and he kissed her briefly on the lips.

"In case there's not a chance in the morning. Thanks, Abby. Good luck."

She put her arms around him and held him very tightly. She held onto him for nearly a minute. Not moving or speaking. Then, breaking away gently, turned and went out of the room.

Bill Faber pressed the starter, and the Rover's engine fired instantly. He looked at Ruth and Jenny seated beside him. "All set?"

They nodded. He turned to the two children in the back. "All right. Settle down, kids."

He eased forward gently, taking up the weight of the trailer. He switched on the windshield wiper to clear the misting rain. "Here we go!" Then, calling to the cyclists through the open window: "See you in ten miles!"

Peter scooted his machine forward and started to pedal rapidly, riding alongside the Rover. Tom Price wobbled badly as he mounted his bike and almost collided with Malcolm. Behind them came Greg, and finally Abby.

As she gained her balance and picked up speed, she looked at the riders spread out across the road in front of her. She started to laugh. They were starting out on an adventure, on a journey of discovery, and they looked ridiculous.

Tom Price was draped in an enormous sheet of transparent plastic that billowed and swirled. Malcolm Christopher wore a bright-red anorak. Overstuffed with kapok, it doubled his bulk, making his legs, in Wellington boots, appear too small for his body.

Greg had split a plastic sack to make a cape to go over his sheepskin jacket. In bold red letters the sack proclaimed POTTING COMPOST.

Abby rode up beside Greg, and they both turned to look back at the house. As they cycled past the last of the buildings, she glanced at the field with its large circle of bare hard soil. It was where Greg had cremated the dead from the village. Nothing had ever grown on the spot.

The high hedges hid the village from their view as they started up the slight incline. The unchecked growth had narrowed the road so that they could not ride more than two abreast. Even on the crown of the road they were not safe from the occasional lash of a whippy branch.

They plodded on up the hill, which was not demanding enough to make them dismount but wearied their legs. They were grateful to reach the crest. Peter was waiting for them at the top. They began to freewheel down the welcome slope.

Abby and Greg paused and again looked back. Across a gate they saw the cluster of houses, barely discernible now in the vaporous morning.

"That's it then," Abby said.

"Yes. That's it then." Greg was determinedly cheerful. "Did you remember to put a note out for the milkman and stop the papers?" He put his palm in the small of Abby's back and gave her a starting shove.

"Come on. We've got a long way to go."

It took them slightly over an hour to reach the ten-mile point where the Rover was waiting. Bill Faber offered to take a turn on a bike and let somebody else drive, but it was finally agreed that they wouldn't make the change until the next stop.

They intended to rest for fifteen minutes, but they found that standing around in the rain, they were getting cold. The Rover set off, and they pedaled on.

The plan was that they should never be separated from the Rover by more than ten miles. One of the men would always be the driver. The two children and Ruth, because of her pregnancy, were to be permanent passengers. Jenny and Abby would take it in turns to ride or cycle. The Rover crew would also be responsible for preparing fires, food and shelter while waiting for the riders to catch up.

The second leg of the journey was more difficult. The roads became hillier, and they had to dismount frequently. The constant drizzle and the squelching mire that surfaced the road made the going hard, and there was little talk.

At various times Tom Price had been warned that his plastic sheet was trailing and was in danger of becoming snared in his rear wheel, but he refused to be parted with his protection. "Old army dodge, this is," he explained. "Keeps the wet out and the body heat up. Don't feel no cold at all. I'm sweating under this. Sweating."

The inevitable happened on a sharp downhill run. The plastic flicked into the back-wheel spokes and locked it solid. The result was spectacular. Man and machine were one, bound together by the plastic. They fell on their side and skidded along the road. First Tom uppermost, then the bike, then Tom again. Greg swerved violently to avoid being hit. He ran into the bank, stopped dead and pitched over the handlebars. Malcolm, who was positioned behind the accident, stopped his bike and stepped away from it, letting it fall. He tottered helplessly across the road, doubled over with hysterical laughter. His great gasping whoops were contagious, and Abby and Peter were caught up in the laughter. She was giggling as she helped Greg to his feet. She began to say, "Are you all right?" but the words became lost in her gurgles.

"It's not bloody funny. I could have broken my neck." He was unhurt and unamused.

Like a mummy, Price had to be unwrapped from the swathe of plastic. He was badly shaken and bruised, but there were no bones broken. When they set out again, he winced painfully as he pedaled and complained unceasingly.

By the end of the day they had made over thirty miles. They spent a cold and uncomfortable night in the workshop of a service station.

The next morning was dry but chilled by a biting east wind. Abby rode in the Rover with Malcolm driving.

The Rover braked on the crest of a hill. The fields of the valley below them were flooded as far as the eye could see. "What do you want to do?" Malcolm asked. "It's bound to be up over the road."

Abby checked the map. "We'd have to go back quite a way. And then it would be a long detour." She considered. Then: "Let's chance it. It can't be all that deep."

They coasted down the hill, then, driving at no more than walking speed, swished forward into the floodwater. Abby hung out of the side window, watching the water level on the wheels. The trailer with its much lower axle base was her main concern. Water getting in through the bottom of the trailer could cause considerable damage to their stores.

For more than a mile the level didn't rise above the rim of the tires; then it began to get deeper. Malcolm stopped, climbed out and waded forward. He walked ten yards, and the water swilled over the top of his Wellington boots. As he advanced, it rose to his knees. He sloshed back.

"If we go through that, the trailer will be awash," he said, sitting on the doorsill and emptying out his boots.

"Will they get through on the bikes?"

"I should think so. But they'll get very wet doing it."

Abby thought. Going back would cost them a lot in time and mileage. "How would it be if we unloaded the trailer a bit at a time? Put the stores in the back of the Rover?"

"Could do it that way. Take six or seven trips I should think."

The rising hills on the far side of the valley looked seductively near. Abby decided.

"Let's do it."

They found it desperately cold working in the water. Even the physical effort of carrying the cartons did little to warm them. They had just finished loading what space was available on the back of the Rover when the cyclists came up.

Abby explained the situation; then Greg took over. "No point in all getting soaked. Leave the bikes. They can go through on the empty trailer. Jenny, Pricey, you get up on the bonnet. Peter, you up on the roof. And hold on tight. Bill and I will stay here and load up. Try and find a place to camp and get a good fire going."

Those directed clambered up onto the Rover. Shivering, Abby squeezed into the front with Ruth and the children. Malcolm started forward, driving slowly and carefully. Even with its heavy load, the Rover rode high out of the water.

Using the tall hedges as a guide, they stayed on the crest of the road and alertly watched for any telltale sign of underwater obstruction.

From his high vantage point on the roof Peter could see across the hedges to where the road rose out of the water on the hill.

"About a quarter of a mile," he shouted excitedly. "Just around the next bend."

"Bloody hell!" Malcolm stopped the Rover. A huge elm tree lay across the road, barring their way. It spanned the narrow track like a bridge, its roots in one field, its topmost branches in another.

"Can we cut it away?" Abby called to Tom Price, who had climbed off the hood and advanced to the tree.

"Never in a million years! Need a power saw to do any good on this!"

She turned to Malcolm. "If we chop a way through the hedge, could we go around it?"

He shook his head firmly. "Couldn't chance it. If we got bogged down, we'd be done for. No, we've got to go back."

They reversed slowly until they reached Greg and Bill. The trailer was rehitched, and they maneuvered awkwardly back along the road.

On the high ground again, they built a fire and dried out. By the time the trailer was reloaded they had lost the whole of the morning.

In the early afternoon they were ready to move. Then, with alarm, Ruth said, "What about Philip? He'll be coming after us this way. If we go another road, he'll never find us."

There was nothing for it but to wait. They drove back to

the top of the hill and made camp in some farm buildings beside the road.

The day had been a total loss. Worse. The new route had added many miles to their journey. They now had farther to go than when they set out.

Philip arrived after dark. He was alone.

18

THE next day went better. It stayed cold, but the sky was clear. The new route proved easier going for the cyclists, and they made good progress. They passed through a number of villages and small towns. The littered cars, the empty shops and houses held a morbid fascination. For some of them, this was the first time they had been out of their own area for almost two years, and they were bewildered by the rapid decay. But though the built-up areas held fascination, they always hurried through them. There still lingered in their minds the dread of disease that might lurk in what were once centers of high population. The specters of the unburied dead still haunted them.

At the end of the third hour the Rover halted on a heavily wooded stretch of road. Tom Price was driving. Jenny was the passenger.

Price said that while they were waiting, he'd take the shotgun and get a rabbit. The children elected to go with him.

Ruth and Jenny took a slow walk along the road. They stopped and looked at a small cottage, now almost buried by its own garden. One section of peg tiles had slipped away from the roof, exposing the rafters. The glass had gone from some of the leaded lights. The front door was open, and the garden had begun to advance into the dark hall.

"Must have been a pretty little place," Jenny said. Ruth agreed.

They walked past the house, then turned to start back for the Rover. Jenny gripped Ruth's arm suddenly and tightly.

"What is it?"

Jenny was staring toward the cottage. Her voice was very quiet. "There was somebody watching us from the upstairs window."

Ruth looked. "I can't see anybody."

"There was somebody there, I tell you." Jenny started to walk more quickly, then halted and pointed toward the side of the house. "Look."

There were two bicycles leaning against the back corner of the cottage. A path, trampled through the dry, brittle overgrowth, led from the road.

"They haven't been there all that long."

An unreasoned fear gripped them both. Low and tensely Ruth said, "Let's get back."

The two women moved quietly, almost skulkingly, past the house, both staring at the dark upstairs windows. They drew level with the gate and began to move faster.

"Hello."

The voice made them jerk with alarm. It came from behind the hedge ahead of them. They halted stiffly. The dry leaves of the beech hedge crackled, and a youth of about sixteen pushed his way through and stood in front of them.

He wore a black fleece-lined leather jacket and heavy knee-high motorcycle boots. His hair hung on his shoulders, and a fair downy beard framed his face. He smiled at them, seeming confident, even arrogant.

"You live around here, do you?"

Ruth said, "No. No, we're passing through. Our car is just up the road." She pointed.

Jenny added quickly, "There are eleven of us altogether."

"Oh, yeah." The youth looked past the women back toward the gate. He called, "Rich!"

A boy stepped out of the gate and walked casually up to join them. He nodded.

"Traveling, are you?"

The first boy answered for them. "Got a car just up the road, they reckon."

Rich looked mildly impressed. "Car. Lucky to have the petrol. We'll walk along with you a bit, shall we?"

The boys took up positions on either side of the two women.

Jenny said, "Our friends will be along in a minute." Then, to stress their strength: "There are eleven of us altogether."

They began to walk slowly.

"My mate there is Clive. I'm Richard. Rich."

"I'm Jenny. Ruth."

"Going far, are you?" Clive asked.

"We're trying to get down to the coast. Somewhere in the Dover area." Jenny forced herself to make the conversation sound relaxed and casual.

"Long way, Dover," Clive said. "Get through a lot of petrol."

They walked in silence until they came within sight of the Rover. Rich nodded approvingly.

"Rover. Good, they are. Where's all these mates of yours then?"

Ruth said, "They're coming behind. They're on bikes. Should be here any minute. Tom is just down there." She pointed to the woods. "He's gone shooting," she added pointedly.

"Oh, yeah," Clive said. He walked ahead a little and stood beside the trailer. He ran his hand over the tarpaulin cover, feeling the outlines of the cases and cartons.

"You're taking a lot of stuff with you."

"Well, we're moving to a new place, you see," Jenny rattled. Then, trying to direct the attention away from the trailer, she said, "Do you live near here?"

"No. No, we don't live nowhere," Rich answered.

"There's us and two other blokes. We stay on the move."

"How do you manage? I mean, it must be hard to find food and things if you're on the move all the time."

Rich shrugged. "We do all right. Things get a bit thin sometimes. Like now. Bad time of year now. There's not much left around in the way of food."

Clive tugged out the knot on the tarpaulin-securing rope.

Jenny felt fear begin to crawl over her. "What are you doing?"

"I'm just having a look, aren't I?" He peeled back the sheet. He reacted, "Gor blimey. You're flush, aren't you?"

Rich peered in through the driver's window. "Bad habit, that, leaving the keys in the ignition. Bad habit."

Clive pinged his finger against the side of one of the five-gallon gasoline drums. It gave a dead, flat note. "Petrol, is it? All full, are they? You're really flush, aren't you? Food in these boxes, is there?"

Ruth said, "Leave it alone."

Rich moved into the middle of the road and stared along the way the Rover had come.

Jenny called at the top of her voice. "Tom! Tom!"

There was a clatter of wings as a flock of pigeons rose from the trees, but no answering call.

Rich moved to stand beside Jenny. He grinned at her. "You're scared of us, aren't you? There's no need, love, we're only trying to be friendly. We don't often meet many people. Specially birds." He put his hand on her arm. She pulled away sharply.

"Now don't be like that," he said. He took her arm again, grabbing it this time and holding it firmly. He wasn't smiling now. He looked across at Clive and nodded toward Ruth. "D'you fancy her, mate?"

Ruth said, "Leave us alone."

Clive stayed where he stood. He looked slighly shifty and embarrassed.

Rich laughed. "He's shy. You know something? He's sixteen, and he's never had a bit. Virgin he is."

"Shut up!" Clive said sulkily.

"Go on, mate. It's your birthday. A couple of good-looking tarts and a trailer full of goodies. Christ Almighty, what more do you want?"

"Stand bloody still!" Tom Price said. "Don't make a bloody move, or I'll shoot your bloody balls off!" He edged out from behind a tree, the shotgun held to his shoulder.

Jenny jerked free from Rich's grip and ran to stand beside Ruth.

The two youths stayed frozen in position. Unkempt and wild-eyed, Tom Price was a frightening proposition from behind a gun.

He moved in closer. "Now you two, piss off," he said. "If you even look back, I'll blow your heads off. Now go. Run!"

They did as they were told, moving at the trot back toward the cottage. As they showed signs of slowing down to a walk, Tom yelled, "Run, I said, you buggers."

The boys disappeared around the bend. Tom nodded with satisfaction. "They won't be back."

Despite the reassurance, Ruth and Jenny stayed tense and guarded until the cyclists arrived.

Greg and the other men went down to the cottage, but the boys and the bicycles had gone.

Midmorning of the next day they reached the motorway, and the cycling became much easier. Greg remembered the road from when he had flown over it in the helicopter. The change seemed incredible. Much of the surface was cracked and broken. The central reservation had bushed into a high wall. The landscaped roadsides were jungles of young trees and bushes. On one high-ridged section, the supporting ground had been washed out, and the road had slipped into the field below.

When they halted for the night, they could see the distant outline of Canterbury Cathedral. When it grew darker, they saw lights from a cluster of houses a few miles away on their left. Perhaps a community like the one they had abandoned. Nobody wanted to investigate.

The Rover tires left a deep and distinctive trail in the wet rotting leaves that surfaced the road. The four youths had no trouble in following it. After Clive and Rich had reported back to their friends, they had all four cycled hard to come within range. In their eagerness to stay close to the group they had once come within a hundred yards of the riders. After that they hung back. They settled for the night at a point where the camp fire ahead of them was in clear view.

They were slowed down by the final barrier of coastal hills. Greg, who was taking his turn at driving, suggested that he should move on down to the coast and make a first reconnaissance of the area, then return and report. Abby was reluctant to break the ten-mile routine but finally agreed.

The cyclists watched with envy the Rover's swift move up the steep hill. Pushing their bikes, they followed.

Later that afternoon Peter gave an excited shout. He pointed. "There it is, look. The sea. The sea!"

They clustered around him and shared his excitement, staring past the two framing hills to the ruled gray line of water that formed the horizon. From this range it looked gently calm.

Malcolm focused the field glasses. With them he saw the choppy white waves. The glasses passed from hand to hand.

"On a clear day you should be able to see France from here," Abby said.

"How far is it?" Tom asked.

"Not much more than ten or eleven miles," Peter told him. "People used to swim it, remember?"

When they started again, it was with new enthusiasm and vigor. They were more cheerful than Abby could ever remember.

They had just begun the long downhill run when the Rover appeared, coming toward them. They were eager for Greg's news.

"There are people down there," he said. "Thirty.

Perhaps more. They're living around the docks area. And they've got boats."

"Did you see them? I mean, did you talk to them?" Malcolm demanded.

Ruth and Bill, who'd accompanied Greg, nodded.

Greg said, "Hang on a minute. We'll go through it as it happened. When we saw smoke, it didn't seem like a good idea to just wander in with all our worldly possessions, so we unhitched the trailer and hid it."

"You left the trailer?" Abby said accusingly. She looked quickly behind the Rover. The trailer was in its usual position.

"We hid it," Ruth said. "Then picked it up on the way back. It's all right. Nothing has been touched."

Greg went on. "Anyway, we went right on into the town, almost down to the sea, and then we got stopped by a couple of chaps with guns. They weren't particularly unfriendly, just wanted to know who we were and what we wanted. Then they said there was a toll charge on the road."

"Toll charge!" a number of voices echoed. Then: "How much?" "What did they want?"

Greg shook his head and made a gesture to silence them. "We never got into that. I told them we wanted to get across to France, and they said they could help us. For a fee, of course. They've taken people over before, apparently."

"Taken people before!" Abby sounded stunned. It had never occurred to her that others might have made the journey before them. "Many?" she asked. "Have many gone?"

Bill answered. "They didn't say. But they didn't seem surprised by the idea. They just accepted it."

"And I thought we were pioneers," Abby said. She felt a sense of disappointment that they would not be the first.

Philip said, "What would they want to take us over?"

"Food and petrol," Ruth replied. "There's nothing else they want. Food and petrol. That's what they said."

"But I'm not sure I trust them," Greg went on. "I didn't let on what we had, but I said we might be interested, and we'd meet them tomorrow. They were keen to come back up here with us. That's what made me wary. What's to stop them just taking everything?"

Greg went through his report again, stopping and patiently answering the questions as they came. When he was finished, Abby said, "Ruth, what was your reaction?"

"Well, first of all it seemed like we'd fallen lucky. But thinking about it since—well, I'm not so sure we should chance it."

"Bill?"

"The same. It's not based on anything concrete. It's a lousy thing to say, but I think we put ourselves at risk by trusting that they're honest."

"Then I don't think we do business with them. And just in case they decide to come and look for us tonight, we'll get off this main road. We'll cut away to the right and hit the coast farther down."

They packed up and moved out, staying together, the Rover moving slowly, at the same pace as the cyclists.

From a hilltop, the four youths watched them turn onto a side road. Dennis, the tallest of the four and evidently the leader, walked across and picked up his bike. "Here we go again then." He adjusted the gun slung across his shoulders, scooted his bike forward and mounted. The other three followed.

19

THERE were no small boats along the coast. Wreckage they found in plenty. Shattered hulls could be seen everywhere. All along the beaches was a litter of spars and rigging splintered and broken by years of heavy seas. There were some ships lodged on rocks and beaches, and farther out, the superstructures of some quite large vessels stuck out of the choppy water; but nowhere was there the size of craft they needed or, indeed, any seaworthy vessel.

Abby was depressed. "Perhaps we should have headed for the Medway. There were always any amount of small boats there."

"There were always any amount down here, too," said Greg. "Don't worry, we'll find something."

On the second day of their search the weather was bright and clear. A sharp wind roughened the surface of the water, and across it they could see France: a smudgy line of sand dunes with hills rising behind them.

"We could always go back and try to do a deal with those people in Dover," Malcolm suggested.

"We might have to," Greg agreed. "But let's give it a day or two more. The way the sea is at the moment I wouldn't risk a crossing in a small boat anyway."

They split into groups and started to search again. Riding in the Rover, Malcolm and Tom went well down the coast. They were excited for a time when they found a boatyard and, hauled up its slipway, a fairly big timber boat sitting in a cradle. When they examined it, they found there were gaping cracks in the timbers, far beyond their ability to repair. The only other complete vessel they saw that day was a tugboat buried to deck level in sand.

They started back as it began to grow dark. Malcolm turned inland, hoping for a shortcut, and after a few miles they found themselves on an involved road system that wound through what had once been a modern housing development. The red-brick semidetached houses showed little sign of dilapidation. There were tiles missing here and there. On one building a chimney stack had fallen. There were rusting cars lining the roadways and drives, and the rank gardens evidenced the neglect. But in the half-light it was possible to imagine that the houses of the development were simply empty and waiting for buyers.

"Stop! Bloody hell, look at that. Stop!" Tom Price shouted the words.

In alarm Malcolm stood on the brakes. "What is it?"

"Back up. Back up. Back up." Tom was leaning out of the window, craning to see behind them.

Malcolm reversed for twenty yards. Tom screamed, "It is. It is. It bloody well is!"

While they were still moving, he opened the door and jumped out. Malcolm braked and leaped to follow him.

In the driveway of one of the houses was a boat. It sat neatly parked on its trailer, hidden beneath a well-lashed plastic sheet.

The two men gazed at the boat. "Would you bloody believe it?" Price breathed. "Don't look for boats in the sea. Look on the housing estates."

"They were nice little status symbols once. Let's have a look at it."

The plastic sheeting was brittle, and it cracked and tore as they cut the ropes that held it. Malcolm smoothed his hand across the hull.

"Fiberglass." Then, surprise in his voice: "It looks all right."

They walked around the boat. "Susan." Price read the name painted on the bow.

She was twenty-two feet long. There was a covered foredeck, then a brief roofed section covering the front of the well that extended almost to the stern.

With rising excitement, Malcolm again said, "It looks all right."

He clambered up on the trailer's wheel and peered into the boat. On the duckboard flooring was a big Mercury outboard motor.

"This is it, Tom. We're there."

They towed it in slowly on the flat-tired trailer. The others, who had been concerned by the late return of the Rover, swarmed around the boat. They were like children with a toy. Malcolm and Tom had their hands shaken by the men and were kissed by the women.

The Mercury was carefully lifted out, and Greg gave it a brief examination. They all waited for his report. "Perfect, as far as I can see. Looks almost brand-new."

They celebrated that night with no prompting from Abby. There was an "eve-of-the-holidays" atmosphere. They were laughing and chatty. In all the time they had been together Abby could not remember a more pleasurable evening.

They had made their headquarters in the small dining room of what had been a seafront café. The beeswax candles gave the room a warm flickering light that made it feel both cozy and safe. They could hear the sound of the sea raking the shingle and the wind gusting through the deserted streets. But they were inside, and they were warm and secure, and they were together.

The whiskey made Abby feel slightly heady, and she went outside. She was buffeted by the wind and leaned against it as she walked across to the seawall. She felt the spray blowing on her face, and when she ran her tongue along her lips, she could taste the salt.

The road was deep with shingle thrown up over the wall by storms. She crunched along it, deeply breathing the cold clean air.

Behind her she heard the door of the café open and then bang shut loudly, caught by the wind. Bill Faber loomed out of the darkness behind her. They stood together, staring at the barely discernible line of foam that marked the sea's edge. They were silent for a long time; then Bill said, "It's cold. You'd better come in now."

Only then did she realize why he had followed her out. He was watching over her, looking after her. The understanding gave her a sudden great surge of sentiment. In all those years of caring and planning and worrying for them she had never recognized that they returned her concern. She had been among them but alone. She had been isolated by the leadership they had imposed on her. Bill's coming outside to make sure she was all right was the gesture of a father, a husband, a friend. She had always felt needed. Now she felt wanted, and it was a good feeling. She pushed her arm through Bill's and stayed very close to him as they walked back.

The next morning they weakened to find the wind at storm force. The great waves were running diagonally to the shore and driving high up the beaches. Long squalls of heavy rain forced them to stay under cover. In an attempt to keep them occupied Abby organized groups to search for ropes, life jackets and a compass. Greg started stripping down the outboard motor, cleaning and oiling. A small cluster stood behind him in a half circle, watching him work. They made him first of all uneasy and then irritable. Finally, he turned and snapped at them, "Haven't you got anything better to do?"

They shuffled off, and Abby was uncomfortably aware that they did have nothing better to do.

Late in the afternoon Greg filled the tank with fuel. He jerked the starting cord, and the motor came to instant life. The propeller raced in a blur. Wreathing exhaust fumes had them coughing through their excited congratulations.

Greg was pleased but dismissive. "We'll see how it does in the water."

It was two more days before they could find out. Then the wind subsided, and the sea settled into a choppy swell. It was still too rought to attempt a crossing, but they could launch the boat for a trial run.

A mile away was a concrete launching ramp. The shingle had banked against it and covered much of it. The men set out early, armed with shovels to clear a path for the boat.

It took four hours of hard digging. They moved forward slowly, and the tide rose to meet them. Finally, they were ready.

Greg reversed the Rover and eased the boat trailer onto the ramp. Malcolm and Bill paced on either side of the boat, holding lines attached to the bows. Tom and Philip stood at the water's edge with improvised boat hooks. The women walked down beside the ramp, keeping pace with the Rover. Peter stood proudly in the well of the boat, feeling very important.

A wave swept in and flooded up over the wheels of the trailer. As it retreated, they creaked in pursuit. Greg inched backward until the Rover's wheels were in the water. Then he stopped and called from the cab, "All right, Abby. Up you go."

She scrambled up into the boat, clumsy and undignified. Peter helped pull her in beside him. As soon as she was on board, Greg backed up again and she felt the stern of the boat lift as it was caught by a high swell. Another backward yard, and the boat rose off the trailer.

"Right! Push her off!" Philip yelled. He and Tom shoved with their boat hooks. The stern began to swing around broadside to the beach, and Philip charged forward into the water to put his weight against the hull.

Abby ran to the stern and stood by, ready to lower the propeller into the water. The swell beneath them subsided, and she heard the keel scrape abrasively on the shingle.

Peter was paddling furiously as the next swell came. Tom was in the water with Philip now, both pushing her out.

Abby tilted the shaft back into the sea and pulled on the

starting rope. The rope recoiled, the engine fluttered, but nothing more. She pulled again, hard and sharp this time. The sudden roar alarmed her, and she throttled back quickly. The motor gurgled, and the prop took a bite on the water.

Peter scrambled forward and hauled in the two lines. Abby swung the engine and, shifting into forward drive, sped up. The prow lifted, and the boat started away in a graceful curve.

The group on the shore gave a ragged cheer. Greg edged up beside Jenny. In a low worried voice he said, "Doesn't it look little now it's in the water? More like a toy."

When the boat had stood on its trailer, parked in the narrow side street, it had looked large and impressive, but now, with much of its bulk beneath the waves, it seemed frighteningly small and vulnerable.

Abby increased the power. The boat moved faster, lifting its bows across the waves, then slapping them down loudly into the next trough. The bouncing motion was uncomfortable and jarring.

She made a wide circle and started back toward the shore. As the cross waves hit, the boat wallowed and became hard to control. A wave broke over the side and soaked them both. It swilled around in the well, lapping their feet.

She aimed the bows of the boat at the ramp. Peter threw the lines out to Malcolm and Bill, and in a well coordinated effort the *Susan* was brought ashore.

Abby rode back with Greg. "Well, what do you think?" he asked.

"She's all right," she answered guardedly. "She's quite nippy, and she responds well. She's all right."

"Will she make the crossing?"

Abby hesitated, then evaded the question. "She's a runabout. A river and estuary boat. She takes water easily."

Greg waited for her to go on and, when she didn't, said demandingly, "Will she do the job?"

"Yes. In flat calm she'd get us there."

"Then we're going?"

"Yes. We just have to be damn sure we pick the right day."
Then she told Greg the rest of the bad news.

She broke it to the others later that evening. "We'll have
to make two trips," she said, "The boat won't carry all of us
and the supplies." She tried to make the change in plan
sound casual and unimportant. "What I think we'll do is get
everybody across first. We'll take the camping stuff and
some food; then I'll start back right away for the supplies.
Oh, and just to be on the safe side, I think it would be a good
idea if two of the men stayed here to keep an eye on the
trailer. Perhaps you'd stay, Tom. And you, Philip. Would
you mind?"

Philip shrugged. "It's all right with me." He said it in a
tone that suggested he didn't care one way or the other.
Since rejoining the group, after failing to get Mary to
accompany him, he had become withdrawn and given to
long periods of morose silence.

Tom was unsure. "Why do we need to stay? I mean,
nobdy is going to nick our stuff. I mean, we haven't seen
nobody, have we?"

Malcolm said, "True. But we know there are people up
the coast. It would be silly to take risks at this stage."

Tom was derisive. "What risk? Hide the trailer away in a
garage, and who is going to find it?"

Abby said quickly, "There's another reason I want
somebody here. I'm not the world's greatest navigator, and
what with winds and tides and currents, it could be tricky
finding this bit of the coast again. I want somebody to light a
big beacon fire so I can come straight to it."

Greg saw that Tom was still hesitating. Making no
attempt at subtlety, he said seriously, "It's a terrific responsibility, Abby. I think I should stay."

It was all that was needed. Tom glared at Greg. "I can
handle it. You think I can't take care of a little job like that?
I'll give you a fire you can see for fifty miles. And let
anybody try and put a hand on our stores. They'd have to
get past me first!"

"Thanks, Tom," Abby said, and meant it. She looked around at their faces. "Well, I think that's about all. Anybody have any questions?"

Ruth said, "When do we go?"

"The moment the weather's right."

It wasn't right for three more days. They filled the time collecting driftwood from along the shore and building it into a mammoth bonfire near the launching ramp.

Philip and Malcolm went to the church that stood on the high ground behind the town. They climbed the iron ladder inside the old stone tower. From the top they had an unrestricted view of the sea.

"If it was clearer, you'd be able to see the other coast from here," Malcolm said. "If you or Tom kept watch up here with binoculars, you'd see Abby coming back and know when to light the fire." Philip didn't answer. Malcolm turned to look at him. He was gazing blankly out to sea.

"Did you hear what I said?"

"Yes. It's a good idea," he said flatly. Then: "I don't know if I'll be coming."

Malcolm's immediate reaction was to try to convince the boy to stay with them. He halted himself before he began and said instead, "You'd go back to Little Barton, would you? Stay with Mary?"

He nodded. "Yes. Mind, I wouldn't leave until Abby gets back. I'd stay and help with the loading."

"Be a help if you would. After that it's up to you, of course. Something you have to decide for yourself. We'd miss you. All of us. But if that's what you want—"

"I'm not sure that it is," he said plaintively.

"It's not a decision I'd like to make. You are going to have regrets whichever course you take."

Neither said any more, and after a few minutes of silence they climbed back down the ladder and started for the beach.

On the way back Philip said, "I'd rather you didn't mention it to any of the others. They'd all start offering advice. I want to think it through on my own."

Abby came awake the moment Greg touched her shoulder. The room was in darkness. "What is it?"

"I've been out to look at the water. I think you should come and see."

She climbed quietly out of her sleeping bag, careful not to wake the others. She pulled on her boots and stood up. "What time is it?" she whispered.

"Going on for five," Greg said, helping her into her coat. They moved to the door and stepped outside. Abby flinched at the sudden cold. The sky was clear and bright with stars. The rooftops were white with frost that sparkled in the light of a half-moon. They crossed quickly to the wall.

Hardly a ripple disturbed the sea. At its edge the waves were so small that they made almost no sound. Beyond, it undulated gently.

"The only time you'll get it flatter than this is if it's frozen over," Greg said.

She hesitated a moment longer and then said, "We'll launch."

The boat was loaded with the camping gear, rations and spare fuel. The early wakening and the imminence of their departure created a tension among them, and they were ill-tempered and snappy. By the time the boat was in the water it was getting light.

With its cargo of seven adults and two children the *Susan* sat low in the water. She lay broadside to the beach about fifty yards out, the sea slapping gently against her hull. It was the only sound that could be heard.

Philip and Tom stood watching from the ramp. "Why the hell doesn't she get going?" Tom muttered. Half an hour had passed since the launch, and Abby still showed no sign of making a start.

She sat in the stern of the boat, staring at the sky to the west, where some night still remained. There was a thin high cloud that seemed motionless. She twisted around to look behind her. The sun was rising and giving a cast of red to the sky. Out to sea the horizon was lost in a light haze.

A breeze came in across the bay, rippled the surface and then died away. Jenny's child started to speak and was quickly hushed by her mother. In the silence they could clearly hear Tom wheezily blowing onto his cold fingers. Again Abby scanned the half circle from east to west. It was fractionally lighter. Nothing else had changed.

"Start her up. We're going."

The suddenness of the order startled them all. Malcolm half stood and called toward the shore to Philip, "I'll see you on the other side," but the words were hidden in the roar of the motor coming to life. There was a flurry of water at the stern, and the boat started toward the shore. Abby swung over hard, and the *Susan* heeled sharply. Malcolm lost his balance and slumped back down. Then, leveling, the bows turned toward the sea, carving a neat angle in the water as the boat picked up speed.

Tom and Philip raised their hands, returning the flutter of waving from the boat. Shouts drifted back to them, the words blurred by the motor and the quickly growing distance.

The two men stayed on the ramp and watched the boat until it was almost out of sight.

Philip said, "Let's go up the church tower. We should be able to keep it in sight."

By the time they reached the top the boat was already lost in the haze.

Abby stared back at the coast, memorizing its features for the return. The others looked back for different reasons. They continued to stare even after the land was lost to sight. Then, reluctantly, they turned and looked ahead.

As they moved out into deeper water, they began to feel the swell. The boat made an uncomfortable rocking motion, and the sea began to break against the bows, sending up bursts of spray.

Their horizon had coiled into a circle around them. As Greg looked around its misty limits, he was amazed at how quickly he had lost his sense of direction. His only reference was the line of their wake. Neither did there seem to be any way of judging speed. The loss of these senses made him uneasy.

A cloud of bow spray broke over the passengers. The children gave shrieks of delighted laughter. Ruth said miserably, "We're getting wet up here."

Abby checked the compass and shifted the tiller to nose the boat more directly into the swell. The rocking motion eased. "There's name for all the movements boats make," Abby said. "There's pitching and yawing, but I can never remember which is which."

"I don't like any of them," Greg answered.

She grinned at him. "People used to do this for pleasure."

He shook his head. "It's not for me." Then, trying to appear unconcerned: "How are we doing?"

"All right, I think. I've changed course slightly, just to make her ride more comfortably. If we stayed on a straight line, we should come out to the west of Calais and east of Cape Gris-Nez. I can't be more accurate than that because I can't calculate drift."

There was murmuring talk now among the others, and every once in a while one of them would stand up and stare forward into the haze for a sight of land. Abby sensed the growing excitement. She looked up. The clear sky and steady throb of the motor reassured her.

"We're going to be all right. We'll make it easily," she said and then felt she was tempting fate and wished she hadn't spoken.

The sun had cleaned the frost off the rooftops and now gave a glitter to the sea. There was more movement in the water now that the tide had changed, and out from the shore the light easterly wind raised flecks of white.

Tom Price had settled in a sheltered position beside the ramp. He watched Philip move toward him, dragging a long spar of timber. The boy reached the bonfire, heaved the spar upright and let it fall against the piled wood. As it struck, it dislodged some of the smaller timbers.

"Careful. Careful! You'll have the bloody lot down," Tom shouted.

Philip glared at him. "Wouldn't hurt you to move your arse and collect a bit more wood."

Tom sounded indignant. "I can't do everything, can I? I'm on watch. Keeping an eye out for the boat. I can't do everything!"

The boy turned and looked out toward the sea. The inshore mists had cleared, but the horizon remained vague. "They should be nearly there by now," he said. "Do you think she'll turn around and come straight back?"

"Oh, yes," said Price confidently. "Nothing to stop her while the weather's like this. I tell you, we'll be over there with them before dark."

Philip's air of preoccupation returned. He was running short of time, and he was still undecided. He slouched off down the beach again and picked up some more timber. When he returned, Price got to his feet.

"Listen, why don't we go and hitch up the trailer and bring it down to the ramp?"

"There's no hurry, is there?" Philip said. He wanted to keep to himself and not have to listen to Tom's chatter.

"Don't want to leave things to the last minute. Come on. We might as well."

Tom started up the ramp to the Rover. Philip followed reluctantly. As they got into the front, he said, "When we get back, I'll go off to the tower. You stay near the fire. All right?"

"Fine with me," Tom said. Then, bright with an idea, he went on, "Tell you what. Take a shotgun with you. Soon as you spot the boat, fire off a shot. Then as I hear the signal, I'll start the beacon. How's that?"

Grudgingly Philip agreed it was a good idea. They started back toward the café.

The landfall came on their starboard side instead of directly in front of them as Abby had expected: Peter saw it first. "Land. Land over there on the right."

Everyone turned to follow his pointing finger. Abby swung the boat toward it. "That must be the cape," she said. "We've drifted farther down than I thought."

"I don't give a damn just so long as it's France," Greg said. He was cheerful now, the sight of land giving him back the dimensions he had lost.

The brightness of the day did little to lighten the drab mournfulness of the coast. Abby looked at it through her binoculars and settled on what seemed like a gently shelving stretch of sand and shingle. She steered toward it.

"That's a good landmark to come back to, Abby," Greg pointed off. About half a mile along the coast was the huge bulk of a supertanker sticking out from the beach like a pier, its stern far up onto the sand.

Ten minutes later, and still fifty yards from the shore, the *Susan* went aground on sand.

"I'm sorry. You're going to have to walk in from here," Abby said.

Bill and Malcolm lowered themselves over the side, gasping at the coldness of the water. "It's freezing," Bill yelled.

"Take the camping stuff first," Greg called. "Keep it dry if you can."

The others handed the equipment down to the waders, who balanced it on their heads and shoulders and then started for the shore.

Abby switched off the engine and looked at the sky. There were clouds in the distant east. The sea was still calm.

"Will you top up the petrol tank for me, Greg?"

"You're going to go straight back?"

She nodded firmly. "I've got to take advantage of it while it's like this. You know how quickly it can change. If it does blow up, I might not be able to cross again for days."

Greg unscrewed the filler cap and began carefully to pour in fuel.

Malcolm and Bill got their first load ashore and started back for more.

"Build a beacon for me, Greg. It's not midday yet. I'll be on my way back well before dark, but just in case, keep it going through the night."

"You'll be here ages before that."

Abby nodded. "Yes, of course."

Bill and Malcolm shouldered the two small children. Jenny came up to the stern and kissed Abby's cheek. "See you in a little while. And don't you start back unless the weather stays perfect."

Abby assured her she wouldn't. Jenny swung herself over and lowered slowly into the water. "Oh, God. It's bitter." She started for the beach.

When she was out of earshot, Greg said, "I'll come back with you, Abby. If you want me to."

"Thanks, but there's no point. It's been much easier than I ever thought. I'll be all right."

"If you're sure."

"I am."

Ruth started giggling when Bill told her to get on his shoulders. Greg helped her climb on, and Malcolm gave a balancing hand. After Bill had made only three lurching, grunting steps, Ruth was helpless with laughter.

Greg went into the water, and Peter passed him the last of the camping things, then followed. When everything was ashore, the three men waded out again to shove the boat off the sand. As they heaved at the bows, Abby started the motor. The *Susan* came free and began to pull backward.

The boat swung around, sending her wake breasting against the men. They stood where they were, waving and shouting. The group on the beach joined in.

Abby looked back at them, returning their waves, then gave her attention to setting her course. When she looked back again, they were all together on the beach.

Tom Price stretched and yawned. With the windows closed it was warm in the cab of the Rover. The slap of the water on the ramp behind him was very soothing. He yawned again, then his eye settled on the rearview mirror. The tide was rising. He stirred himself and looked back. The water had almost reached the end of the trailer. He sighed and shuffled himself across into the driver's seat. "I told him he shouldn't have run it so far down," he muttered. He started the engine and drove forward up the ramp for five or six yards. As he reached to switch off the ignition, he noticed the gasoline gauge. It was reading quarter full. "Can't waste that," he said aloud. Grunting with the effort, he got out and collected the tools and containers he needed to drain the tank.

In the tower window Philip looked at the sun. If Abby was coming back, he should see her before long. He scanned the sea again with the binoculars. The haze, shimmering now in the afternoon ligh, still obscured the opposite coast. Nothing moved on the water. He turned and sat on the floor with his back to the wall. His head in his hands, he thought about returning to Little Barton. He tried to imagine his future there with Mary and then to set it against a future in a warmer and, he hoped, easier land. There seemed no way of balancing one thing against the other. He stood up again and looked out of the window. He saw the boat immediately. A tiny spot of white, still well out to sea and far, much too far off to the right. He used the binoculars to confirm his first view. Even with the glasses he could see no detail other than that it was the boat. The course it was running would take it miles off its landfall. He picked up the shotgun and pointed it out of the window.

Price put the drum of gasoline in the trailer and started to stow the tools. The blast from the shotgun made him start. Then he spun around and stared out to sea. From his position he could see nothing of the boat. He moved quickly across to the beacon fire.

As Abby saw the unfamiliar details of the coast ahead of her she realized that she had been drifting to port. She swung right to run along the shore. She was still about a mile and a half out from land when she saw the smoke. With the glasses she pinpointed the red glare of its source. She felt enormous satisfaction as she steered in toward it.

Clive saw the smoke first. He and his companions were camped on the hill behind the town. They had lost sight of the Rover and its treasure-laden trailer after it had turned away from Dover. Since then they had gone more than fifty miles down the coast in search of it. Defeated, they were returning.

"Rich, what d'you reckon that is?"

His friend moved up beside him. Dennis and the fourth boy joined them. They stared for a moment, and Clive asked again, "What d'you reckon it is?"

"Don't know," Dennis said. "Worth having a look, though, isn't it?"

They mounted their cycles and started down the hill.

The beacon was burning brightly when Philip ran breathlessly up to join Tom.

"Can you see her yet?" he gasped. Tom grinned and pointed. The little boat was curving in toward them, leaving a broad wake. Both smiling, they watched the approach. Then Philip said, "Come on. Let's get the covers off the trailer."

As they loosed the ropes, the unsure wind swirled smoke around them. They felt the glow of heat from the beacon fire. Tom glanced at it proudly. "Not a bad little bonfire," he said above the crackle of the flames.

"It did the job all right," Philip said. He glanced out to sea again. He could hear the motor now. He felt elated. "Another half hour, we'll be on our way." Only as he said it did he realize he had made up his mind.

They peered carefully over the seawall. "It's the bloody Rover. It's them," Dennis said. His voice was tight with excitement.

"I can only see two of them. Where are the others?" Clive asked softly. Then, shading his eyes against the sun, he said, "Perhaps they're in that boat that's coming in. I can't see properly."

Dennis said, "Then let's get it before they arrive. Take your guns." He gave his orders quickly and efficiently. "Rich, you drive. Me and Clive'll keep them off until you've got it up on the road." He turned to the fourth boy. "You cover us all the time from here. Then put the bikes in the back of the Rover, and off we go. You all got it?" They nodded. Dennis said, "Good. Then let's go and collect."

Abby was still a thousand yards out. She saw the youths before Tom and Philip. For a moment she couldn't understand who they were or what they were doing, but she instinctively felt the danger. Then she recognized they were carrying guns. She started to shout and wave. Tom and Philip waved back. They didn't hear their attackers until the boys were directly behind them.

"Stand still!" Dennis screamed. His voice was wild with his excitement and fear.

Tom cringed backward from the guns. He remembered Clive from their earlier encounter. Philip felt sick with terror.

Rich was already in the Rover and pressing the starter. As the engine fired, he slammed into gear and spun the wheels by revving too hard. He sent a hail of shingle spitting around the four behind him. He eased off the throttle, and the tires bit. The Rover and trailer raced up and turned onto the coast road.

Keeping their guns aimed, Dennis and Clive moved backward; then they turned and started to run to the road.

Abby could see all the action now, more clearly than anybody. She pushed the throttle over hard, driving the boat directly for the beach.

Dennis and Clive were at the top of the ramp now and ran to start and lift the bikes into the back of the Rover. The fourth boy moved into clear sight, his gun trained toward Tom and Philip.

Philip saw the shotgun he had used to signal still lying on the shingle beside the ramp. He knew that if he moved to get it, he was an easy target for the boy who still covered them.

The engine of the Rover coughed and died. On the beach they heard the shout of alarm. "The bloody thing's out of petrol."

The boat hit the beach and drove high up onto the shingle. Abby threw herself over the side and fell into the water on her knees. She scrambled up and, slipping again, crawled forward.

Her arrival took the boy's attention away from Philip. He ran forward and scooped up the shotgun. He got it to his shoulder as the boy fired. The shot took Philip in the chest and carried him backward almost to cannon into Abby as she came up the beach. He was dead as he fell. She saw the blood pumping out of the blackened hole.

Knowing only rage and fear, she picked up the gun from beside his body and started forward. She began running up the ramp with the gun raised. She halted to take aim and looked up at the boy. She saw his face, and she knew him. Peter fired as she started to say her son's name. She was dead before she finished it.

Tom stayed crouched beside the ramp long after the boys had fueled the Rover and the sound of its engine had died. When it was dark, he stood up and considered the boat. Then he turned and started to walk away toward Dover.

The weather stayed fine for a week. Throughout that time they kept the fire burning on the beach. Despite their desperate hunger, they waited until the first storm and knew for certain Abby wasn't coming. Then they started inland. As they straggled off the beach, Jenny walked beside Greg.

"What'll happen to us now?"

He shook his head. "I don't know, Jen." Then: "But we'll survive. We'll survive."